THAT'S NOT WHAT I HEARD

THAT'S NOT WHAT I HEARD

STEPHANIE KATE STROHM

SCHOLASTIC PRESS / NEW YORK

Library of Congress Cataloging-in-Publication Data

Names: Strohm, Stephanie Kate, author.
Title: That's not what I heard / Stephanie Kate Strohm.
Other titles: That is not what I heard
Description: First edition. | New York: Scholastic Press, 2019. | Summary: High-school seniors
    Kimberly Landis-Lilley and Teddy Lin have been together since kindergarten, but then
    someone starts a rumor that they have broken up, and suddenly the whole William Henry
    Harrison High School is taking sides, somebody is putting up posters supporting Kim and
    criticizing Teddy, there are incidents of artistic vandalism, people are talking about having
    separate proms, and even teachers and parents are getting involved—and nobody is more
    confused about the chaos then Kim and Teddy themselves.
Identifiers: LCCN 2018031382 (print) | LCCN 2018033490 (ebook) | ISBN 9781338281828
    (Ebook) | ISBN 9781338281811 (hardcover)
Subjects: LCSH: High school students—Juvenile fiction. | Rumor—Juvenile fiction. |
    Dating (Social customs)—Juvenile fiction. | Interpersonal relations—Juvenile fiction. |
    Malicious mischief—Juvenile fiction. | CYAC: High schools—Fiction. | Schools—Fiction. |
    Rumor—Fiction. | Dating (Social customs)—Fiction. | Interpersonal relations—Fiction. |
    Vandalism—Fiction.
Classification: LCC PZ7.S9188 (ebook) | LCC PZ7.S9188 Th 2019 (print) | DDC 813.6
    [Fic]—dc23

10 9 8 7 6 5 4 3 2 1   19 20 21 22 23

Printed in the U.S.A. 23
First edition, February 2019

Book design by Maeve Norton

For all the teachers who somehow got me through my spectacular fail of a career in education: the L3 lunch squad, ninth-grade English '15, Senior Advisors '16, and everyone who made Room 117 an incredible place. Thanks for never minding when I hid in the copy room to cry. That's one. (One dedication, not one demerit.)

PART ONE: RUMOR

CHAPTER ONE

KIM LANDIS-LILLEY
DAY ONE

Kim had always thought that the day everything changed would be more of a Day Everything Changed, with capital letters. Like maybe there would be a blinding flash of green light in the sky, and then a bunch of dead birds would fall out of it, and before she knew it she'd be running through the woods with a bow and arrow, trying to defend her little sister from an alien invasion or a totalitarian regime or something like that.

Even though Olivia could definitely defend herself, as she was now taller, faster, and stronger than Kim, despite being four years younger. Probably, this just meant that Kim had been reading too many books from her best friend Jess's extensive dystopian collection. But anyway. She'd thought it would be more dramatic.

The day hadn't started off dramatically. It started off just like most of senior year had, which wasn't, honestly, really all that different from freshman, sophomore, or junior year. Not that Kim was complaining. She liked routine. Which was why she was sitting at the same table in the cafeteria she always sat at, with Jess and Elvis, waiting for Teddy, as she ate a turkey sandwich with lettuce, tomato, and honey mustard—the same sandwich she'd been eating every day for lunch since her moms packed her very first lunch way back on the first day of school.

(Mama K made the sandwiches back then. Mama Dawn was such a bad cook that even sandwiches, which were really more construction than cooking, somehow turned to messes in her hands.)

"I'm not gonna call you that," Jess said.

This was one routine Kim could have done without. Jess and Elvis had been having this fight every spring for the past three years. This was now year four of the fight, and it hadn't changed at all.

"Babe," Elvis said. "Babe. Come on. If you don't call me E-Rod, no one will. It takes one drop of ocean to start a tidal wave. That tidal wave starts with you."

"Tidal waves are massive forces of destruction," Jess argued. "This line of reasoning is disrespectful to people who have lost their lives in natural disasters."

"It's the last baseball season *ever*," Elvis whined. "I've spent the past four years as Elvis Rodriguez, moderately successful third baseman. But imagine if that moderately successful third baseman was transformed into . . . E-Rod. Can't you give me this? For my last season as a Mighty Flying Arrow?"

"I have zero allegiance to the Mighty Flying Arrows. And there is literally nothing you can say that would entice me to call you E-Rod."

"Kim?" Elvis asked hopefully.

"Hey, Junior." Kim's boyfriend, Teddy, dropped a kiss on top of her head, barely ruffling her long brown hair, which stayed stick-straight no matter what she did to it. Teddy slid into the seat next to her, saving her from having to tell Elvis, again, that she just couldn't call him E-Rod with a straight face. "You can't forcefully create a nickname, Elvis," Teddy said, turning to talk to his best friend. "It has to come up organically."

"Like Junior?" Kim asked.

"Doesn't count as a nickname if it's on your birth certificate," Teddy replied as he unpacked his lunch.

Kimberly Dawn Landis-Lilley Jr. was, in fact, her full legal name.

"God, I can't wait until it's warm enough to eat outside." Jess looked longingly toward the door out of the cafeteria as she peeled a clementine. "It always smells like fish in here."

"Spring's just around the corner." Elvis patted her on the back consolingly.

"It's already spring. The weather just didn't get the memo that it's supposed to warm up."

"Spring and . . . baseball season," Elvis continued. "A season for rebirth. New beginnings. New nicknames."

"Let it go, Elvis! Or I'll give you a nickname you *really* don't want!"

Teddy and Kim exchanged a look. Elvis and Jess were always fighting about *something*. Kim could count on one hand the number of times she and Teddy had fought, and most of those weren't real fights, just disagreements. Like that time Kim's phone died and Teddy thought she was ignoring him. Or that time Teddy ate all the M&M's Kim was saving to eat on the bus after her away game. They were both, generally speaking, conflict-averse people. Natural pacifists. One of the many reasons they were meant to be together.

Teddy was her destiny. On the first day of kindergarten, they'd lined up alphabetically, and Kimberly Landis-Lilley had been right next to Teddy Lin. They'd been best friends immediately, and boyfriend and girlfriend since sixth grade.

(Technically, Teddy was still her best friend, but Jess was her *girl* best friend, and Kim found they were both essential. Just like Elvis was Teddy's *boy* best friend.)

So the fact that the alphabet had united them was totally destiny. But Teddy was doubly her destiny because Kim's parents had met *exactly the same way*. Kimberly Landis and Dawn Lilley had met at their freshman seminar in college, when the professor had taken attendance alphabetically. And maybe one day Kim and Teddy would get married—Kim Landis-Lilley-Lin was a bit of a mouthful, but she'd think of something—and then maybe *their* daughter would sit next to her soul mate on the first day of kindergarten, and it would be like a chain of destiny. Kim leaned over to kiss Teddy, because he just looked irresistible eating an apple. Most people didn't know that there was a cute way to eat an apple. But most people hadn't been eating lunch with Teddy Lin for the past twelve years.

"PDA!"

Kim and Teddy broke apart, and she looked up to see her theater teacher standing over them.

"Sorry, Mr. Rizzo," Teddy said.

"Consider that your official PDA warning of the day." Mr. Rizzo swirled a red coffee stirrer around in a mug that read LIKE A BOSS, BUT WITH LESS MONEY. "Carry on. Dustin Rothbart!" Mr. Rizzo boomed as he moved toward the table behind them. "That's one for throwing garbage on the floor. I don't care that you were aiming for the trash can!"

Teddy put his arm around Kim and carried on eating his apple. Kim knew it wasn't just the alphabet that was responsible for bringing her and Teddy together—although she was totally grateful for the alphabet. It was destiny.

"Are you even coming to the game today?" Elvis wheedled.

"No way," Jess said. "You know I have a strict no-games policy."

"It's senior year! There aren't even that many games left!"

"And yet my policy remains unchanged."

"I wish I could come to *your* game." Teddy squeezed Kim just a little tighter.

"Me too. I hate it when we have games on the same day."

Kim really did hate having to miss Teddy's game because she had a game of her own. It was hard balancing both of their schedules during the spring sports season. Sort of like if Wei-Yin Chen and Monica Abbott had been dating while Chin was pitching for the Orioles and Abbott was pitching in the Olympics. Of course, this metaphor didn't really hold up, since Wei-Yin Chen and Monica Abbott had never dated. And neither Teddy nor Kim was a pitcher, but Kim thought they looked a little bit like younger versions of Wei-Yin Chen and Monica Abbott. Except Teddy was way cuter. Teddy was so cute in his baseball uniform, it should have been illegal. He was even cuter in his uniform than he was eating an apple.

"Baseball is the longest, slowest, most boring sport in existence," Jess said. "It's self-preservation. Nobody can sit through that."

"But you go to Kim's softball games!" Elvis protested.

"That's different. I gotta support my girl. You know women's sports don't get the respect they deserve."

Kim held up her fist for a pound, and then she and Jess exploded it, perfectly in sync.

"Great, Jess. Thanks," Elvis said. "I feel really supported."

"Be your own support, dude." Jess shrugged. "That's not my job."

"Kind of is, though."

And then they were off again. Kim wondered if they'd stay together through prom. She hoped so; otherwise it would make their pictures super awkward. And she'd have to redo the whole Limo Matrix, never mind the fact that she'd already put down a deposit on an MKT ten-passenger stretch limo. The fact that her best friend was dating Teddy's best friend was definitely convenient, but sometimes Kim wasn't sure if Jess and Elvis actually liked each other, or if they'd found themselves thrown together so often by hanging out with Kim and Teddy that they got together out of a sense of inevitability rather than genuine affection. From the way they were arguing—from the way they always argued—it sure didn't *seem* like they liked each other.

"Fine!" Elvis exploded. "Don't come! Just give E-Rod a chance! That's all I'm asking!"

"You know when's a great time to get a new nickname started? College," Jess said. "Not right now. College."

Kim cleared her throat warningly.

"Oh, calm down, Kim." Jess jostled Kim's shoulder good-naturedly. "I'm not violating any terms of the sacred Landis-Lilley-Lin Collegiate Accord. I can still *mention* the c-word."

Kim and Teddy had made a pact not to tell each other where they were going to college. They hadn't even talked about where they were applying. They'd agreed it was the only way they could each make sure they ended up at the best possible school for them. This way, neither one of them would be tempted to sacrifice anything for the other one. They'd choose their schools in a vacuum, and they'd work out whatever came next. Kim knew she'd love Teddy just as much whether he was right down the hall or across the country.

It was a good plan. It was a *smart* plan. It was the kind of plan that ensured their futures, that had made Mama K nod with approval when Kim had first come up with it as they scrolled through the Common App's website together in Mama Dawn's home office. But sometimes, Kim was so desperate to know if she'd be anywhere near Teddy she wanted to abandon the plan altogether and demand he produce a list of every single school he'd applied to, preferably organized geographically.

That was why she couldn't even mention the c-word. Her resolve wasn't nearly as firm as Jess thought it was.

"Want to hit up the vending machines before lunch ends?" Teddy asked as Jess and Elvis continued to bicker. "M&M's on me."

"I think you know the answer to that one."

Kim loved M&M's the way she loved Teddy. She literally could not imagine her life without them. Good thing she'd never have to.

Ready for M&M's and ready to be done with the whole E-Rod thing, Kim finished the last bite of her turkey sandwich and zipped up her lunch bag. Jess didn't even break stride in her argument with Elvis, but still managed to wave goodbye to Kim as she and Teddy left the table, arms wrapped around each other's waists.

"You know Ms. Johansson's trying to get them to take all the candy out of the vending machine," Teddy said casually as they headed out of the cafeteria toward the gym, like that wasn't going to totally ruin senior year.

"No way. She wouldn't."

"She was talking to Principal Manteghi about it outside the lounge. Healthy choices. All that stuff. But I don't think Manteghi'd go for it. She's got that huge jar of candy on her desk."

"She better not go for it."

"Don't worry, Junior." Teddy squeezed her hand—once, twice. Kim squeezed his hand back, just once. The three squeezes—that was their thing. One of their things, anyway. "I know the vending machine is your favorite thing at William Henry Harrison High."

"*You're* my favorite thing at William Henry Harrison High."

But then something weird happened. Teddy didn't say, "You're *my* favorite thing at William Henry Harrison High." He didn't say anything.

As Teddy trailed to a halt in the middle of the gym, Kim looked up at him, wondering if maybe he'd stopped to kiss her. But Teddy looked like kissing her was the last thing on his mind.

"I'm not . . . I'm not *really* your favorite thing about high school, right?" he asked.

"Of course you are."

Kim had never felt more confused. Not even when the substitute had walked into English class and accidentally started doing a unit on *As I Lay Dying* when they were actually reading *Mrs. Dalloway*, and that had been extremely confusing.

"But, I mean, there's lots of other stuff." Kim was staring at Teddy talking like he was a substitute teacher going on about William Faulkner. "I mean . . . softball . . . community service . . . Jess . . . You do, um, lots of other stuff."

Kim was still staring at him. She had absolutely no idea what he was saying.

"It's senior year," Teddy continued. "It's almost the end of senior year, and I just don't want—"

"Am I not *your* favorite thing at William Henry Harrison High?" Kim interrupted him, because although she was still confused, she had a dawning feeling that all was not well. Never mind that he had brought up the fact that it was almost the end of senior year, which sounded like he was veering dangerously close to talking about *next* year, which was absolutely, 100 percent, full-on forbidden.

"No! I mean yes. I mean no?"

Maybe Teddy had confused even himself.

"I guess I just mean . . . that I just want to make sure you know that there's more to high school than just Teddy-and-Kim. There's more to *life* than just Teddy-and-Kim."

Kim recoiled like she'd been splashed by icy cold water. Of course she knew there was more to life than her relationship! That was the exact reason she'd proposed the Secret College Plans Plan in the first place! Teddy—*her Teddy*—couldn't possibly have said that. He couldn't possibly *mean* it. But Teddy never said things he didn't mean, so he must have meant it.

"I know there's more to high school than 'just Teddy-and-Kim.'" *Just.* Kim couldn't believe he was describing them as a *just*. Before this very moment, Kim hadn't known that it was possible to air-quote coldly, but boy, she was air-quoting in the coldest way possible. "I have a very full life, Teddy. You just happen to be my favorite thing about it. But if you don't feel that way, then you should just break up with me."

What was happening?! The words had tumbled out of Kim's mouth before she even really knew what she was saying. Had she just told Teddy to break up with her?

"Wow." Teddy took a couple steps back, away from her. "Uh . . . okay, then."

Now it was Kim's turn to stumble back a few steps. Her brain was malfunctioning. Okay? *Okay?!?!* She'd kind-of-accidentally told Teddy to break up with her, and he'd just said *okay*?!

A breakup? It seemed impossible—a doomsday scenario Kim had never prepared for, but here it was, happening. Her destiny, all five foot ten of him, *okay*-ing her into a breakup she hadn't wanted at all. This was it. The end. No solar flare, no sonic boom, just an *okay* and nothing more.

She had to leave. She couldn't even *look* at him anymore. But where could she go that wasn't haunted by a memory of her-and-Teddy? Even right here in this gym, they'd survived running sprints together. Outside this room was the vending machine where he'd bought her more M&M's as an apology for eating all of hers—the vending machine where he'd been about to buy her M&M's before everything had gone so horribly, horribly wrong. And then out into the hallway where they'd held hands so many times. Nowhere was safe.

But standing here, Teddy looking at her like she was a stranger, was the least safe place of all.

So Kim ran. She ran faster than she'd ever run the bases in softball, even faster than she ran during that game in Elgin last year that went into extra innings. Kim flew out the door, past the vending machines, and down the hall, with no other thought than getting away as fast as she possibly could.

Kim ran so fast she didn't notice Phil Spooner, frozen in front of the vending machine, his fingers poised to press A3 so he could get a bag of Garden Salsa Sunchips.

CHAPTER TWO

PHIL SPOONER
DAY ONE

Very few people *did* notice Phil Spooner, as a matter of fact. First of all, he was a freshman, which already made him basically invisible to the senior class. Second of all, Phil had the kind of face that was best described as forgettable. The kind of face that someone had once described as "a white guy with . . . hair?" The kind of face that meant the office was unable to locate his school pictures this year because nobody could quite remember what he looked like. And third of all, Phil Spooner didn't really have a "thing." He wasn't particularly brilliant in any of his classes, didn't play any sports, couldn't be described as artistic or musical or anything like that. He was just a guy. And there wasn't anything wrong with being just a guy.

But Phil Spooner wouldn't be "just a guy" for much longer.

Because Phil Spooner had inadvertently witnessed something *monumental*.

The doors to the gym were propped open, like they usually were. And just as Phil had been about to press A3 and get those Sunchips, he heard someone say, clear as day, "If that's how you feel, then you should break up with me!"

And then *Kim Landis-Lilley*, of all people, had run out of the gym, *crying*.

It didn't take a Sherlock Holmes to deduce what had just happened. Even a Phil Spooner could figure it out. As impossible as it was to believe, Kim Landis-Lilley and Teddy Lin had just broken up. And Phil Spooner was the only one who knew.

There was a rumor that Kim and Teddy had been together since the day they were born. According to this rumor, their moms had given birth at the same hospital, and the nurses had found the two babies holding hands in those little plastic tubs people put newborn babies in. Phil didn't buy that for a second. He'd visited his cousin Eva in the hospital when she'd been born, and Eva certainly couldn't have reached an arm out of her little plastic baby tub to grab another baby's hand. The whole idea was ludicrous, not to mention physically impossible. But maybe the rumor was more of a metaphor. Because Phil did know that Kim and Teddy had been together long, long before he had arrived at William Henry Harrison High, and he had assumed they'd be together long after he left.

Phil pressed A3, and his Sunchips tumbled out of their appointed place. This was very interesting information, he mused as he retrieved them. This was quite possibly the *most* interesting information Phil Spooner had ever learned, and Phil Spooner certainly knew his way around interesting information. For example, he had learned a lot of interesting information when he'd visited the National Air and Space Museum with his parents in Washington, DC, last summer. But he wasn't sure what, exactly, to do with his newfound knowledge.

And just as he opened his bag and popped a Sunchip into his mouth, Jess Howard walked into the vending machine vestibule, cementing this as the most dynamic snack purchase Phil Spooner had ever made. Jess, Phil knew, was Kim's best friend. Phil had seen Kim and Jess eat lunch together every day, a lunch that Jess always finished off with a single clementine. He also knew Jess had a great love for dystopian fiction and pink Starbursts, because she frequently spent her free period—the same free period Phil Spooner had—reading in the library and would often leave behind a pile of Starburst wrappers. Phil believed this to be accidental littering and not malicious, but he had no proof of this.

Only a belief that someone who read that much couldn't possibly be bad.

"Are you looking for Kim?"

Phil Spooner had spoken aloud to Jess Howard. They had been in the library for the same free period all school year—Phil tried to do some quick mental calculations to figure out how much time they'd spent together, but failed—and in all that time, he'd never once spoken to her. He'd admired her elegant hands as they unwrapped Starbursts, he'd noted her astounding focus as she read, but he'd never, ever spoken to her. As if a lowly freshman like Phil Spooner would talk to a senior like Jess Howard, but here he was: talking.

"Yeah." Jess looked at Phil like she hadn't noticed him standing there. Probably, she hadn't. That happened to him a lot. "Yeah, I am looking for Kim, actually. Who are you?"

"Phil. Phil Spooner."

He held out his hand for her to shake, but she didn't take it. Probably because there was visible Sunchip dust on it. Phil wiped his hand on his pants.

"Okay, then, Phil Spooner. Have you seen Kim?"

"She ran that way." Phil pointed down the hallway with his still-orange finger. The Sunchip dust was more tenacious than he'd anticipated.

"'Kay. Thanks."

Jess Howard turned to go. No! She couldn't leave, now that they were actually talking!

"Kim was crying," Phil blurted out. Was that too negative? Should he have led with something nicer? So Jess Howard could see he was a positive, fun-loving guy? Well, maybe it didn't matter. "Kim and Teddy broke up." Phil saw quickly that this had stopped Jess Howard in her tracks.

"No, they didn't," Jess scoffed. Phil had never heard someone scoff quite so thoroughly as Jess Howard scoffed in that moment.

"They did. I heard it. And then Kim ran out, crying."

"No way."

This, Phil had not anticipated. That Jess—or anyone else— might not believe him. But why *would* she believe him? Who was he to her but an anonymous freshman with a forgettable face who had once been to the National Air and Space Museum?

"They broke up. Seriously."

"Okay, *Phil Spooner*," Jess said, like that was allegedly his name, although it was definitely his name. "Why did they break up?"

Hmm. Well. As his theater teacher, Mr. Rizzo, liked to say, ah, there's the rub. Phil didn't *know* why they'd broken up. But he felt convinced that he *had* to know, or at least pretend he knew, or no one would ever believe he'd heard what he'd heard.

As a general rule, Phil was not a liar. In fact, he considered himself a very honest, straightforward sort of person. When he'd read *Divergent*, because Jess Howard had been reading *Divergent*, he'd wondered if he might have been part of the Candor faction, because up to this point, Phil had really prided himself on his honesty.

(Jess Howard, in case anyone was wondering, was Dauntless through and through, although Phil suspected she was probably Divergent as well.)

But in this very moment, all Phil Spooner could do was lie.

"He didn't like any of her Instagrams!"

Phil didn't know *why* that was the sentence that came out of his mouth. But it was, and there was nothing he could do about it now.

Jess Howard took a few steps closer to him. She was close enough that Phil could see how long her eyelashes were as she narrowed her large brown eyes.

"Kim broke up with Teddy because he *didn't like her Instagrams?*"

He'd blown it. Phil had totally blown it. But he couldn't do anything else but nod, solemnly, because once you'd started to improv, you had to go with it. He could hear Mr. Rizzo in his head shouting, "Yes AND, Spooner! YES AND! For the love of Leslie Howard, stop contradicting your scene partner!"

(Phil didn't know who Leslie Howard was. And he definitely didn't love her.)

"That scruffy-looking nerf herder," Jess growled, of all the improbable things to growl. "I knew it. I *knew* that bothered her. But she can never admit that anything is wrong with perfect Teddy. But something's gotta give eventually, right, Spooner?"

"Right," Phil agreed, unable to believe that this was, miraculously, working.

"That was a really big win for them last weekend, and Kim was so proud of that pic with her and the rest of the team after the game. Do you know how hard it is to take a cute Insta in a softball uniform, Spooner? Do you know?"

"I do not."

"Can you imagine having literally *hundreds* of likes and *your own boyfriend* isn't even one of them?"

"I literally cannot."

@The_Philver_Spoon had exactly two Instagram posts, both of which Phil had taken at the National Air and Space Museum last summer. He'd then abandoned Instagram after that brief experiment.

"This is emblematic, honestly. It's emblematic of the

whole thing." Phil had never been part of anything emblematic before. It was all happening so fast. "With Teddy and Elvis, it's always *baseball season* this and *baseball season* that. You know, it's *softball* season, too! That's got bats! Bases! Balls! Hats! What about equality, Spooner? What about Title IX? What about *respect*?"

"Oh, most definitely."

Phil didn't even know what he was saying. But he knew he agreed with Jess Howard 100 percent, and that was what mattered.

"Thank you, Phil." Jess Howard placed a hand on his arm. A part of Jess Howard was touching a part of Phil Spooner. Phil stared at the hand, far more elegant up close than it was when he'd observed it from across the library, almost mesmerized by her warm brown skin and the bright pops of turquoise nail polish. Phil felt that same sense of wonderment and awe he'd experienced when he'd stepped through the doors of the National Air and Space Museum and hadn't experienced since. "Thank you for letting me know," she said seriously. "I have to go find Kim."

She disappeared then, but Phil swore he could smell a sweet, fruity scent lingering in the air.

Like a clementine.

CHAPTER THREE

OLIVIA LANDIS-LILLEY
DAY ONE

There were a lot of injustices about being a freshman, but having a locker on the third floor was the worst of them all. And it wasn't that Olivia Landis-Lilley minded climbing three flights of stairs, because she didn't. Stair work was a good, challenging form of cardio, and she'd definitely noticed more definition in her calves since the beginning of freshman year. What she *did* mind was how much time it took. Sure, most of her classes may have been on the third floor, but lunch wasn't. And making the trek down from the third floor to lunch meant the freshmen were always last to lunch, and therefore had the shortest lunch period, which was just rude. Never mind the sprint she'd have to do to come up here and get all her softball crap before practice at the end of the day. And again, the sprint up the stairs was good cardio, but if she was late to practice, she'd have to do *more* sprints, and she didn't want to build up too much lactic acid. Olivia tried to stay positive, tried to remember the calf definition, but it was hard not to be grumpy anytime she'd made the climb to the third floor.

"Olivi-aaaah." Olivia's best friend, Daisy, liked to address her like that, emphasis on the *aaaah*. Daisy popped around Olivia's open locker, her topknot quivering from the sudden movement as she peered into Olivia's space. "Did you do the Adverb Intro thing for Powell?"

"Obviously." Mama K still checked her planner to see what her homework was and *then* checked her homework to make sure she'd done it right. Annoying. Olivia probably could have forged a fake planner to throw her off the scent, but that seemed like more work than just doing her homework.

"Well, Powell didn't do a great job of introducing them, because I have no idea what an adverb is."

"Modifies a verb. Describes *how* you do something. Usually ends in *-ly*," Diamond Allen said from down the hall, where she was stuffing books into her bag. "Can also be used to modify an adjective, but that wasn't on the homework."

"Gracias." Daisy scribbled on the blue worksheet.

Another group of freshmen came up from lunch. Daisy scooted out of the way as Evan Loomis came over to open his locker, nodding at Olivia. In nearly a year of having lockers next to each other, the nod was the only form of communication they'd exchanged. Which was totally fine with Olivia. Unlike her older sister, Kim, Olivia did not believe you were forced by destiny to fall in love with someone just because they happened to come next to you in the alphabet. Of course Olivia loved Kim, in the way all sisters were kind of obligated to love each other, but she definitely didn't understand her.

"Can we help you?" Daisy must have been talking to someone behind Olivia. Olivia turned to see who it was.

"Oh, hi, Phil," Olivia said. Phil Spooner looked nervous—which was weird—as he shuffled from side to side in front of the lockers. Olivia hadn't had a ton of interactions with Phil Spooner, but he'd been a totally serviceable partner in PE this morning. Usually, Olivia preferred to pick her own partner, but she knew Coach Mendoza wouldn't stick her with a dud. Phil had done an A+ job of holding down her feet while she knocked out fifty-four sit-ups in a minute—a new personal best—and that made him more than all right in Olivia's book.

Phil still hadn't said anything while Olivia had gone on that mental jog back to PE. He coughed once, awkwardly, but didn't form any words.

"Can I, um, help you?" Olivia asked, though not as rudely as Daisy had.

"I have something to tell you," Phil said gravely.

Had he counted her sit-ups wrong? Had Phil fudged the numbers, for unknown reasons, and maybe she *hadn't* broken her record? No. She'd counted, too. That couldn't be it. So why was Phil Spooner standing in front of her, looking like he'd run over her dog?

Olivia didn't *have* a dog. She had a guinea pig named, stupidly, Baby Ruth, who everyone called Baby. And she really doubted Baby could have gotten out of her cage, out of the house, and onto the road. But that was the kind of devastation she imagined as she heard Phil Spooner's awkward cough.

"You're being weird, Phil Spooner." Daisy narrowed her eyes and stuck her purple pen right through the middle of her topknot. "Spit it out."

Gabe Koontz arrived to open his locker, the one on the other side of Olivia's, jostling Phil and Daisy and Olivia closer together.

"Sorry," Olivia said as she bumped into Evan Loomis.

"No worries," he said, and just like that, their months-long streak of only nodding to each other was over.

"Kim and Teddy broke up," Phil mumbled.

"Kim Landis-Lilley and Teddy Lin *broke up*?!" Diamond Allen shouted from down the hall. She really had remarkable hearing.

"I thought you should know," Phil mumbled again.

Maybe Phil had thought just Olivia should know. But now *everyone* knew. Olivia could hear them all talking, conversations traveling down the hall, a waterfall of "Kim-and-Teddy Kim-and-Teddy Kim-and-Teddy."

"Kim and Teddy really broke up?" Evan Loomis asked. Someone was being remarkably chatty today.

"Really." Phil nodded. "I'm sorry, Olivia," he added, like he had actually run over her guinea pig, instead of announced that her perfect sister had parted ways from her equally perfect boyfriend, for some unknowable but undoubtedly perfect reason.

Phil was looking at her like she should be upset, but she

wasn't. It's not that Olivia had *wanted* Kim and Teddy to break up. Teddy was always really nice to her. And Kim and Teddy were never gross, like Sophie Maeby and Nico Osterman, who were also in Kim's class. For example, Olivia had never seen Teddy's tongue before, thank God, and she had seen Nico Osterman's tongue *multiple* times, which told you everything you needed to know about the depth and breadth of Sophie Maeby and Nico Osterman's crimes against PDA.

No, Kim and Teddy were only gross in the way that sometimes things are so cute they become gross, like a folder with a picture of kittens sitting in flowerpots on it. Ms. Powell had this exact folder in her room, and sure, it never actively bothered Olivia during English, but she didn't exactly love sharing a space with it, either. Which is why she usually hid in her room when Teddy came over, and left him and Kim to do gross things together like bake cookies or play catch or paint picture frames for displaying printouts of their selfies.

It was like they were running a summer camp for codependency.

"Why would you know this?" Daisy asked. "Like, I gotta be honest, Phil Spooner, this is pretty random, coming from you."

"Yeah, Phil," Diamond Allen chimed in. Olivia hadn't realized she'd come over. Olivia hadn't realized an entire crowd of freshmen had formed around her locker. Or that even Gabe Koontz and Evan Loomis were looking at her. After a lifetime of anonymity, Olivia was finally interesting. Not because she was the only freshman on the varsity softball team, not because she had the fastest mile time for girls in her class, not because she'd knocked out fifty-four sit-ups this very morning, but because of her sister. Awesome. Exactly like Olivia had always dreamed it would be. "Who told you this?"

"Nobody told me this," Phil said, his voice getting louder. "I was there. I was there when it happened. I heard it myself."

All around Olivia, all she could hear was shouts and shrieks and "What!" and even more "Kim-and-Teddy Kim-and-Teddy Kim-and-Teddy."

"What did they *say*, Phil?" Diamond asked eagerly as more voices from the crowd joined in.

"Yeah!"

"What did they say?"

"Who broke up with who?" Evan Loomis, again? Olivia stared at him in bewilderment. He'd finally decided to speak, and *this* was what he wanted to talk about?

"It's *with whom*, Evan, and you should know that!" Diamond Allen said. "Is nobody else paying attention in English?"

"I am," Olivia muttered, but no one could hear her. She'd found herself somehow pushed away from her locker as the crowd pressed eagerly toward Phil Spooner, her backpack abandoned among the teeming masses. She couldn't even hear what Phil was saying anymore. Not really. Something about Instagrams, maybe? That didn't make any sense. DMs? That made less sense. A Mercedes-Benz? Definitely not. Now she was just rhyming random words. Olivia couldn't even make out who had broken up with whom. As if Kim could ever break up with Teddy.

Kim. Olivia thought about her sister, *actually* thought about her sister, for the first time. If Teddy had broken up with Kim, she was going to be devastated. Like, someone-ran-over-her-nonexistent-dog devastated. Olivia couldn't even remember a time before Teddy. Kim and Teddy had been best friends since before Olivia could remember. Maybe even since before she was *born*. There were pictures of a tiny Teddy next to an infant Olivia! Teddy was even more integral to Kim's life than *Olivia* was, which was kind of depressing. What would Kim *do* without Teddy? She didn't do anything without him now. Even when they were separated, which was rarely, they were in constant communication. When they'd gone to the Bahamas on vacation this year, Kim had set up a FaceTime with Teddy so he could watch her eat breakfast. It was way more embarrassing than all the people taking pictures of the buffet. What if Kim was physically unable to function without him? Would Olivia have to feed her, like a baby?

Olivia was already the sole caretaker for Baby the guinea pig. She wasn't sure she had time for the care and keeping of a distraught older sister. Olivia had a *lot* going on. Not that anybody else seemed to notice. Or care.

BANG! The door to the third-floor copy room slammed open with such force that Diamond Allen screamed. Standing in the doorframe was a shocked Ms. Powell, clutching a folder that was mercifully free of cats.

"Loitering!" Ms. Powell said, the giant statement necklace on her chest quivering with indignation. "Loitering is strictly prohibited by the Student Code of Conduct. I suggest you get a move on if you want to avoid detention!"

Everyone started to disperse, and the "Kim-and-Teddy Kim-and-Teddy Kim-and-Teddy" was more of a murmur than a roar, but it was still going. Could Phil Spooner be right? Had Kim and Teddy really broken up? Obviously, Phil Spooner had no reason to lie, but the whole situation was so unbelievable, Olivia was having a hard time processing any of it. Like when Daisy showed her that video of a guinea pig on a skateboard. It just didn't make any sense. Guinea pigs didn't have the mass necessary to steer a skateboard. And Kim didn't have it in her to break up with Teddy. Which meant *Teddy* must have broken up with *her*. Although that made about as much sense as a guinea pig on a bicycle. *Nothing* made sense.

"Are you okay, Olivia?" Ms. Powell asked urgently, now that they were almost alone in the hallway. Phil Spooner had gone, taking his news with him. Only Daisy and Evan Loomis were waiting in the hallway, standing by Olivia's locker. Evan was holding Olivia's backpack. He must have picked it up to save it from trampling, since it didn't look trampled at all. "Olivia. Are you okay?" Ms. Powell asked again.

"Um. Yes?"

Olivia knew that yes wasn't a question. It was supposed to be an answer. But she did question why all these people thought *she* was so upset. Maybe they'd assumed Teddy Lin had been the brother she'd never had.

Oh, for Pete's sake, Olivia thought as Ms. Powell patted her arm comfortingly. It's not like Kim and Teddy had gotten divorced. They'd broken up. And it had nothing, nothing whatsoever to do with Olivia.

"Carry on, Olivia!" Ms. Powell proclaimed, like she was Winston Churchill or something. Olivia felt reasonably optimistic that she'd have no problem carrying on. With one final pat, Ms. Powell shut the door to the third-floor copy room firmly behind her and sprinted down the hall. Ms. Powell ran like she'd never heard of lactic acid buildup in her life, and if she hadn't been weighed down by that statement necklace, Olivia suspected she might have made pretty good time.

CHAPTER FOUR

MS. POWELL
DAY ONE

Ms. Powell, in general, did not run. She believed exercise was for people who had time, and time was emphatically a thing Ms. Powell did not have. A math teacher, for example, might be able to exercise. Math teachers could never understand how time-consuming it was to grade essays, dozens and dozens of endless essays. Ms. Johansson, for example, was always going on about her Zumba marathons or her HIIT intervals or her CrossFit box, whatever that was. If Ms. Powell had the kind of time Ms. Johansson did, maybe she'd have a CrossFit box, too. Maybe she'd run. But Ms. Powell ran today. She ran like she didn't know running in the hallways was expressly prohibited by the Student Code of Conduct.

God, these stairs are brutal. Ms. Powell hated being stuck up on the third floor with the rest of the ninth-grade team.

It was always a thousand degrees up there, except in the winter, when it was negative a thousand degrees, and it took her forever to get down to the teachers' lounge. But today, it took her no time at all. Because even though the door to the third-floor copy room had been closed, and even though both copiers had been noisily printing away, Ms. Powell had heard every word Phil Spooner had said.

Well, she'd heard almost every word. But she'd heard more than enough.

CHAPTER FIVE

MS. SOMERS
DAY ONE

On good days, Ms. Somers saved her Light 'n' Fit Strawberry Cheesecake Greek yogurt for last. Today, she whipped off the lid and dug into it first.

Was it summer yet? So far, the last quarter of the year felt longer than the other three put together. It had been worse than the stretch from Columbus Day until Thanksgiving break, which Mr. Rizzo liked to call Awful-tober.

Clearly, she wasn't the only one feeling the strain. As she looked around the teachers' lounge, she saw purple bags under everyone's eyes and giant mugs of coffee in everyone's hands. Ms. Somers's eyes met Coach Mendoza's, and he nodded at her sympathetically from his table where he sat with the other PE teachers, each of them demolishing their own rotisserie chicken. Ms. Somers wondered sometimes if maybe they all shared a Costco membership—they'd gone through a staggering amount of chicken this year. A chicken every day for lunch, for how many school days so far this year...? Well, she wasn't a math teacher. Yes, there was plenty of math involved in teaching orchestra, but none of it, luckily, involved word problems.

"You're not gonna believe this." Ms. Powell burst into the teachers' lounge like she'd run all the way there from the third-floor copy room, frizz escaping from her bun and papers escaping from the manila folder she was carrying. Maybe she *had* run all the way from the third-floor copy room. "Kim Landis-Lilley and Teddy Lin broke up."

"They did not," Mr. Rizzo scoffed from over by the Keurig machine. "Did someone use up all the Donut Shop K-Cups?"

"They *did*, Rizzo."

"Who did? Who used them up?" he demanded, eyes darting around the room. "Everyone knows I need my lunchtime Donut Shop!"

"Not the K-Cups. I'm talking about Kim Landis-Lilley and Teddy Lin!" Ms. Powell slammed her folder down on the table where Ms. Somers was sitting. Ms. Somers jumped at the force of the slam and watched a purple worksheet fly across the table to land on top of her quinoa salad. Carefully, she removed the Advanced Adverbs! worksheet from her lunch and put it back on top of Ms. Powell's folder.

"They did *not*, Powell." Evidently giving up, Mr. Rizzo grabbed a regular dark roast K-Cup from the wicker basket in the cabinet under the Keurig machine. "I literally just gave them a PDA warning."

"Well, the times, they have a-changed since then. I heard

Phil Spooner telling a group of people just outside the third-floor copy room."

"That's your source? Really? Phil Spooner?" Mr. Rizzo asked skeptically. "Come on, Powell. You're better than that."

By this point, everyone in the lounge was watching Ms. Powell and Mr. Rizzo face off. Even the PE teachers had stopped eating their rotisserie chickens.

"Who's Phil Spooner?" Mr. Dykstra jumped in, the Major Battles of World War I quizzes he'd been grading pushed off to the side.

"Phil Spooner's a freshman. That's the kid whose school pictures got lost," Ms. Johansson clarified. "He doesn't know Teddy or Kim. Why would he have any kind of valuable information?"

"Spooner and Landis-Lilley—Olivia Landis-Lilley," Coach Mendoza clarified, "were partners in PE this morning. He might have picked something up."

Ms. Somers shot Coach Mendoza a look. She would have thought he'd be above gossiping about students. He shrugged at her, grinned, and then ripped a leg off his chicken.

"Irrelevant." Mr. Rizzo popped his K-Cup in the Keurig and turned to face them as he brewed his coffee. "Teddy and Kim were kissing in the cafeteria *after* whatever block of PE Phil and Olivia have together. So I don't care how many partner sit-ups they did. It's got nothing to do with anything."

"Olivia Landis-Lilley has everything to do with everything," Ms. Powell shot back. "Because she was in the group of freshmen Phil Spooner was talking to. And when Phil said Kim and Teddy broke up, *Olivia didn't deny it.*"

The lounge was stunned into silence for a moment. All they could hear was the sound of Mr. Rizzo's K-Cup finishing its final brew, and then Ms. Johansson taking a very slurpy sip of Diet Coke.

"That doesn't necessarily mean anything," Ms. Somers was surprised to find herself saying. Coach Mendoza winked at her. Shoot! She didn't want to get involved! She always thought it was *weird*, the way all of her coworkers knew which students were dating each other, and now here she was, just as bad as they were. She frowned at Coach Mendoza. He shook his head and laughed, quietly, as he grabbed the communal bottle of Frank's RedHot and dumped some more on his rotisserie chicken. "I mean. Maybe Olivia just didn't want to gossip about her sister."

"You have a sister, Somers?" Ms. Powell asked.

Ms. Somers shook her head. She did not, in fact, have a sister.

"I rest my case," Ms. Powell said.

Ms. Somers wasn't sure what the case was. Then again, she didn't have a sister. Maybe that was exactly Ms. Powell's point.

"So?" Ms. Johansson took another extraordinarily slurpy sip of Diet Coke. "What happened?"

"Well." Ms. Powell cleared her throat. "Phil Spooner wasn't *exactly* clear on what *exactly* happened . . ."

"Oh, color me shocked." Mr. Rizzo tossed the empty K-Cup into the trash can.

"Two points!" Coach Mendoza said quietly. He got up and walked over to the whiteboard. Ms. Somers had to scoot her chair in so he could squeeze past her to put two new hash marks next to Mr. Rizzo's name on the K-Cup Basketball scoreboard. For a PE teacher, Coach Mendoza really didn't smell like sweat at all.

"What, exactly, is your problem with Phil Spooner?" Ms. Powell asked.

"Have you ever tried to put Phil Spooner into an improv group?" Mr. Rizzo stirred his coffee aggressively. "He is *dead weight* onstage. Not even Diamond Allen could save him, and that girl was born to *yes, and.*"

"Hello? Who cares about Phil Spooner's improv group? What did he *say?*" Ms. Johansson pressed. "Spill it, Powell. What did Teddy do?"

"Why are you assuming it was Teddy?" Shoot! Ms. Somers had already forgotten her vow to *stay out of it.*

"He's a guy." Ms. Johansson shrugged.

"Teddy Lin is a sweet kid," Ms. Somers argued. *Staying out of it* was out the window, apparently.

"Landis-Lilley's a great kid, too," Coach Mendoza said. "Kim Landis-Lilley," he added, for clarification.

They were both great kids. Kim and Teddy were really sweet together, too. Not like some of the other couples in the senior class, like Nico Osterman and Sophie Maeby, who were always in detention for excessive PDA, or even Jess Howard and Elvis Rodriguez, who argued all the time.

Ms. Somers would never admit it out loud, but if Kim and Teddy *had* broken up . . . Well, the very idea of it had her a little shook. Ms. Somers knew she certainly shouldn't place her faith in true love in a high school relationship, but they were just so cute together. She didn't even give them a PDA warning that time she saw them holding hands while they watched an abbreviated version of *The Merchant of Venice* performed by a visiting theater group at an all-school assembly at the end of the first semester. She couldn't. It had been too adorable.

"Let's have it, then, Powell," Mr. Rizzo said. "What did Phil Spooner say? Which one of these perfect specimens screwed up?"

"Now . . . I can't be exactly sure . . ." Ms. Powell sounded nervous, almost. "But it sounded like Phil Spooner said something about Kim sliding into someone else's DMs."

Mr. Rizzo burst out laughing.

"What's a DM?" Mr. Dykstra asked, his mustache twitching.

"Oh God, Dykstra, you don't need to know." Rizzo was still laughing. "Powell, check your ears. There's no way that's what it was. The kids aren't even on Twitter anymore."

The kids weren't on Twitter anymore? This was news to Ms. Somers. What were they on, then? When did she get so old?

"That's what he said!" Ms. Powell exclaimed.

"Come on. What's a DM?" Mr. Dykstra insisted.

"Direct message." Ms. Johansson popped open another can of Diet Coke. Someone was going into fifth period well caffeinated. "It's a way to communicate privately on Twitter. It's how all the former *Bachelor* contestants hook up with one another. Or how regular people hook up with pro athletes."

Ms. Johansson knew a lot about hooking up with famous people. Ms. Somers eyed her curiously. Had Ms. Johansson been hooking up with famous people all year and holding out on them? Now *that* would have been a really interesting conversation. Usually, at lunch Ms. Johansson talked about

That Time She Went to Cabo with Her Girlfriends, or the fact that Old Navy had really good activewear at a great price point, and neither of those was a particularly interesting conversation.

"Is Kim Landis-Lilley hooking up with a former *Bachelor* contestant or a pro athlete? Somehow, I have a hard time picturing either one," Mr. Rizzo said. "Especially considering that she is a *high school student.*"

"I'm just telling you what I heard!" Ms. Powell collapsed into the empty chair next to Ms. Somers, narrowly avoiding dunking her elbow into Ms. Somers's quinoa salad. Ms. Somers quietly scooted her salad out of dunking range.

"Maybe you misheard. Maybe they were talking about a different kind of sliding," Coach Mendoza suggested. "You know. Baseball. Softball. Lin and Landis-Lilley are both in the middle of pretty intense seasons."

"Oh, it's always balls and bats with you boys!" Ms. Powell sighed.

Coach Finn, who was not a boy, shot Ms. Powell a very pointed look before polishing off the last of her rotisserie chicken.

"Listen," Ms. Powell said. "I know what I heard. Kim Landis-Lilley and Teddy Lin broke up. And it sounds like it was all Kim's fault."

"Watch it, Powell." Coach Finn stood up and stretched. Ms. Somers could hear her vertebrae crack from across the room. "No smack talk about my best outfielder. Or I'll have you, and anyone else who says anything about Kim, running laps around the diamond."

"I'd like to see you try," Ms. Powell muttered.

Ms. Somers would also kind of like to see her try. Not that she had anything *against* Ms. Powell, not really, but Ms. Powell had a tendency to ask really long-winded questions at after-school all-staff meetings when Ms. Somers would rather be headed home. Watching Coach Finn boss her around the softball field would be pretty satisfying.

Coach Finn picked up her empty rotisserie chicken container and hurled it across the room, where it landed neatly in the trash can.

"How many points is that?" she asked.

"It's called K-Cup Basketball, Finn." Coach Mendoza shrugged. "You don't get any points for plastic chicken tubs."

The bell rang, startling Ms. Somers like it always did.

"You'll see!" Ms. Powell called as the teachers filed out of the lounge, hurrying to class. "They broke up, and I told you first!"

"Hey, Somers." Coach Mendoza stopped on his way out of the room, leaning over Ms. Somers's table. She watched the stopwatch around his neck swing back and forth. "You get all your chaperone credits yet?"

"Not yet." Ms. Somers put the lid back on her Tupperware and zipped it into her lunch bag.

"You should chaperone prom." She looked up from her Tupperware to see Coach Mendoza wink at her. "It'll be fun."

He sauntered out of the room, leaving Ms. Somers standing alone, clutching her lunch bag to her chest.

Maybe today wasn't such a bad day after all.

CHAPTER SIX

SOPHIE MAEBY
DAY ONE

Ms. Somers could be so cute if she just *tried* a little. That's what Sophie Maeby always thought, and today was no exception. Ms. Somers liked to wait outside the orchestra room and welcome them all into class one by one, which was kind of cute, but mostly annoying, unlike her wardrobe, which was not at all cute, and too bland to even *be* annoying. As Sophie waited in line to head into class, she took in today's tragedy. Way-too-big khaki chinos—classic teacher pants— a William Henry Harrison High polo—*ugh, no, Ms. Somers, you're better than that!*—and the same lumpy, ill-fitting cardi-gan that Ms. Somers always wore, the one she kept in her classroom for when it got cold. Hair in a messy ponytail. Sensible shoes. Random pencils sticking out of her pants pockets. Sophie wondered if there was a makeover show she could secretly submit Ms. Somers to. But that would probably embarrass Ms. Somers, and she'd never want to do that. Ms. Somers was the only teacher who didn't treat Sophie like she was a total waste of space. And it wasn't because Sophie was anything special at the violin. She wasn't. Ms. Somers was just nice to everybody. But maybe she needed to be a little nicer to herself. Sophie wondered if Ms. Somers was familiar with the term *self-care*. Her split ends suggested she probably wasn't.

"Babe." Nico slid both his arms around Sophie's waist, hugging her from behind, cutting in front of Josiah Watkins. "Babe. Hey. Hey, babe."

"Nico, what are you doing here?" Recently, Sophie felt like she'd had a hard time keeping the annoyance out of her voice when she talked to Nico. "You're gonna be late for English."

Orchestra was a Nico-free zone. It was one of two classes they didn't have together. Sophie wondered when she'd started thinking about things in terms of *Nico-free zones*.

"Relax, babe." Nico licked the side of her face. At one point, she might have found this endearing. Passionate, even. But now Sophie just hoped that Ms. Somers hadn't seen. Sophie felt pretty confident that Ms. Somers would never let anyone lick the side of her face, not even her boyfriend of ten months. Sophie wondered if Ms. Somers had a boyfriend. Probably not, based on her pants. Although Sophie immediately felt mean for thinking that.

"What do you want, Nico?"

"You."

Sophie made a noise. It kind of sounded like *engh*. Nico didn't seem deterred by it.

"Just learned something major, babe." Nico was managing to hug her as they moved forward in line. It would probably have been impressive if it hadn't been so inconvenient. Nico was like a sloth, like a heavy, six-foot-two sloth, and Sophie was the immobile tree branch forced to bear his weight. "Guess who just officially became prom king and queen."

"No one." Sophie dragged Nico forward a few steps. "Prom's not until May."

"But it's all set now. Babe, you're gonna look so hot in that tiara."

Sophie snorted.

"Nico, I'm not getting any tiara. Teddy and Kim are going to be prom king and queen. Everybody knows it. Everyone's known it since, like, the dawn of time."

"Not anymore they're not," Nico said smugly. "They broke up."

Sophie froze in her tracks. The line advanced ahead of her, leaving a gap. From behind her, Josiah Watkins tutted his disapproval, but tuts or no, Sophie couldn't keep the line going.

First of all, Josiah Watkins could wait. He and Chris Foster had held up the line yesterday discussing tux options for prom that wouldn't clash, and had then exchanged the kind of romantic goodbye that suggested they were about to be separated for much longer than a class period. And had Sophie tutted once? Nope. Sophie would never tut about love, no matter how long it held up the line for. But second

42

of all, and most importantly, Nico had just broken the kind of news that necessitated a pause. She needed to process what she'd just heard.

She couldn't believe it. Could. Not. Believe. It. Sophie couldn't have been more surprised if Ms. Somers had turned up for class today with a professional blowout and a gel manicure.

"Seriously? They broke up?" Sophie asked.

"Seriously."

"But *why?*"

"Not sure." She could feel Nico shrug behind her. "Sounded like something about Firenze? But that's not a word."

"Firenze is a word, Nico," Sophie snapped. "It's what Italian people call Florence. In Italy."

"Yeah, okay, yeah," he said equably, apparently oblivious to her snapping. "Yeah, that makes sense. Teddy's moving to Firenze, I guess. Not sure why that means they had to break up . . ."

"Of course they had to break up. Of course! Don't you see?" Sophie shook Nico off her. "Don't you see, Nico? Don't you see how romantic this is?"

"Um . . ." Nico stared at her blankly. "No?"

"He broke up with her *because* he loves her!" Sophie cried.

"Um . . ." Nico said again. "What?"

"He's ending things so he doesn't hurt her! So they don't have to do long distance! Because it would hurt him too much to be with her and not be *with* her! That's love, Nico! That's what *love* is!"

"Sophie?"

Sophie turned around to see that there wasn't anyone left in line anymore. Even Josiah Watkins must have walked around her at some point. There was only Ms. Somers, looking at Sophie with concern.

"You ready for class?" Ms. Somers asked.

The bell rang, meaning Nico was late for English, like Sophie knew he would be. She didn't even look behind her as Nico ran off down the hall. She was done looking at Nico Osterman.

Sophie was going to break up with him. Today. She couldn't spend another day as Sophie-and-Nico, not when she'd witnessed real love, *true* love, in the form of Kim-and-Teddy. Nico Osterman wouldn't know what romantic sacrifice looked like if it bit him in the nose ring. God, Kim was lucky. Sophie would give anything to experience the love of a true romantic like Teddy Lin. It was better to have loved and lost than never to have loved at all, Sophie was sure. And she was also sure she'd never really loved Nico. Not really.

Not like Teddy loved Kim.

CHAPTER SEVEN

NICO OSTERMAN
DAY ONE

As Nico fled down the hall toward English, he turned around to see Sophie disappear into the orchestra room as Ms. Somers shut the door behind her. Huh. That was weird. Usually, after they'd said goodbye, Sophie would kiss her fingers and then wave them at him, and then he'd do the same thing. That was, like, their *thing*.

She was being weird today. Nico had told her not to eat the hot lunch at school. He was pretty sure that there were mood-altering chemicals in there, maybe added in by the government, to try to keep the youth population docile. And the way Sophie was acting? Well, it was basically solid proof. But Sophie had a weakness for the crispy chicken sandwich in the cafeteria, no matter how much Nico warned her about what might be in there.

"Move it, Osterman!" Jess Howard barked as she stalked down the hall. Nico slid out of her way.

"Hey, Jess," he said. "Did you hear about Teddy and Kim—"

"Yeah, I *heard*," Jess snapped, cutting him off. "I can't believe it. Well, I *can* believe it. I just can't believe *him*. How could he do this to her?" Jess said that last part more like she was talking to herself, but Nico heard it anyway.

"Well, sometimes people have to do things."

"People don't *have* to do things." Jess Howard was glaring at him so fiercely that Nico quickly abandoned what he was *going* to say, which was that it wasn't exactly Teddy's fault that his family was moving to Firenze. "It's called free will, Osterman. It's called *choice*. Aren't you supposed to be in English right now?"

How did everyone know he was supposed to be in English? He watched Jess as she continued her march down the hall. Man, Nico would *not* want to be Teddy Lin right now.

CHAPTER EIGHT

JESS HOWARD

DAY ONE

Jess Howard was probably the only person at William Henry Harrison High who had thought that Kim and Teddy's breakup was inevitable. And it wasn't because she'd seen some secret flaw that was invisible to the outside world because she had the closest seat to view this paragon of a relationship. Well, Elvis also had the closest view, since he was usually right by her side when she hung out with Kim and Teddy, but Elvis didn't really count. Elvis was so oblivious he'd forgotten her birthday, their anniversary, and Valentine's Day every year since they started dating.

(People seemed to think Jess Howard was the kind of person who would be mortally offended by this, but honestly, she couldn't have cared less. They were just *days*. All holidays were a human construct. So were days of the week. Just a symptom of the human drive to impose order on a meaning-less universe. In a way, she almost respected Elvis's complete disregard for the calendar.)

So, no, Jess Howard wasn't privy to some secret flaw in the seemingly perfect union of Teddy and Kim that only she knew about. But that was exactly *why* she'd always suspected they'd break up. Because nothing was perfect. Perfect didn't exist.

People always thought she and Elvis were on the brink of breaking up. Yeah, they argued a lot, but who wouldn't argue with someone who had spent the past four years trying to rebrand himself as E-Rod? Someone who had a totally baseless and bizarre aversion to corn kernels, but was fine with eating it off the cob? These kind of illogical imperatives necessitated argument! Arguing was *normal*. What *wasn't* normal was dating someone since the dawn of time and then having one minor disagreement about who ate all the M&M's before an away game and absolutely nothing else.

Jess couldn't find Kim anywhere. She'd checked the girls' locker room, thinking that might have been a smelly safe haven, a decidedly Teddy-free zone. She'd stopped by Coach Finn's desk, thinking Kim might have gone to her softball coach for comfort. She'd even popped into the nurse's office, to see if Kim had tried to get sent home from school. And now Jess was just pacing around and around the building, wondering if she'd find Kim curled up in a ball somewhere, hiding beneath a bulletin board decorated with pictures of the track team.

Eventually, Jess's feet led her to the library. Maybe because this was her free period, and she always spent her free period in the library. It was as good a place to go as any. She did a quick scan—no Kim. Jess pulled out her phone to check again—no response to any of Jess's texts, missed calls, or voicemails. That's right. Jess was worried enough to *actually leave a voicemail*. For the first time, Jess considered the possibility that Kim might have left the building, that she could be wandering down the side of the road, alone, like a broken-hearted deer.

Kim *was* like a deer. Like a sweet, trusting, innocent, very speedy deer. And Teddy had blown her up like she was Bambi's mom and he was a hunter with a grenade launcher. And all Jess wanted was for Teddy to feel some of the pain that she knew Kim felt. So maybe that was why she passed through the library and into the computer lab. Maybe that was why she opened Facebook and clicked on Teddy's profile. Unbelievable! It still said he was in a relationship with Kim. And his profile picture showed Kim and Teddy cheering with Popsicles. Jess had taken that picture this summer. They'd been in Elvis's backyard, eating Popsicles and running through the sprinkler like they were seven instead of seventeen. Looking at it now, you'd never know what a snake Teddy was. And Jess wanted everyone to know.

Honestly, Teddy was lucky Jess's only weapon was a computer and not a spear, like Okoye in *Black Panther*. Although she didn't consider herself a violent person, right now, Jess wished she could summon the Dora Milaje and face down Teddy with an army of other Wakandan warrior women.

"Uh, Jess?" Elvis was now sitting at the computer next to her. Jess had no idea how long he'd been there.

"What are you doing here?" Jess was busy cropping Kim out of Teddy's profile picture. She didn't have time for Elvis.

"What are *you* doing?"

"It's my free period," she said. "I belong here. Aren't you supposed to be in AP Spanish?"

"I came to look for you. I heard this crazy rumor that Kim and Teddy—"

"Not a rumor." Perfect. Jess had gotten the crop just right. She sent the picture to the printer.

"Are you serious? Wait. Jess." Jess ignored him as she got up to wait by the big printer/copier in the corner. "Seriously? What happened?"

"He *broke her heart*, Elvis," Jess said fiercely. "And now, he's dead to us."

The printer spat out a picture of Teddy's giant face, grinning like he was the nicest guy in the world. Jess knew better. She grabbed a black Sharpie out of the cup of random pens sitting on the computer lab table.

"He's dead to us?" Elvis repeated. "Jess, he can't be dead to us. Teddy's my best friend."

Not a Teddy bear, Jess wrote at the top of the picture. *He's a SNAKE,* she wrote in huge block letters across Teddy's smiling face. Maybe it wasn't her best work, but Jess could always come up with something else later. She fed the picture back into the copier, wondering how much paper was in there. Two hundred copies seemed like a good start.

"Jess, what are you doing?"

"Just letting everyone know exactly who Teddy Lin is."

Jess pushed the big green start button, and the copier whirred to life.

"We know who Teddy is. He's my best friend. And he's your friend, too."

"Not anymore he's not." Jess turned and looked at Elvis, really looked at him, for the first time. "When Teddy broke up with Kim, he broke up with us, too. You have to pick a side."

"Can't I be Switzerland?" Elvis asked weakly.

"There is no Switzerland. There's only Team Teddy and Team Kim. And I know where *I* stand."

Jess picked up a hot copy of her Teddy snake poster, grabbed a piece of Scotch tape off the computer table, and taped it to Elvis's shirt.

"Now everyone will know where *you* stand, too," she said smugly.

Elvis gulped.

Jess pretended she didn't hear it.

She had a war to win.

CHAPTER NINE

ELVIS RODRIGUEZ

DAY ONE

Elvis had two problems. The first problem was that he was insanely, egregiously late for Spanish. The second problem was that he was wearing a snake-ified picture of his best friend on his chest.

Elvis decided to ruminate on the second problem while he walked his way down the hall to resolve the first problem.

Did Elvis *want* to be wearing a snake-ified picture of Teddy on his chest? No. Absolutely not. And the easiest way to fix that would be to remove it. But then that opened him up to a whole host of other problems . . .

Obviously, Elvis was an independent being, capable of independent thought and actions. He didn't *have* to agree with Jess. He rarely did, in fact. But above all things, Jess

Howard valued loyalty. Real, true, ride-or-die, I've-got-your-back-no-matter-what, I'll-be-there-when-the-chips-are-down loyalty.

It was the thing he loved most about her.

And Elvis had a feeling that Jess would view this whole thing as the ultimate loyalty situation. Not *just* the whole Teddy-snake-on-chest thing, but everything it symbolized. Taking sides. Choosing Kim. Turning against Teddy.

Because Jess was loyal, above all else, to Kim. And Elvis knew that Jess expected *him* to be loyal, above all else, to *her*. Which meant, essentially, choosing loyalty to Kim over loyalty to Teddy. And that just felt wrong. But not being on the same side as Jess felt equally wrong . . .

The snake-Teddy was still on his chest as he rounded the corner toward Señora Parrilla's room. Elvis passed a couple freshmen girls who stared at it, giggled, and then started whispering furiously as they hurried down the hall, reminding Elvis that the wearing of the snake-Teddy posed *another* problem, one that was more practical and tangible than the betrayal of his best friend.

The Student Code of Conduct was fairly liberal on the subject of dress code. There were only two things that were expressly prohibited. The first was revealing clothing, detailed in a short paragraph couched in sexist language. (Elvis hadn't even realized it was sexist until Jess had pointed it out. One of the many reasons he was so lucky he had her! Not that he *had* her, obviously. That was sexist, too.) The other was anything containing violent images or hate speech, and Elvis was pretty confident that calling Teddy

Lin a snake was much closer to hate than love on the speech spectrum.

He was now standing in front of Señora Parrilla's door, and he still hadn't figured out what to do. Wear the snake, and betray Teddy and risk violating the Student Code of Conduct? Or remove the snake, and betray Jess and risk her terrible wrath?

This was the kind of problem Elvis usually went to Jess with. But he obviously couldn't do that now. And that was the whole problem.

By the time Señora Parrilla opened the door, Elvis still hadn't made a decision.

Which meant the decision was made for him.

"Hola, Elvis," Señora Parrilla said wryly. "Gracias por acompañarnos."

"Lo siento," Elvis replied. "Baño." He grimaced and rubbed his stomach.

"Uh-huh." Señora Parrilla rolled her eyes, but she let him into the room anyway. She probably wouldn't mark him down as tardy, either. Señora Parrilla was cool like that.

She was also not wearing her glasses. Which was probably why she didn't notice the giant Teddy on Elvis's chest.

But from the gasps, giggles, and shocked whispers as Elvis walked into the room, he was willing to bet she was the only one who *hadn't* noticed.

Alea iacta est. Elvis didn't take Latin, but Jess did. And she said "Alea iacta est" often enough that he knew what it meant. Usually she said it after he'd ordered loaded potato skins and then decided he actually wanted mozzarella sticks but the waitress had already walked away. Or after he told

Jess to click on the pair of sweatpants but then decided he meant jeans on the "Build Your Perfect Outfit and We'll Tell You Which Disney Prince Is Your Soul Mate" BuzzFeed quiz she'd made him take. (Elvis had gotten Prince Naveen. He felt like he could have done a lot worse.)

Alea iacta est meant "the die is cast." He had passed the point of no return. What was done could not be undone. What was seen could not be unseen. And from now on, Señora Parrilla's AP Spanish class could not unsee the smiling, happy face of Elvis's best friend, the word *SNAKE* writ large across Teddy's forehead.

Elvis slumped into his seat, trying to sink as low as possible, trying to hide the hallmark of betrayal emblazoned on his chest, way worse than Hester Prynne's scarlet *A* back in tenth-grade English.

But it didn't matter how much Elvis slumped. They had all seen it.

Alea iacta est.

CHAPTER TEN

PRINCIPAL MANTEGHI
DAY ONE

There were a couple different games Principal Manteghi liked to play while she was talking on the phone. One of which was seeing how quietly she could unwrap and eat one of the Hershey's Special Dark Kisses she kept in a giant glass jar on her desk. She had gotten so good at this she could have qualified for the Olympic team, if there had been an Olympic event in Silent Chocolate Eating.

"Absolutely," she said into the phone as she unwrapped her third Kiss of this phone call, the superintendent none the wiser as he droned on about his plans to repave all the parking lots in the district.

Another game she liked to play was trying to think of all the famous principals in pop culture. There was Mr. Belding, obviously, from *Saved by the Bell*. She couldn't quite remember if Mr. Feeny had become principal on *Boy Meets World*, but the only rule of the game was, obviously, no googling. Her favorite was Principal Duvall in *Mean Girls*. Tim Meadows was perfection. It always kind of bummed her out that the only female principal she could think of was Principal McGee from *Grease*, and she might have been even less competent than Mr. Belding.

But again, that was pretty much the point of her whole career. Exactly the reason she was here—to prove that accomplished, capable women thrived in positions of authority. Principal Manteghi said "Mm-hmm" into the phone as she adjusted the framed photo on her desk, looking at her twenty-one-year-old self grinning, arms around two of her fellow Teach For America corps members.

And look at her now. Saving the youth of today, one school parking lot at a time.

"Absolutely, Tim." *Absolutely* was Principal Manteghi's favorite phone word. She really thought it conveyed a sense of commitment. "I've already got the date circled on my calendar. The first weekend in May sounds like the perfect time to repave the parking lot. Yes. Mm-hmm. Uh-huh. Absolutely."

Tim Harwood was good at his job—no, *great*. He was a fantastic superintendent. But he was awfully hard to get off the phone.

"Sounds good, Tim," Principal Manteghi said firmly. You had to be firm with Tim or you'd be on the phone until graduation. "Yup. Mm-hmm. Absolutely. I've gotta jump—new hire interview. Yes. Okay. Sounds good, Tim."

Principal Manteghi hung up the phone as she slipped

her feet back into her heels, checking her hands for any chocolate stains. None, obviously. She was a chocolate-eating Olympian. Hopefully, this would be her last interview, and she'd be able to tell Señora Parrilla today that they'd found someone to sub during her maternity leave. This candidate *seemed* like a good fit. Good on paper, anyway. But that had also been true of the last three she'd interviewed . . .

After a quick smoothing of her hair to make sure no frizz or flyaways were escaping her neat bun, she was ready. Of course, Lois at the front desk could have sent the new hire interviewees directly to her office, but Principal Manteghi liked to greet them at the front and walk them back herself. She felt like it gave a nice, personal touch. It let prospective staff members know that she was the kind of hands-on principal who was invested in every aspect of her school, and it let them know exactly the kind of place William Henry Harrison High was.

But as soon as she opened the door, Principal Manteghi started to doubt that she had any idea what kind of place William Henry Harrison High was. The walls were covered—absolutely covered—with black-and-white photocopies that had been scrawled on with markers. What was this? A burn book? Was this her own personal *Mean Girls*?! Principal Manteghi may have loved Principal Duvall, but that didn't mean she wanted to *be* him! Was she supposed to get a baseball bat? She didn't even know where Coach Mendoza *kept* the baseball bats!

Principal Manteghi ripped the nearest photocopy off the wall. Was that . . . *Teddy Lin*?! Principal Manteghi would have been less surprised to see the Easter Bunny in a burn book!

Teddy was one of the good kids. One she *never* had to worry about. Of course, Principal Manteghi cared deeply about the educational well-being of each and every one of her students, but there were some who caused her more stress than others. Teddy Lin wasn't one of them. She'd never heard anyone—teacher or student—with anything bad to say about Teddy.

Principal Manteghi prided herself on having an almost complete mental Rolodex of all her students—except for that one freshman with the unfortunate situation on picture day. *What was his name again?* She *still* couldn't remember. Maybe she shouldn't have stopped taking those ginkgo biloba supplements.

But Teddy Lin... Principal Manteghi flipped through her mental Rolodex. Teddy Lin: No serious disciplinary action in the past four years—just one phone call home about tardies his freshman year. Decent GPA. Baseball team. Homecoming king. Probably future prom king. Attached at the hip to Kim Landis-Lilley... Kim Landis-Lilley... who was suspiciously absent from this photo.

Cropped, by the looks of it. That shoulder could definitely have been Kim's. But what was Principal Manteghi doing, focusing on the shoulder?! There were words here!

"Not a Teddy bear," Principal Manteghi found herself reading out loud. "He's a SNAKE."

Crisis. This was officially a crisis. Of course, William Henry Harrison High wasn't some kind of idyllic Eden. Principal Manteghi had witnessed bullying before. She herself had even been the victim of a widely liked Instagram post where someone had photoshopped her head onto a series of Hillary Clintons in a rainbow of pantsuits. (Honestly, Principal Manteghi had kind of enjoyed that. She did appreciate a good pantsuit. But she'd still put up a halfhearted hunt for the perpetrator for appearances' sake.)

But this was no pantsuit Instagram. This was a full-on smear campaign targeting one of her school's kindest students—someone who had volunteered, repeatedly, to give tours to new kids, a job Principal Manteghi always had difficulty filling! She had to get these down. Now. Before anyone saw. And she had to find out who could possibly have done it.

"Principal Manteghi?"

She looked up at the sound of her name. An unfamiliar man was standing in the hallway. She found herself momentarily distracted by the shine of his dress shoes, the crease in his chinos, and the way his tie coordinated perfectly with the checks in his gingham button-down. Now *this* was how a teacher should dress. She was fairly certain Ms. Johansson had been wearing leggings on Tuesday. Athletic leggings. Appalling.

"Chris Guzman?" he said. "We spoke on the phone. I'm here for the long-term sub interview? But I can come back if you're . . . busy."

It was a *busy* of doom. Because with that *busy*, Chris Guzman, her afternoon interview appointment, couldn't help but cast his eyes toward the Teddy posters. Well, he certainly wasn't going to want to work here anymore. And Principal Manteghi would have to rip down the bulletin board that proudly proclaimed WILLIAM HENRY HARRISON: A SCHOOL THAT CARES! because that certainly wasn't true anymore, as evidenced by the Teddy Lin snake posters that were, ironically, covering it up at the moment.

"Mr. Guzman," Principal Manteghi said. "I'm so sorry. This isn't—"

The earsplitting ringing of the end-of-fifth-period bell interrupted Principal Manteghi's apology. It was all she could do to keep from screaming as students poured out of every door, filling the hallway with their shrieks of scandalized delight and their phones. Oh no, not their phones. Everywhere Principal Manteghi looked, there was another phone, shooting pictures of Teddy Lin the snake off to the internet, recording this incident for all of posterity. Oh God. Why hadn't she banned all phones on school grounds? Was that even a thing she could do? She'd call the superintendent. The superintendent . . . That sent Principal Manteghi down an even lower spiral. Tim, she was sure, would have plenty to say about this.

"Is this a bad time?" Chris Guzman shouted over the din of the students gossiping and immortalizing Principal Manteghi's lowest moment as an educator. "I can come back later."

It was, in fact, a very bad time.

CHAPTER ELEVEN

DAISY DIAZ
DAY ONE

The freshmen missed *everything* because they were sequestered on the third floor. It was honestly unconscionable. At every single assembly they had, Principal Manteghi was always going on and on about school culture and their shared community values, which were apparently the spirit of inclusiveness and honor or something like that. Principal Manteghi was super into the idea of the William Henry Harrison High "family." Daisy suspected Principal Manteghi was so into this idea because she was an only child. In Daisy's experience, families were noisy agents of chaos, and that sounded exactly like the kind of thing a high school principal would want to *avoid*, not embrace.

But even if Daisy was willing to go along with Principal Manteghi's metaphor—William Henry Harrison High as family—the construct totally fell apart when it got to the freshmen. You didn't stick your family up on the third floor, where they were boiling in the summer and freezing in the winter, where they were always late for lunch, and most importantly, where they missed all the gossip. Or maybe Principal Manteghi's idea of family was the Rochesters, from *Jane Eyre*. Because that meant the freshmen were Bertha Mason, Mr. Rochester's first wife he kept locked up, banging around the attic.

"Teddy Lin set a bunch of snakes loose on the first floor," Diamond Allen projected from all the way down the hallway as she burst out of history with panache.

"Diamond." Daisy tried not to roll her eyes as she maneuvered around Evan Loomis, escaping from math and ready to be done for the day. "Save the drama for Drama Club, okay?"

Honestly. Theater kids. Usually they were just textbook overreactors, but now it looked like they'd started just making stuff up out of nowhere.

"It's not drama!" Diamond protested, affronted. "It's *news*."

"Fake news, dude." Daisy readjusted her backpack strap, shifting her heavy load of books from one shoulder to the other.

"Nope. I heard it from Sam Akitis. He has math on the first floor because he skipped ahead to calculus."

Daisy paused. Sam Akitis, their class's resident math genius, *had* skipped ahead to calculus and did, in fact, have math on the first floor. He also wasn't a theater kid. He was a Mathlete. Didn't they deal in cold, hard facts, those math people? Could Sam give them some quantifiable data on the snakes? Then Daisy might be more likely to believe it . . . but no. It was too ridiculous for words.

"Are the snakes all gone?" Chloe Baker asked timidly, peeping over Diamond's shoulder. Now Daisy actually rolled her eyes. Typical. Chloe Baker was afraid of everything. When they'd gone on that choir trip to Six Flags, Chloe had spent the whole time sitting with the teachers because she was too scared to go on the roller coasters and she thought that log flume water would give you pinkeye.

Daisy had ridden the log flume four times and was totally pinkeye-free, so there.

"Coach Mendoza corralled all the snakes," Diamond reported. "You know he coaches wrestling in the winter sports season, so it wasn't a problem for him."

"Do you even hear what you're saying? Coach Mendoza *wrestled a bunch of snakes?* He's not Hercules!" Daisy jumped as Olivia banged open the locker next to her—she hadn't even realized she'd stopped in front of Olivia's locker. "Think about this logically, Diamond. Where would Teddy get a bunch of snakes?" Daisy paused, then asked Olivia in an undertone, "Teddy doesn't have a snake, right?"

"Nope." Olivia was hurriedly getting all of her softball stuff out of her locker, jamming it into her Adidas gym bag.

"I'm just glad all the snakes are gone," Chloe said.

"He's clearly deranged. Teddy, I mean," Diamond clarified. "I bet he released the snakes as some kind of revenge on your sister, Olivia."

Olivia grunted in response. Daisy thought it looked like she was trying to hide her head inside her gym bag.

"Kim doesn't care about snakes. It's not, like, an Indiana Jones thing." Daisy tried to think about what Kim was afraid of. Nothing came to mind. She was pretty tolerant of all kinds of creepy-crawlies—Daisy had watched Kim shepherd a gross bug to safety out of the Landis-Lilley household on more than one occasion. "So it doesn't even make sense as a revenge plot."

"The heart doesn't make sense, Daisy!" Diamond proclaimed. "Love is chaos! Like a hallway full of snakes!"

Oof. Maybe they should trap all the theater kids up on the third floor instead of the freshmen. Then they could spout their dramatic metaphors at one another and leave the rest of the school in peace.

"Hey! Wait!" Daisy called, noticing that Olivia was already poised at the top of the stairs. She stopped, but Daisy swore she could see every muscle in Olivia's body tense, like she was desperate to run down the stairs. Daisy popped open her locker, chucked her math book in there, grabbed her science homework, and ran to join Olivia on the stairs. They *always* walked down to the first floor together after school. Had Olivia really been about to leave without her?

"I don't wanna be late for practice," Olivia grumbled as they started walking.

"You never are." Daisy had to hustle to keep up with her. What was going on? Olivia wasn't really worried about the snakes, was she? First of all, there was no way that was real. And even if Teddy Lin had somehow actually unleashed a serpentine terror on the first floor, Kim probably would have sung them a song and escorted them out the front door like she was Snow White, only for reptiles instead of chipmunks and birds or whatever. "Can you believe Diamond?" Daisy prompted Olivia, hoping that might get her to open up. "Like, if there had been snakes on the first floor, they definitely would have stopped class or made an announcement or something."

Olivia only grunted in response. Daisy eyed her best friend critically. Something was definitely up with her. Maybe she *was* really upset about the Kim and Teddy breakup. Maybe Daisy had been foolish to think it wouldn't affect their lives that much. First Phil Spooner, now Diamond and the snakes . . . As Daisy stepped off the staircase onto the first floor, something drifted gently down from the ceiling, like a giant, eight-and-a-half-by-eleven snowflake. Daisy reached out and grabbed it out of the air.

It was a picture of Teddy, grinning behind black marker calling him a snake.

What the . . . Had *Kim* released the snakes?! Daisy wouldn't have thought her capable of that, not in a million years. But Daisy would never have thought Kim capable of *this*, either. Daisy tried to reconcile the Kim she thought she knew—Olivia's sweet older sister, who was always happy to drive them places, always asking if they needed help with their homework, always making them hot chocolate topped with ridiculous mountains of marshmallows—with a Kim who could cover the whole school with posters insulting her formerly beloved boyfriend.

Maybe Kim had been *too* sweet. Daisy's sisters never made her hot chocolate. And whenever she asked Rafa for a ride— her only sibling with a driver's license—he laughed in her face. Maybe Kim's sweetness had been hiding her diabolical side. Or maybe she'd snapped, and the breakup had released a font of heretofore hidden darkness.

Daisy wouldn't have believed it. But she looked down and saw a Teddy poster with a dirty footprint right on top of his smiling face. Unbelievable things were happening today.

Someone covered in Teddy posters walked by her like an Abominable Paper Snowman. Three girls trailed behind him, laughing and taking videos on their phones.

"Olivia," Daisy said suddenly, realizing that Olivia wasn't there anymore. "Hey! Olivia!" Daisy shouted.

But Olivia didn't respond.

Wherever she'd vanished to, she was long gone.

CHAPTER TWELVE

OLIVIA LANDIS-LILLEY
DAY ONE

There was something about the dirt of a softball diamond that grounded Olivia. It wasn't quite dirt, and it wasn't quite clay, but it was some magical substance in between. She dug her cleats into the ground and smiled, thinking there was nothing better than the faint stain of the diamond dirt that colored her socks all spring and summer long. If Olivia could have dug a hole in the diamond and buried herself up to the neck in the red dirt, she would have. Now *that* would be the kind of spa treatment Olivia would be interested in.

Olivia shifted back and forth, feeling her calves flex as she bounced up and down, keeping her muscles warm after running laps around the field. They were supposed to be tossing the ball around the diamond, but Wendy, their pitcher, was up talking to their catcher, the ball snug in her glove and tucked under her arm. Olivia looked around her. First and second base were gossiping, too. Molly Santos was hovering over at third base, looking desperate to run up to home plate and join in on their conversation. Clearly, Molly knew better than to try to talk to Olivia during practice. Olivia looked behind her to the outfield—there were two of them talking, too. Kim still hadn't shown up.

"Come on, Wendy," Olivia growled, annoyed. Were they going to do anything or just stand here chatting? Olivia looked to her right, where she could see the baseball diamond in the distance, close enough that the outfields might have overlapped if William Henry Harrison High ever produced a real powerhouse of a hitter, but not close enough that Olivia could discern anything beyond small figures around the bases. Were they having as many problems over there? Was Coach Mendoza content to let the team spend all of practice chatting, like Coach Finn apparently was?

Olivia was pretty sure it was Teddy over at second base, like always. Unlike Kim, Teddy must not have been distraught enough about his romantic problems to miss practice. Olivia couldn't believe Kim hadn't shown up. So irresponsible. The whole point of being on a team was that you couldn't let the team down. Nothing was more important than the team. Nothing.

Olivia was trying to think of a way she could tell Kim off that wouldn't result in Mama K forcing them to have a "deliberative dialogue" about dealing with sibling issues in a constructive way. Olivia didn't want to have any kind of dialogue. She just wanted to yell at Kim.

"Phan!" Coach Finn yelled at Wendy. "What are you doing up there? It's not social hour!"

Finally. Shamefacedly, Wendy scuttled back to the pitcher's mound and tossed the ball to Olivia. Olivia caught it easily, loving the smacking sound as the ball slid neatly into her glove. She threw it back to Wendy, who tossed it off to first.

"Landis-Lilley!" Coach Finn was jogging down the third-base line toward Olivia. She passed Molly and joined Olivia in that no-man's-land between second and third that had become her home. A freshman, playing shortstop on varsity softball. Olivia still couldn't believe it sometimes. "You heard anything from your sister?"

"Nope." Olivia deflated a little. Why did everyone only want to talk about Kim? Like, yes, boo-hoo, the breakup was tragic and all, but didn't everyone have better stuff to talk about? Coach Finn especially. They had a game against Jonathan Jennings High this weekend, and they'd only *barely* beaten them last game. Way too close for comfort.

"It's not like her to miss practice," Coach Finn said. "She's only missed two in the past four years, and she had doctor's notes for those."

"Maybe the snakes scared her off," Olivia muttered.

Coach Finn shot Olivia a look. Wendy threw the ball to Olivia and she caught it, grateful to have something to focus on besides Coach Finn. Even the softball field wasn't safe from Kim-and-Teddy anymore. Olivia threw the ball back to Wendy, hoping Coach Finn realized the conversation was over.

"Car!" Molly screamed.

A gray Honda Accord was barreling down the field,

headed straight toward the softball diamond. What was happening?! Instead of slowing down, it seemed to be speeding up.

"Run, ladies!" Coach Finn commanded, and the team scattered for the safety of the dugout.

But Olivia didn't run. She had a feeling, somehow, that the car was coming for her. She watched, instead, as Coach Mendoza started sprinting toward the car from the baseball field, waving his arms and shouting. She thought he might have been shouting, "The grass was just reseeded!" but he was too far away for her to be sure.

The car certainly didn't pay Coach Mendoza any attention as it drove onto the diamond. Olivia winced as it skidded to a halt, sending up a spray of red dirt onto her sweats. She had no info on when the grass may or may not have been reseeded, but tire tracks could *not* have been good for the field. The passenger door popped open to reveal Kim's best friend, Jess, sunglasses pushed up on top of her head and a crazed look in her eyes.

"Get in," Jess demanded. "We have to find your sister."

CHAPTER THIRTEEN

TEDDY LIN
DAY ONE

Usually, Teddy liked baseball practice. He liked it even when Coach Mendoza made them run sprints, like he had today. But today, no matter how fast he sprinted, he couldn't outrun the fact that everyone—including the entire baseball team—had seen all those posters. He swore that every time he turned around, all the outfielders were clustered together, staring at him. Talking about him, probably.

Man, today just needed to end. First, Teddy had accidentally broken up with Kim. Or she'd broken up with him? He still wasn't sure what had happened. But before he could *talk* to her about it, she'd run away. And then she hadn't been in English after lunch. And then when he got out of class, the entire senior hall was wallpapered with posters calling him a snake. A *snake*. He couldn't believe it. Apparently Kim *had* wanted to break up with him. Because the snake poster thing seemed like a pretty nuclear option after what he'd thought had just been a misunderstanding.

Corey Brooks, over at shortstop, turned to Teddy and pulled up his sweatshirt, flashing the snake poster he'd taped to his T-shirt. Awesome. Corey had now flashed Teddy four times, and Coach Mendoza hadn't noticed one of them. Coach Mendoza *had* noticed Elvis flipping Corey off from third base in retribution and made him run five laps around the field. Teddy appreciated Elvis's show of solidarity, but he couldn't help but be bothered by a small sliver of doubt that poked at the back of his brain. A poke that wondered why Elvis's sweater had looked oddly rectangular as they walked to the locker rooms—that wondered why Elvis had insisted on changing inside a bathroom stall—almost like Elvis had been trying to conceal a hidden snake poster . . .

No way. Teddy gritted his teeth and kicked the side of second base. Elvis wouldn't do that to him. And Principal Manteghi had promised that all the posters would be gone before tomorrow, and that whoever had put them up would be issued serious consequences. Kim, issued a consequence. Teddy couldn't even imagine it. The only consequence Kim had ever gotten was because of an overdue library book, and she'd been distraught until the librarian realized she'd reshelved the book wrong and Kim had of course turned it in, right on time. Because that was how Kim did things: right on time.

He wondered if she'd scheduled this breakup, too. If she'd penciled *Print Posters* into her planner right after lunch.

Teddy had bought that planner with her at Target. He'd

stood with her patiently for what had felt like hours as she flipped through the different planners and smoothed their shiny surfaces. Believe it or not, he used to think her planner thing was *cute*, loving the way she got so excited about a new calendar, her color-coded pens, her plethora of Post-it notes. Well, it was a post-Kim world. And Teddy would never use a planner again.

Not that he used one now anyway.

Kim had gotten him a planner, on that same Target trip. His didn't have metallic polka dots on it, like hers did. It was just plain black on the front, but Kim had printed out a picture of the two of them at the Target photo center and then taped it carefully into the inside cover. Was that why Kim had broken up with him? Because he never used the planner she got him?

No. Nobody liked planners that much. And Kim had been buying Teddy planners he didn't use since sixth grade. They were all in his closet, stacked up one on top of the other. If it had been the planner, she would have broken up with him a long time ago.

Maybe that was the worst part of all of it. Not knowing *why* she'd broken up with him. It was worse than never again hearing Kim laugh so hard she snorted, and then watching her cover her nose with shock, like it was still surprising to her, somehow, even though she *always* snorted when she laughed. When she *really* laughed, not pretend-laughed to be nice. Like she'd really laughed last weekend, when they'd gone to the Dairy Star after their games, and Teddy had done an impression of Mr. Dykstra eating soft-serve and getting it all up in his mustache . . .

A baseball whizzed right past Teddy's left ear and sailed into the outfield.

"Catch those, Lin!" Coach Mendoza shouted from where he stood by the dugout. "You've gotta catch those!"

"He's distracted, Coach!" Corey Brooks shouted back, smirking. "Girl trouble!"

"I could not care less, Brooks!" Coach Mendoza shouted back. "I'm sensing a distinct lack of focus today, Flying Arrows. Would running laps help us focus up?"

"NO!" Elvis screamed, while everyone else muttered something to the same effect. Elvis really hated running. He always said if he wanted to run, he'd have played soccer. Usually that statement meant five more laps from Coach Mendoza.

"Poor Kim must be awfully lonely," Corey mused, quietly enough that Coach Mendoza couldn't hear him, but Teddy definitely could. "She was looking hella cute this morning, too. There's something about that red sweater, man, am I right?"

Teddy had given Kim that red sweater for her birthday a couple months ago. It made her dark hair look shiny and her brown eyes enormous and whenever she wore it, Teddy couldn't quite believe someone that gorgeous was with him. *Was* with him. Emphasis on the *was*.

"Or maybe it's what's *under* the sweater, if you know what I mean . . ."

Teddy did not consider himself a violent person. He had, in fact, never been in any kind of a physical fight, unless you counted the time that he pushed Elvis jokingly and Elvis fell off a picnic table, but that had more to do with Elvis's lack of balance than Teddy's violent shoving abilities. And so Teddy couldn't explain why he launched himself at Corey, tackled him to the ground, and started slapping him with his baseball glove.

"Lin!" Coach Mendoza shouted. "What are you *doing*?! Get off him!"

"Dude! Stop! Ow!" Corey yodeled in pain. Teddy realized that slapping his teammate with a baseball glove was kind of an absurdist maneuver, but it was what he'd started with, and he was sticking to it.

"Aaaaaaaa!" Teddy heard Elvis scream, and before he knew it, Elvis had materialized next to him, vigorously slapping Corey's calves with his own baseball glove. Teddy assumed the calves were the only body part Elvis could reach, and Elvis wasn't inflicting some kind of special calf-muscle torture, but you never knew.

"Rodriguez! Are you kidding me?" Coach Mendoza was now running over to them, probably about to pull them off Corey by physical force. Teddy knew he should stop, but he couldn't. All he did was slap Corey harder.

"What is *wrong* with the two of you?" Corey whined. "At least hit me like a normal person!"

Before Teddy could decide if he was going to hit Corey like a normal person, deafening sirens filled the air.

"Teddy! Stop, man!" Josiah Watkins must have made it in from the outfield before Coach Mendoza could get there from the dugout, because it was Josiah who shook Teddy's slapping arm and pulled him off of Corey. "It's the police!"

Teddy froze, crouched in the dirt of the baseball diamond, Josiah's arm still restraining him gently. He was vaguely aware of Elvis still slapping away at Corey's legs. The police?! This was bad. This was so, so, so bad. Could you be arrested for slapping someone with a baseball glove? Would Teddy's parents *murder* him if he got arrested, and then they, in turn, would *also* be arrested? It seemed like the most likely scenario.

"Don't drive on the—are you kidding me? A *second* car on the field? What is going *on* today?" Coach Mendoza was now running across the baseball diamond, waving his arms over his head at the police car barreling through the field and straight toward them. "WE JUST RESEEDED THE GRASS!" Coach Mendoza yelled. "Does no one understand the fragility of an ecosystem that's recently been introduced to soil conditioner?!"

With a well-placed kick, Corey shook Elvis off him and struggled up to a sitting position.

"You guys are so lame," Corey said, brushing the dirt off his track pants.

"You're the lame one, you . . . uh . . . lame-o!" Elvis retorted.

"I get why Kim dumped you." Corey narrowed his eyes at Teddy. "Work on your anger, man. And she was way too hot for you, anyway."

Teddy tensed. Kim *was* way too hot for him. But he didn't like hearing Corey say it.

"Not worth it," Josiah muttered, keeping a calming hand wrapped around Teddy's arm. "You've gotta relax, man. The police are here."

Despite Coach Mendoza's frantic waving, the police car pulled right up onto the diamond, its flashing lights casting red and blue shadows over Corey's face as he leaned in toward Teddy.

"Slap me all you want," Corey hissed in Teddy's face. "I'm asking Kim out. And there's nothing you can do to stop me."

"She won't say *yes*," Elvis protested. "No way. Not in a million years."

"We'll see."

Teddy wanted to get his baseball glove back out and slap that smug smile right off of Corey's stupid face. But Josiah must have taken it away from him at some point, because Teddy no longer had a glove. Probably for the best. Because the police car—well, technically, it looked more like a police truck—had parked, and the driver's door opened. Teddy was conscious suddenly of the entire team clustered around him, like they were forming a protective shield. He wondered if he should make a run for it, or if that would make things worse. Evading arrest probably wouldn't earn him any points with the judge.

"Dude." Elvis slapped Teddy's arm and pointed at the police truck. "It's not the police."

Teddy followed Elvis's pointing arm to the gold lettering on the side of the police car that spelled out ANIMAL CONTROL.

"Animal Control?!" Corey laughed. "They didn't even send the real police for you, Lin! They sent Animal Control!"

"That wasn't even a good burn, man." Josiah shook his head. "That was weak. That was like the kind of burn you get from a hot glue gun."

Teddy didn't know why Animal Control was here. But he knew that the guy walking toward him in a uniform, complete with glinting badge, certainly looked like a police officer.

"Can I help you, Officer?" Coach Mendoza asked, positioning himself between Teddy and the cop. "Maybe I could help you find the parking lot?" he added in an undertone.

"I'm looking for Teddy Lin," the officer said. Teddy's stomach plummeted into his cleats. "I was told I could find him on the baseball field."

"May I ask why?" Coach Mendoza hadn't immediately given him up. Maybe there was hope for Teddy after all. Maybe they'd form some kind of baseball brotherhood and refuse to turn him in, shielding him forever from the long arm of the law.

"Got an anonymous tip that a student named Teddy Lin released a bunch of snakes on the first floor of William Henry Harrison High." Teddy exchanged a bewildered glance with Elvis. Someone thought he'd released *snakes* into the school? Why would he do that? Where would he even get a snake? "Now, I've examined the property and I've found no reptiles," the officer continued, "but I'd like to ask Mr. Lin a few questions."

"Seems unnecessary." Coach Mendoza crossed his arms. "I was in the school myself all afternoon, and I didn't see a single snake. No crime. No guilty party. So I see no reason you need to talk to Teddy."

The Animal Control guy seemed to consider this, shifting his weight from side to side as he scratched the stubble on his chin.

"Seeing as there's no reptiles," the cop said, "I suppose

that's fine. But if I even see so much as a garter snake, I'm coming back. Gentlemen."

The cop nodded at them, then climbed back into his truck. Teddy could practically feel Coach Mendoza wincing as the vehicle tore up the grass on his way out of William Henry Harrison High's athletic fields.

"There's only one snake here," Corey hissed. "And his name is Teddy Lin. Ow!" he squawked in distress.

Teddy was pretty sure Josiah had just slapped Corey with a baseball glove.

It was always nice when the outfield had your back.

CHAPTER FOURTEEN

KIM LANDIS-LILLEY
DAY ONE

Kim had done A Very Bad Thing.

Kim had not *intended* to do A Very Bad Thing, which is probably what most people who did Very Bad Things would say. But Kim hadn't intended to do anything, and certainly nothing as bad as skipping school. She'd just started running.

And she hadn't stopped running. No one had seen her sprint through the doors by the gym, cut through the soccer field, and keep going down the driveway that would be filled by parents in the pickup line in a couple hours. And none of the cars she passed as she headed down Mariner Drive, away from school, seemed to notice her. And if anyone driving down the John J. Crittenden Memorial Highway thought it was weird that a teenage girl was sprinting down the side of the highway wearing jeans—not exactly high-tech performance gear—they didn't do anything about it.

Kim hadn't intended to go to the Dairy Star, either. But that's where she found herself when she finally stopped running, four miles later. The neon soft-serve ice cream cone at the top of the small roadside stand blinked beckoningly at her, like the beacon of a safe haven. Even though it *wasn't* a safe haven. She'd gone here with Teddy more times than she could count. But she'd been here with her moms and Olivia *first*, and at least that was something. Even if she'd been here with Teddy just this weekend. Back when things were *normal*, and everything was right with the world.

There was nowhere in this town that hadn't been tainted by memories of Teddy. To get away from him, she'd have to move to a different county. Maybe a different *country*. For the first time, Kim felt like none of the colleges she'd applied to were far enough away. And now, of course, she was desperate to know where Teddy had applied.

But for very, very different reasons than she'd had not so long ago. How had everything changed so quickly?

Still. Kim wasn't going to *not* eat ice cream just because she *used* to eat ice cream with Teddy. If she applied that logic, she'd have to stop eating altogether. She couldn't think of a single food she'd ever eaten without Teddy. Except, like, baby food? But Kim wasn't going to revert to an infant state just because she'd been dumped. Even if curling up into the fetal position sounded pretty good right about now.

Well. She was here, right? Might as well get something. As soon as everyone realized Kim was gone, she was going to be in major, major trouble—with school, but even worse, with her moms. Mama Dawn might like to think that she was more laid-back than Mama K—she was definitely more of the Good Cop—but both of Kim's parents were going to lose it. They wouldn't believe Kim had left school. She'd never skipped class. Ever. Come to think of it, Kim couldn't even think of a single rule she'd ever broken. She studied for quizzes and turned in permission slips on time and never missed curfew and only stayed home from school when she was actually sick, with a note from her doctor in hand. She did everything right. And everything had gone wrong anyway. So what did it matter? She might as well have some ice cream.

Kim pulled the five-dollar bill out of her pants pocket that her moms made her take with her everywhere "for emergencies," although she wasn't sure how much five dollars would help in an emergency. Five dollars wouldn't get you very far. Although it *would* get you a small butterscotch dip at the Dairy Star.

Butterscotch is for old people. That's what Teddy said. Every time she ordered it. He'd said it last weekend when they'd been at the Dairy Star, and Teddy had done his famous impression of Mr. Dykstra getting ice cream in his mustache. The memory of it hit her like a softball to the face, like the time she'd fractured her orbital rim. Was this what life was going to be like, forever? Unexpected memories assaulting her constantly, wherever she went? Kim wasn't sure she was strong enough to handle it. Kim wasn't strong at all. Olivia could already bench-press nearly twice as much as Kim could, and Olivia was still a baby. Basically a baby, anyway.

Kim walked up to the window and waved at Mrs. Schuster

behind the counter. Last summer, Nico Osterman had worked at the Dairy Star. But now he was back in school, obviously, where Kim was supposed to be, and the Schusters, the owners, took turns manning the counter.

"School get out early, Kimmy?" Mrs. Schuster asked.

"Something like that." Kim tucked her hair behind her ears self-consciously, unable to meet Mrs. Schuster's eyes. "Butterscotch dip in a cake cone, please."

"Coming right up."

Kim slid the five-dollar bill onto the counter as Mrs. Schuster busied herself with the soft-serve machine. Kim crossed her arms, hugging herself, wishing she had something warmer than her red sweater. Her red sweater . . . that Teddy had given her for her birthday. She wanted to rip it off, but then she'd probably freeze to death. Sometimes spring still felt an awful lot like winter.

"Butterscotch cone!" Mrs. Schuster announced.

Kim took her ice cream and her change and sat at one of the metal picnic tables, the seat so ice-cold she could feel it through her jeans. At least ice cream was still delicious. Even in a world where nothing made sense, one thing still did.

Kim finished her cone and wiped the melting drips of ice cream off her hands with a small paper napkin. She sighed and looked up at the sky. It was the kind of gray day that prevented Kim from having any idea what time it was. She could have checked her phone, but that would have opened up a whole different set of issues. If Kim checked her phone, everything would be real. Teddy breaking up with her. Her skipping school. The fact that she didn't turn in her history paper and Mr. Dykstra would only give her partial credit, at best. Nope. Better to just sit here in the cold at the Dairy Star and pretend nothing was real.

Shivering, Kim wrapped her arms tighter around herself. She had purposefully chosen a picnic table where Mrs. Schuster couldn't see her through the Dairy Star window, because if someone asked Kim what was wrong right now, she'd lose it. All she could do was trace her hands over the indentations in the table, scuff her feet in the gravel beneath them, and watch the sky.

At first, Kim thought maybe the darkening sky was a reflection of her mood. She remembered when Mama Dawn had decided to repaint the dining room, and she'd brought home all those paint cards. Kim and Olivia had loved looking through the different colors, even if Mama K had insisted on Seattle Gray instead of the brighter color Mama Dawn had initially wanted. Kim watched the sky now like it was changing through all the different colors on the paint card, from Cloud to Flint to Dove to Pewter to Slate. It was definitely getting darker. Had Kim been here long enough that the sun had started to set? She shivered, but more out of trepidation about what was waiting for her at home than out of actual cold. Kim couldn't feel much of anything anymore. Not the cold from the metal bench, and not her broken heart, either.

A gray Honda Accord tore into the parking lot, tires squealing as it almost knocked over the trash can.

"Kim!" Jess catapulted herself out of the car, leaving the driver's door open in her rush to hug Kim. "Did you run all the way here? Are you crazy? Are you okay? Should we murder Teddy? Do you want *me* to murder Teddy? How can I help?"

"We're missing practice." That sounded like Olivia. Kim didn't think it could possibly be Olivia—there was no way she'd ever miss practice—but there she was, standing by the car, kicking a rock. It scuttled along the parking lot and came to rest right by Kim's left foot. "I never miss practice."

"You didn't have to come," Jess said.

"Yes, I did," Olivia replied mulishly. "You drove up onto the field—which is terrible for the grass, by the way—and forced me into the car. I was worried you were going to dislocate my shoulder."

Kim exchanged a glance with Jess. She should have known Olivia wouldn't have wanted to come find her. Not that she needed Olivia to rescue her. Or Jess, even. Kim had been totally fine at the Dairy Star. She could have run home eventually. It was only about three miles from here.

"What happened?" Jess asked.

"I don't really want to talk about it," Kim said. She still didn't even know what had happened. One minute she'd been totally, completely, head over heels in love with her best friend, and the next . . . it was like she didn't even know him. Maybe she'd *never* known him. Because if she wasn't his favorite thing, what were they even doing together? Teddy had been her favorite thing. Full stop. Not just in high school. But her favorite thing—her *person*—everywhere. And now that was all over.

"Absolutely," Jess said. "You got it. No talking. Just doing."

"Doing what?" Kim asked.

"Don't worry about it. I've got it all under control. Now, let's get in the car," Jess said. "It's way too cold for ice cream."

Kim tossed her napkins in the trash, and within minutes they were cruising down the highway, heading straight toward what would almost definitely be a series of dire consequences.

"Where are we going?" Olivia asked from the back seat. "Can you drop me off at school so I can finish practice? Or at least run some sprints or something?"

"No!" Jess glared at Olivia in the rearview mirror. "How can you even think of softball at a time like this? There's only one team you need to worry about right now. And that's Team Kim."

Team Kim.

Kim knew Jess was there for her, no matter what. And she was grateful for that. But Kim wasn't even sure what team *she* was on yet. Mostly, she just missed this morning, when she and Teddy were on the same team.

But Kim had heard what he'd said in the gym. Seen the look in his eyes. And there was no going back.

"Team Kim," she murmured.

"That's right, baby," Jess said. "Team Kim. And we are going to bring that dumb ex of yours—and anyone else on Team Teddy—a pointy reckoning that will shudder them."

"You guys are so weird," Olivia muttered.

Jess and Kim ignored her.

PART

TWO:

RECKONING

CHAPTER FIFTEEN

SOPHIE MAEBY
DAY TWO

Sophie didn't have a lot of crafting expertise, per se. But she did have a hot glue gun, a lot of babysitting money she'd saved up, and a ton of coupons for Joann Fabrics her mom had found online. Sophie's mom was a coupon genius. She could find at least 20 percent off of literally anything.

"Support Teddy Lin!" Sophie called at a group of students coming down the hall—probably sophomores. They still seemed young but they walked down the hall like they owned the place, not like the freshmen, who scuttled nervously from class to class, like they were afraid of making accidental eye contact.

"How much?" One of the sophomore girls broke away from the pack and paused at the folding table Sophie had set up outside of Ms. Somers's room. She picked up one of the teddy bear headbands Sophie had spent all night making and turned it over in her hands, examining the adorably fuzzy ears.

"We're purely a donation-based service." Sophie gestured to the shoebox she'd covered with construction paper and written *JUSTICE FOR TEDDY* on in black marker. "It's pay-what-you-can. The Teddy Bears are a nonprofit organization dedicated to restoring Teddy Lin's good name and fighting back against the smear campaign that targeted him unfairly during fifth period yesterday. All proceeds go toward the construction of more teddy bear headbands."

Wow. That sounded pretty good. Maybe Sophie should write, like, a mission statement or something.

"Cool." The girl turned to her friends. "Do any of you guys have cash?"

One of the sophomore girls unearthed a crumpled twenty from her pocket, and they each got a pair of ears. And then more people started coming over—and more, and more, and more. Pretty soon Sophie was engulfed in a mad dash for teddy bear ears, handing them out as fast as she could, stuffing donations in the shoebox, giddily wondering if she'd run out of ears before she had time to go home and make more tonight.

"Babe! Hey, babe!" Nico was pushing his way through the crowd of people. "What's going on? I texted you, like, a million times last night."

Oh. Right. Nico. Sophie realized she'd forgotten to break up with him.

She'd also forgotten he existed.

"What's going on?" Nico looked around, bewildered, at

the mass of people stampeding for ears. "Are you a mouse, babe?"

"I'm a teddy bear! Duh!" Sophie snapped with exasperation, pointing at her ears. "And I'm breaking up with you."

"You're breaking up with me because you're a bear?"

"No, not because I'm a bear!" Sophie watched Josiah Watkins from her orchestra class pick up a pair of ears and slip them solemnly onto his flattop. She and Josiah exchanged nods of solidarity. Now *this* was a get. Josiah wasn't some silly sophomore. He'd probably bring in the whole baseball team. And the Model UN. The rest of orchestra. And then his boyfriend could bring in the track and field team. And the student council. And who knew what extracurriculars Sophie was forgetting! Between the two of them, they could probably get every guy in the senior class!

"Then *why*?" Nico asked, anguished. A girl Sophie didn't recognize elbowed Nico in the throat in her eagerness to get her ears on. He staggered back a few steps, his hands covering his Adam's apple protectively.

Sophie almost would have felt bad for him if she hadn't evolved so completely past him.

"*Why* doesn't matter. It's over, Nico. Accept it. Move on."

"Do you do custom orders?" a junior girl asked Sophie as she stuffed a wad of cash into the shoebox. "Like if I wanted my ears to match my hair?"

"We may be expanding our options in the upcoming days." At this moment, Sophie felt like anything was possible. Because as she looked down the hallway, all she could see was a sea of adorable brown teddy bear ears, stretching from locker to locker, as far as the eye could see.

And then she saw *him*. Teddy. The real one. He was walking down the hallway with Elvis Rodriguez, looking from ears to ears like he had no idea what was going on. Well, he'd know soon enough. He'd know exactly what Sophie had done for him, and he'd see that they were two of a kind. They were two equally romantic souls, wandering the halls of William Henry Harrison High alone. And Sophie was definitely alone now. Nico must have finally gotten the message, because he'd disappeared from the cluster of teddy bears in front of her.

Sophie didn't care that Teddy was moving to Firenze. Well, like, she *did* care that he was moving to Firenze, because his selfless act of breaking up with Kim had shown Sophie just exactly who Teddy Lin was. He was a passionate, caring romantic, like a cowboy in a Nicholas Sparks movie who would give up all his cowboy-ing dreams if that's what his lady love wanted.

He was everything Sophie had ever wanted.

And she was going to make him *hers*.

CHAPTER SIXTEEN

MS. SOMERS
DAY TWO

Ms. Somers usually made it to her room right before the first bell rang, which gave her all of homeroom to do any last-minute lesson planning, finish the coffee in her Oberlin travel mug, and eat a Nutri-Grain bar. But today, she'd somehow slept through her alarm and was racing down the hall with wet hair, clutching an armful of sheet music as the bell rang.

Something was different about the students Ms. Somers ran by. They were all wearing... cat ears? No, that wasn't right. They weren't pointy. Dog ears? Was this some kind of spirit week thing? Ms. Somers thought spirit week only happened before homecoming, but maybe there was a spring sports spirit week she'd missed on the calendar. They'd probably gotten an email about it. But they all got *so* many emails. It was hard to read every single one of them . . .

Ms. Somers pushed her way through the throng of dog-bear-whatever students. As she got closer to her classroom, the dog-bear horde only got thicker and thicker.

"Justice for Teddy!" Sophie Maeby, Ms. Somers was almost positive. Ms. Somers could recognize all of her students' voices. Sometimes she pictured them almost like music notes: some low and lyrical, some high and trilling, like Sophie's. "Join the Teddy Bears!" Sophie called out.

Teddy bears. *That's* what the ears were. Now that she knew what they were, Ms. Somers could absolutely see it. Finally, Ms. Somers squeezed through a small gap in the crowd and found herself standing in front of a small table right outside of her classroom. Sophie Maeby beamed from behind the table.

"Buongiorno, Teddy!" Sophie Maeby said, looking right past Ms. Somers. Ms. Somers realized she was standing right next to Teddy Lin. Did the ears have something to do with him? "Come stai?"

"Uh . . . what?" Teddy said. He looked as confused as Ms. Somers felt. They were Italian teddy bears?

"What's going on, Sophie?" Ms. Somers asked. "The first bell already rang."

"I'll take a pair of ears!" Elvis Rodriguez poked his head out from behind Teddy. "Oh—sorry, Ms. Somers," he added quickly.

"The students are wearing teddy bear ears in support of Teddy," Sophie explained as she handed Elvis the last pair of ears on her table. "We know he's not a snake. And we want

96

Teddy to know that we all support him. Especially after *someone* put up all those awful posters."

Sophie raised her eyebrows significantly on the *someone*. Did she know who did it? There had been an emergency all-staff meeting after school yesterday to discuss the posters. Ms. Somers knew that Kim Landis-Lilley was the primary suspect, but she just didn't believe Kim would do something like that, never mind that it would have been physically impossible, since everyone knew Kim had left the building long before the posters had shown up. Which is what Ms. Somers had said in the meeting. But it hadn't seemed to dissuade Principal Manteghi from her resolution to question Kim about them today. If Kim ever returned. She'd left school grounds in the middle of the day yesterday, which was already a punishable offense, even if her absence should have exonerated her from anything related to the posters—poor Kim. Ms. Somers couldn't help but feel bad for her. But she felt bad for Teddy, too. Those posters certainly hadn't been nice. The whole thing was such a mess!

"Gotta go," Elvis Rodriguez said as he slipped through the crowd, clutching his ears.

"Everyone should go," Ms. Somers said firmly. "You're all going to be late for homeroom."

"Homeroom bell will be ringing in approximately forty-five seconds!" Coach Mendoza's voice boomed through the hallway. The crowds parted, and students started scurrying in every direction, revealing Coach Mendoza standing in the middle of the hallway with his stopwatch. "Forty-four! Forty-three! Rodriguez, do you want a demerit for being tardy? Lin? Looking for a demerit? Rothbart, that's one for running in the halls!"

Within moments, they were all gone. Even Sophie. It was just Ms. Somers and Coach Mendoza and a small folding table, alone in the hallway.

"Is this your table, Ms. Somers?" Coach Mendoza asked.

"Kelly," she said automatically. "I mean, don't call me Kelly," she amended, remembering where they were. "I mean, you can call me Kelly outside of school. Not that you see me outside of school. I mean. Um. Yes? This is my table?"

It *was* her table. She wasn't sure why it had come out as a question. The whole Kelly thing had thrown her. Ms. Somers took a desperate sip of coffee. Clearly, she hadn't had enough.

"Got it." Coach Mendoza flipped the table onto its side and easily folded it flat. Usually, Ms. Somers could only accomplish that feat with a lot of kicking and some definitely not-school-appropriate language. She followed Coach Mendoza as he walked it into her room, trying not to notice how nice his biceps looked in his William Henry Harrison High baseball shirt as he lifted the table.

"Behind the last row of chairs is good," Ms. Somers blurted out, pointing to the back of her classroom.

"Sure thing, Kelly." Coach Mendoza dropped off the table, then turned to look at her. "Oh, I'm sorry," he said. "That was only for outside of school, right?"

"Right." Ms. Somers was suddenly conscious of the fact that her wet hair was dripping down the back of a shirt she was fairly certain was on inside out. And she couldn't remember whether she'd brushed her teeth or not. And as Coach Mendoza stepped closer to her, she had a deep fear that she hadn't remembered to put on deodorant, either. Why had today, of all days, been the day her alarm hadn't gone off?

"I kind of like Kelly," he said. "So maybe we should see each other outside of school?"

"Um, Ms. Somers?" Sophie Maeby was hovering in the doorway, pulling anxiously on a lock of her curly hair, a construction-paper-covered shoebox tucked under her arm. "I'm sorry about the table. I should have asked first."

"It's okay, Sophie." Ms. Somers leapt away from Coach Mendoza and started vigorously erasing the whiteboard. "It's school property! Not, you know, my personal table. Ha-ha!" Why was she laughing?! That wasn't even a joke. Ms. Somers took such a big slug of coffee she choked on it, spluttering as she attempted to regain her equilibrium.

"Sure." Sophie looked back and forth from Ms. Somers to Coach Mendoza. Oh God. Had she heard the whole Kelly thing? Definitely not school appropriate. Ms. Somers erased harder, determined not to look at Coach Mendoza. "Okay. Well, thanks for the table. I should probably get to homeroom."

"And we should probably let Ms. Somers get ready for first period. Do you have any ears left, Sophie?" Coach Mendoza asked as he walked her out of the room. "Maybe I should wear them to practice this afternoon."

Ms. Somers didn't hear what Sophie said. She half collapsed against the whiteboard, clutching the eraser to her chest.

Had Coach Mendoza just *asked her out?*

The homeroom bell rang, startling Ms. Somers into action.

Coffee. Nutri-Grain bar. Lesson plan. Right.

Coach Mendoza would have to wait.

CHAPTER SEVENTEEN

ELVIS RODRIGUEZ
DAY TWO

Elvis was sweating.

A lone bead of sweat traveled down his forehead, skimmed the ridge of his nose, and plopped onto his lower lip.

"Elvis. Gross," Jess said, the disgust evident in her voice as they waited in line in the cafeteria. "I'm not going to be able to eat if you keep sweating like that."

"Hot in here." He pulled at the collar of his T-shirt, trying to get some air.

This was the moment he'd have to declare his allegiance. He'd stalled, saying he needed to get hot food, even though he had a perfectly good PB&J waiting in his locker. But he needed a minute to think. Or the couple minutes it would take for him to get a rather unappealing chicken fajita plopped onto his tray.

Elvis couldn't believe he'd gotten away with it so far. At this exact moment in time, with an unappetizing flour tortilla waiting wanly on his plate, Jess thought he was firmly anti-Teddy, as he'd worn the snake poster yesterday. Teddy thought he was his bro, his BFF for life, since he'd joined in on the Corey smackdown.

Also: Were they going to get in trouble for that? It seemed like Coach Mendoza hadn't reported it, which was unexpected, but nothing was going as expected right now. It felt like William Henry Harrison High was entering an era of lawlessness, and Elvis wasn't sure he was ready for that. So far, the only consequence had been Corey glaring at them in the halls, and that wasn't much of a change from his typical expression.

If it hadn't been for lunch, Elvis probably could have kept playing for both sides. He didn't have a single class that both Kim and Teddy were in—or Teddy and Jess, for that matter, as that was the more pressing issue. Was Kim even in school today? He hadn't seen her since lunch yesterday.

But now, Jess and Teddy would no doubt converge in the cafeteria.

And Elvis would have to prove, once and for all, where his loyalties lay.

As they walked toward their table, Elvis white-knuckled his tray, the fajita plate rattling ominously against his silverware. Was it even their table anymore? Who would sit here? Kim or Teddy? Jess had made it pretty clear that she wouldn't, under any circumstances, share any amount of space with Teddy. Someone would take custody of the table.

And someone would take custody of Elvis.

"Elvis. What are you doing?" Jess was already sitting down, staring up at Elvis like he'd lost it. Maybe he had. He could hear roaring in his ears and the thumping of his heart and, above it all, the rattling of his fajita plate. "Sit down. You're being weird."

Elvis put his tray down on the table to at least stop the rattling. He swallowed, hard, as he watched Teddy walk over to their table and put his lunch bag down on it.

"Hey, Jess. Have you seen Kim?" Teddy asked. "I'm worried about her."

"You're worried about her." Jess put down her yogurt, almost in slow motion. Elvis was pretty sure that Teddy had never seen Jess go nuclear before. Elvis, of course, had. He'd been at Jess's house when her uncle had said that the problem with women is that they think differently than men. Jess had put her drink down in super slow motion then, too, right before she'd exploded into a white-hot ball of rage. "You, my former friend, no longer have the right to be worried about her."

"Well, that's not . . ." Teddy trailed off and took half a step back, probably scared off by the ice in Jess's voice. "I mean, I don't think—"

"That's right," Jess interrupted him. "You don't think. And you didn't think. And you lost the best thing that ever happened to you. And you lost this table, too. And I don't care *how* many desperate girls are wearing teddy bear ears. You're dead to me, and to Elvis, and to everyone who matters at this school."

"Elvis?" Teddy turned to Elvis with hurt in his eyes, and in that moment, Elvis didn't see a seventeen-year-old. He saw the Teddy he'd met in kindergarten, the one who'd helped him build an enormous Lego rocket ship and was always up for kickball and never hesitated to share his snack. The Teddy who had been by his side as they graduated from T-ball to Little League, and who hadn't made fun of him when Elvis had cried after missing an easy out that would have earned them a spot in the Little League World Series qualifiers. He saw the sixth-grade Teddy who'd helped him muster up the courage to ask Molly Santos to dance with him at the Spring Fling, the seventh-grade Teddy who'd encouraged him to kiss Wendy Phan, and the freshman Teddy who'd told him to stop mooning over Jess and just ask her out already.

"Find yourself a new table," Jess said. "Because this one's ours."

Teddy turned to go.

"Wait!" Elvis cried. As Teddy turned back around, Elvis was vaguely conscious of the cafeteria hushing around them. This was it. This was his moment. With that "Wait!" Elvis had chosen, and now he needed everyone to know his choice.

"What are you doing?" Jess hissed as Elvis climbed up onto the table.

"I'm making my stand, Jessica!" Elvis said, steadying himself as the uneven table rocked under his weight.

"Get down. You look like an idiot."

"I'm not an idiot!" Elvis unzipped his hoodie. Under his sweatshirt, nestled against his stomach, were the teddy bear ears he had gotten from Sophie Maeby this morning.

"You *didn't*." The betrayal in Jess's voice was almost enough to make Elvis reconsider. But then he looked at Teddy, smiling up at him hopefully, and he knew this was the path he was destined to walk. "Elvis. No. You're supposed to be on my side."

"My name is Elvis Rodriguez!" Elvis shouted, although there was no need to shout. The cafeteria was totally silent. "But you can call me E-Rod. And I. Am. A. TEDDY BEAR!"

As the cafeteria roared its approval, Elvis lifted the ears dramatically up to the sky and placed them on his head. Teddy grinned at him, and Elvis knew he'd done the right thing.

"Elvis, get off the table!" Mr. Rizzo was on lunchroom duty again. He ran over to Elvis so quickly coffee sloshed out of his NOTORIOUS RBG mug, leaving a trail of sludgy brown caffeine in his wake. "That's one!"

"One what?" Elvis asked.

"One *demerit*. Get down!"

"I can't, sir!" Elvis said. He was pretty sure he'd never called anyone *sir* before, but Elvis was doing a lot of things he'd never done before.

"Dustin Rothbart, put your phone away!" Mr. Rizzo snapped. "That's one for filming this. And, Elvis, feet on the floor. Now!"

"I can't! I'm scared!"

"Rodriguez, you're three feet off the ground." Coach Mendoza was now standing next to Mr. Rizzo, his arms folded.

"It's not the height, Coach." It wasn't, of course. It was Jess, staring up at him with murder in her eyes.

"You realize we're done, right?" Jess was standing now,

right next to Coach Mendoza. "You and me. We're done. Finished. Over. And you're dead to me, too. And you'd better get the hell away from my lunch table."

"It's *my* lunch table!" Elvis stamped his foot.

"That lunch table is the property of William Henry Harrison High, and now you're at two, Elvis," Mr. Rizzo said. "Get down within the next thirty seconds or it's four and an automatic detention."

Elvis clambered off the table and went to stand by Teddy, trying to put as much space as possible between himself and Jess.

"Thanks, man." Teddy squeezed Elvis's shoulder. "We'll get a new table."

"That's right you will," Jess said. "This table—this entire side of the cafeteria—is ours now. And I better not see *any* Teddy Bears on this side of the line!"

There was, in fact, a bright yellow line directly down the middle of the cafeteria. The tile work in the school's colors—gift of the class of '94—bifurcated the entire room. And from a quick scan, it looked like Jess had claimed the better side.

"Your side of the cafeteria has the hot food line!" Elvis protested.

"Then I guess you'll be bringing lunch from home for the foreseeable future." Jess shrugged.

"No student can prevent another student from sitting anywhere they choose," Mr. Rizzo said.

"Of course not," Jess agreed. But the malice glinting in her eyes was anything but agreeable.

Elvis knew he wouldn't be crossing that line. Ever. And it

wasn't like he was giving up on stellar fajitas. So they had a new table. So what?

Everyone in the cafeteria must have been listening. Because a sea of Teddy Bears moved out of one side of the cafeteria and gravitated toward Teddy and Elvis. And then another sea of people—did Team Kim have a name? A mascot? Anything?—came to cluster around Jess.

"No one has to move!" Mr. Rizzo announced. "Stay where you are!"

"We're moving because we want to," Sophie Maeby said as she strode confidently across the cafeteria, her pink polka dot lunch bag slung over her arm, an army of girls in teddy bear ears surging behind her. "Ciao, caro," she added as she came to stand by Teddy, winking at him.

"Do you speak Italian?" Elvis whispered to Teddy.

"Not at all," he whispered back.

"So what—"

"I don't know, man." Teddy shrugged. "Nothing makes sense anymore."

Wasn't that the truth? Elvis was dressed like an anthropomorphic bear. Jess had dumped him. He'd been booted off of his lunch table—out of an entire half of the cafeteria! And he still didn't even know *why* Kim and Teddy had broken up, only that their breakup had turned his whole world upside down.

"It's fine, Mr. Rizzo," Teddy said loudly. "Come on, Elvis. Let's sit down. Over here."

There was an empty table on their side of the yellow line that had been vacated by a group of Kim supporters. Teddy and Elvis took a seat, and Elvis was surprised to see Sophie

Maeby sit right next to Teddy. Did Sophie and Teddy even know each other? Elvis had never seen them speak before, and now here she was, making animal ears and sitting next to them at lunch.

The doors at the front of the cafeteria swung open, and Kim walked through. There was something different about her. As she moved through the silent cafeteria, walking through the tables of staring students, Elvis couldn't quite put his finger on what it was.

Kim came to stand at their table—no, it was *her* table now, it wasn't Elvis's anymore—and looked across the yellow line, right at Teddy.

She wasn't smiling. That's what was different. Elvis couldn't remember ever seeing Kim without a smile on her face. But now, she looked cold, and hard, and maybe even scarier than Jess.

"Kim Landis-Lilley," a voice boomed from over the loudspeakers. The entire cafeteria hushed and turned toward the corner of the cafeteria ceiling, where the speakers hung. "Please see Principal Manteghi in her office immediately."

For once, no one made a sound.

CHAPTER EIGHTEEN

PRINCIPAL MANTEGHI
DAY TWO

"So you *didn't* put up the snake posters," Principal Manteghi said for the third time.

"Correct. I wasn't even in the building when that happened."

Kim Landis-Lilley sat perfectly upright in the chair across from Principal Manteghi's desk. The principal was used to slouchers. Usually, people called into the principal's office slouched desperately, like they were trying to disappear into the faux-leather chair. But Kim Landis-Lilley had been in this office only once before, when she'd received a commendation for collecting gently used sports equipment to donate to a local women and children's shelter. Principal Manteghi hadn't ever expected to see Kim in this office for any reason other than a commendation.

But a lot was happening this week that she hadn't expected. Including, miraculously, Mr. Guzman taking the job. So at least Señora Parrilla's maternity leave was covered. But that seemed like a very, very small win when compared to the Teddy Lin snake posters and her lack of a culprit.

The email notification on her desktop pinged. Anxiously, Principal Manteghi clicked on an email with the subject line "RIOT":

I have single-handedly prevented a small riot from fomenting in the cafeteria. No need to send backup. Lunch will now proceed as usual for the remaining eighteen minutes of the period.

Sent from my iPhone—please excuse typos

Matthew Rizzo
WHHHS Theater Teacher

All emails and phone calls returned within two business days

Even coming from a drama teacher—and one with a propensity for exaggeration—the word *riot* was troubling. All of a sudden, it seemed that Principal Manteghi's well-maintained kingdom was toppling. Had it been so fragile all along that one insignificant breakup was enough to bring it all crashing down?

Principal Manteghi took a deep breath and fixed Kim with her most significant stare, the one that had cracked the case of the Freshman Fart Bandit.

Kim stared right back.

Clearly, she was made of stronger stuff than any Fart Bandit.

"And you don't know who put up the snake posters, either?" Principal Manteghi asked.

"Also correct."

Principal Manteghi didn't totally buy that one. She rubbed her temples, wondering if she needed glasses, or if constant headaches were just part of the job description. Ms. Powell had spent all of yesterday's emergency all-staff meeting insisting that Kim Landis-Lilley was the only possible perpetrator of SnakeGate.

(Principal Manteghi should have shut it down faster when Mr. Rizzo had called it SnakeGate. She was pretty sure everyone was calling it SnakeGate now. Before long, Mr. Rizzo would probably be calling whatever happened in the cafeteria CafGate. Urgh.)

But despite Ms. Powell's insistence, Principal Manteghi was positive it couldn't have been Kim. There was security footage of her sprinting out of the building right at the end of lunch—well before the posters went up—and she never came back. Of course, if the school board had sprung for security cameras inside the building as well, like Principal Manteghi had asked for, none of this would even have been an issue.

So who else could it have been? Someone who was defending Kim—maybe her sister, or a softball teammate, or a friend? Or maybe these posters were more of an artistic statement and had nothing to do with Kim and Teddy at all. Toby Neale, William Henry Harrison High's resident art genius, had been demerited on multiple occasions for what he saw as street art and Principal Manteghi saw as vandalism. In fact, only a couple months ago, he'd wallpapered the school with hand turkeys that were protesting either the romanticizing of colonialism or the lack of funding for arts education in the American public school system, depending on whom you asked. Last year he'd stickered the building with tiny, misshapen cartoon cacti he'd created using the art room's InDesign account—Principal Manteghi still didn't know what that one meant. Maybe the Teddy Lin snake posters were a Toby Neale commentary on the dangers of toxic masculinity or the spread of information in the age of social media or something like that. Toby was a senior, too. It was entirely possible that he'd been inspired by the breakup. What had he said when the school had stopped serving chocolate milk, and Principal Manteghi had confronted him about hanging milk cartons with expertly photoshopped protest labels from the cafeteria ceiling?

"In times of crisis, art bears witness." Right. That's what it was.

And this whole situation was certainly a crisis for Principal Manteghi.

She'd have to bring in Toby Neale for questioning. But right now, she had Kim Landis-Lilley. And all Principal Manteghi could do was try to get her talking.

"Bullying is a very serious offense, Kim."

"I know. I'm in the Anti-Bullying Coalition. We meet on Tuesdays after school, if you want to join us."

Principal Manteghi gritted her teeth. Was that *sass*? She doubled down on her serious look.

"So you understand, then, exactly how serious this is. And why it's so important that we find out whoever did this, and issue them the consequences they deserve."

Silence. But Kim was now looking down and seemed to be having trouble meeting her gaze. Perhaps Principal Manteghi was making slight inroads here.

"Maybe when you're in detention on Friday for cutting class, something will come to you."

"Maybe."

Principal Manteghi doubted it. These kids were loyal to a fault. She respected the way they stuck up for one another, the way they acted as one another's secret keepers.

Made her job quite a bit harder, though.

"You know, Kim." Principal Manteghi sighed and leaned forward. "Breakups can be hard. At your age, it can feel like the end of the world. But I wouldn't want you to jeopardize everything you've accomplished here—and everything you're going to accomplish in college after successfully graduating—because of some boy."

"Because of some boy." Kim laughed. "Because of some *boy!*" she said again, the phrase barely audible through her laughter. "Principal Manteghi, Teddy Lin isn't *some boy*. He's been my best friend for twelve years. He's been my boyfriend for six. He knows me as well as—maybe better than—my own mothers. He's the first person I go to when I'm sad, or happy, or lonely, or scared, or proud of myself, because he's the person I share everything with. He's the person who makes me feel like I should *always* be proud of myself, because he loves me completely. Loved me completely," she amended sadly. "Loved me."

Principal Manteghi had never seen a sadder use of the past participle.

"So don't tell me he's just *some boy*, okay?" Kim was standing up now, and Principal Manteghi couldn't shake the feeling that *she* was now the one in trouble. "Teddy Lin may be a lot of things. But he's not *some boy*."

Kim left without being dismissed, but Principal Manteghi didn't have the heart to chase her down and issue the demerit.

CHAPTER NINETEEN

PHIL SPOONER
DAY TWO

"Hey! Spoony! Over here!"

The call of "Spoony!" rang through the cafeteria almost musically, shattering the silence that followed Kim Landis-Lilley's departure. Phil Spooner looked around the room. Could Spoony, perhaps, be referring to *him*?

It must have been. Because Diamond Allen was looking at him—making direct eye contact and looking at him—and waving him over to a table on the Team Kim side of the cafeteria.

(Phil Spooner was obviously Team Kim. Jess Howard was the captain of Team Kim. And Jess Howard could do no wrong.)

"Sit right here, Spoons," Gabe Koontz said, patting the seat next to him.

Phil slid into the vacant chair next to Gabe and across from Diamond. Today was proving to perhaps be even *more* interesting than yesterday had been. First, Phil usually ate lunch alone, or at a table with other freshman guys who didn't talk to one another, which was basically like eating alone. Phil didn't even know most of their names. Second, he'd acquired not one but *two* nicknames in the span of the last several minutes. He wasn't even sure which one he preferred! There was something rather endearing about Spoony, but Spoons had a rugged masculinity that Phil quite liked.

"Can you believe how dumb all those bears look with their DIY ears?" Diamond asked him. "Sophie Maeby is not a crafter."

"Totally dumb," Phil agreed.

(Actually, the ears were kind of cute. But Phil wasn't going to jeopardize his seat at a table where people actually *talked* with something as controversial as an opinion.)

"Do we need ears?" Chloe Baker asked between nervous nibbles of a baby carrot. "Something that lets people know we're Team Kim?"

"We are *not* wearing animal ears." Diamond sniffed disdainfully. "This isn't the first-grade play."

(Phil had played a pig in the first-grade play. Diamond Allen had been Old MacDonald herself. Some people were destined for stardom from an early age.)

"Can someone remind me why, exactly, we're Team Kim again?" Gabe Koontz poured the last of his Cool Ranch Doritos crumbs straight out of the bag and into his mouth. Phil wondered what Gabe's feelings on Sunchips were.

"We're supporting Olivia," Evan Loomis said from down at the end of the table.

"Right. Of course we're supporting Olivia," Diamond said. Phil turned to look behind him. He could only see Olivia's hunched shoulder blades as she bent over her lunch, sitting across from Daisy Diaz. Did Olivia need support? It was hard to tell from only looking at her shoulder blades. "Freshmen solidarity. We have to stick together. And, you know, feminism."

"And Teddy released *snakes* into the school," Chloe practically whispered.

"And it was all Teddy's fault they broke up in the first place. Right, Phil?" Diamond asked, and now everyone at the table was staring at him. "Phil was there when it all happened, you know."

"Right. Uh, right." Phil cleared his throat. "It was all Teddy's fault."

"You would not *believe* the stuff Teddy was getting up to on Instagram." Diamond leaned in conspiratorially, and the rest of the table leaned with her. "Phil told me all about it. It started because Teddy hadn't been liking any of Kim's posts. But apparently there was also this girl who had just qualified for the US Olympic softball team . . ."

Phil hadn't said anything about the US Olympic softball team! He certainly hadn't intended to paint Teddy Lin as some kind of philanderer! What if it got back to Teddy that Phil had been spreading rumors about Teddy? And he hadn't been, not really. He'd only sort-of-kind-of-*barely* made something up. It hardly even counted! It was all *based* on a true experience Phil had definitely witnessed. He had just . . . filled in the blanks.

"So that's why he's moving to Italy?" Chloe asked as Phil drifted back into the conversation. "To try to avoid further international incident?"

"Exactly." Diamond nodded. "They're still not sure if the US will be able to participate in the Summer Games."

Teddy Lin had canceled the Olympics?! Or wait—none of this was true. Or maybe it was true now? Had *Phil* canceled the Olympics?! No! Phil *loved* the Olympics! Especially the Summer Olympics! Phil only got to watch gymnastics once every four years, and if he'd ruined that for everyone, he wasn't sure he'd be able to live with himself.

"Team Kim. Got it," Gabe said. "Hey, I'm just happy we have the side of the cafeteria with the hot food line."

"That's because Team Kim has the best of everything." Diamond smiled.

"Are you sure we don't need a better name?" Chloe asked. "Or, like, a mascot? An outfit? Something?"

"We don't *need* all that flash because we are on the side of righteousness," Diamond said. "Those Teddy Bears are trying to disguise their moral turpitude with adorable animal ears."

"Heh-heh. Turpitude," Gabe said.

"What does that even sound like, Gabe?" Diamond asked. "Why is that funny?"

"I dunno. Turd?" he offered.

"Not even remotely." Diamond shook her head. "Spoony, this is why we need you on Team Kim. You see what I have to work with here?"

Spoony. There it was again. Man, it felt good to be Spoony.

"Can we at least have a team color or something?" Chloe asked. "Obviously I'm Team Kim, and I'm not saying I *want* to wear the ears or anything, but..." From the covetous look Chloe was shooting across the cafeteria, Phil was pretty sure she *did* want to wear the ears.

"Well, Phil, you know her best," Diamond said, and the entire table turned to face him again. Phil couldn't remember the last time this many people had looked at him so often. "What's Kim's favorite color?"

"Red," he answered with a confidence he did not feel. He was pretty sure she'd been wearing a red shirt yesterday. So that made sense, right? "So maybe we should wear ... red ... headbands?"

Did Kim Landis-Lilley even like the color red? Phil didn't know! Phil didn't know anything! This was why you should never go off script! On the day Phil graduated, he'd have several choice words for Mr. Rizzo about the dangers of improv and why it should be banned from the theater curriculum.

"Headbands aren't really as cute as teddy bear ears..." Chloe said.

"So wear something else red in your hair. There are lots of hair options," Evan Loomis said.

"I love it, Spoony. Yes. Absolutely." Diamond was nodding, and so was everyone else. "We won't look like animals like those flashy, desperate Teddy Bears."

"In that case, I can get us what we need," Chloe volunteered.

"What if I don't look good in a headband?" Gabe asked.

"This isn't about you, Koontz! Use your *brain*." Diamond

looked over at Phil, like, *Can you believe this guy? Wow.* It felt almost like Phil and Diamond Allen had an inside joke or something. Just last week Diamond had lodged a formal petition with Mr. Rizzo to never have to be Phil's improv partner again, and now look at them. Practically best friends. And was it him, or was Chloe Baker nibbling that carrot almost flirtatiously in his direction?

"I'm gonna get some more Tater Tots." Gabe pushed himself away from the table. "Spoons, you want?"

Phil nodded in agreement. He did, in fact, want.

Phil wanted everything.

CHAPTER TWENTY

TEDDY LIN
DAY TWO

Teddy looked around the cafeteria. Everyone on his side of the line except for him was wearing bear ears.

"So why is everyone dressed like an animal?" he asked Elvis.

"It's for you, man. To support you or something."

"We're wearing the ears to show you we love you, Teddy," Sophie said from his other side. "We want you to know that William Henry Harrison High is on your side."

"Half of William Henry Harrison High, anyway," Elvis said quietly, casting a wary glance over the yellow line.

Kim was gone—presumably off to Principal Manteghi's office. Maybe this meant she really *had* put up the posters. He wondered what Principal Manteghi was going to do to her. Teddy couldn't imagine Kim getting in trouble. She'd only been to the principal's office once, and that was to get some kind of award for community service.

"The Teddy Bears are a nonprofit organization dedicated to restoring your good name and fighting back against yesterday's smear campaign," Sophie said, like she was reciting something.

"You're a *nonprofit*? Seriously? Can I see your articles of incorporation?" Elvis asked. "Do you have a 501c3 number?"

"What Kim did to you was just awful, Teddy." Sophie placed a hand on his forearm. He stared at her soft pink nail polish. Kim *never* wore nail polish. She said it chipped too quickly, especially during softball season. She'd gotten a manicure just once in all the time they'd been together, when she was a bridesmaid in her cousin's wedding. It had chipped immediately. "Especially when you were so clearly trying to protect her feelings. It's crazy how some people just don't get it."

Sophie stared meaningfully at him. Teddy wondered if she was trying to prove that she *got it*. Whatever *it* was.

Was that what Teddy had been doing? Trying to protect Kim's feelings? Teddy stared into his lunch bag like there were answers hiding in there. All he'd done was ask a question—a simple question—and it had blown up in his face. He hadn't wanted to break up with Kim. Absolutely not. He'd just been wondering if maybe . . . well, maybe there was more to them than just being Kim-and-Teddy. He wanted to make sure that they were still a fully formed Kim and a fully formed Teddy. He hadn't realized asking that was such a crime. Especially since it had seemed like that was important to Kim, too, what with her whole we-can't-talk-about-college-ever ban.

But the ban's days were numbered, because it was getting closer and closer to the time where they'd have to make their decisions about college. And Teddy hadn't necessarily wanted to break up with Kim if they ended up at different colleges, even if those colleges were at opposite ends of the country, but now, it didn't matter what he wanted. They were broken up.

Even if Teddy still wasn't exactly sure *why* they had broken up.

And he definitely didn't *want* to break up with her.

But again: It wasn't exactly up to him. It was Kim's decision, and he had to respect that.

"Take all the time you need, Teddy," Sophie crooned. Her hand was still on his arm. Teddy watched Elvis's eyebrows waggling at him. They seemed to say *What is going on???* and also *We need to talk about this ASAP* and definitely *Is Sophie Maeby petting your arm???*

Yes, Teddy tried to eyebrow back. *We need to talk ASAP because Sophie Maeby is definitely petting my arm.*

"Whenever you're ready," Sophie continued, "I'm here for you." She squeezed his arm. "Ti voglio sempre avere al mio fianco."

No idea what that meant. Teddy only really spoke English, despite his grandma's best efforts to teach him some basic Mandarin and the school district's best efforts to teach him Spanish for the last six years. Teddy wanted to ask Sophie what was up with the Italian.

But asking questions hadn't been working out so well for him recently.

"Ciao, ciao, ciao," Elvis said as he peeled the lid off a pudding cup.

That, Teddy was pretty sure, meant goodbye.

Teddy hadn't been ready to say goodbye.

But maybe that was part of saying goodbye—you were never really ready.

CHAPTER TWENTY-ONE

NICO OSTERMAN
DAY THREE

Darkness. All was darkness.

And pain.

And sadness.

And . . . like . . . depressing-ness . . .

No more Sophie.

"WHYYYYYYYYYYYYYY!" Nico howled up toward the heavens.

"Nico, that's one for howling in environmental science," Ms. Thurber said. "Dustin, you're at one for laughing. Anyone else?"

Nico pulled the hood of the sweatshirt over his head, pulled the drawstrings tight, and retreated back into his world of darkness.

It hurt too much to look at the light.

It hurt too much to do anything.

CHAPTER TWENTY-TWO

JESS HOWARD
DAY THREE

It was the first really nice day of the year.

There was a point in spring where it felt like winter would never actually relax its grip, and they'd be stuck with forty degrees and rainy for the rest of time. But today, finally, it felt like spring was here. Jess had seen crocuses peeking out of the grass near the school doors this morning, and she'd paused there a moment, closed her eyes, and tilted her face to the sun, letting it warm her. Jess could almost forget that there seemed to be just as many Teddy Bears—maybe even more—than there had been yesterday. She could almost even forget that she'd bought an orange prom dress specifically to match this orange vest Elvis was dead set on wearing, despite the fact that it was butt-ugly. What would happen now that they weren't going together?

Jess didn't want to get a new dress, but she didn't want to match Elvis, either.

"Jess?"

"Huh?" Jess opened her eyes. Kim was staring at her. Jess wasn't outside anymore, or back home staring at the prom dress in her closet, but under the fluorescent lights in the cafeteria, waiting in the hot lunch line with Kim.

"You okay?" Kim asked.

"Totally." If anything, Jess should have been the one asking Kim if *she* was okay. This was Kim's first time back in the cafeteria since Principal Manteghi had dramatically summoned her yesterday. Undoubtedly, this was going to be the most difficult lunch of Kim's life so far. People weren't even trying to hide the fact that they were talking about the breakup. Jess glared at a couple of gossiping Teddy Bears, but it didn't help. "Just thinking about how nice it is outside."

"I know."

Kim smiled, and Jess felt like she hadn't seen Kim smile since she broke up with Teddy. Kim had been practically catatonic when Jess had found her outside the Dairy Star. She hadn't said much on the drive back to her house, and she hadn't mustered up any kind of defense when her moms started asking Kim what on earth she was thinking. Kim hadn't even protested the major grounding they'd put on her.

"It'll be so nice to eat outside today," Kim continued.

"Finally." Jess *loved* eating outside. Getting to escape the fluorescent, fetid halls of school made lunch even more of an escape than it usually was. And the fact that eating outside was one thing that made Kim smile made it even better. It couldn't have been easy, watching all those clowns roam the halls with their teddy bear ears. Jess's fingers itched to rip them right off people's dumb heads whenever she saw them bobbing blissfully down the hallway. Didn't these people know they were on the wrong side of history?! They were supporting a total butt! Jess wanted to distribute pamphlets to educate all these misinformed people. But that seemed like a risk after she'd luckily gotten off totally free from the poster thing. Poor Kim—Jess couldn't believe Manteghi had interrogated her. Jess was beyond grateful Kim hadn't ratted her out. Not that she'd expected Kim to—because the two of them understood what loyalty meant. Not like Elvis, that rat.

Jess couldn't believe how fast Elvis had turned on her. Once the first fit of blinding, white-hot rage had passed, she could understand a bit that Elvis had some loyalty to Teddy. They went back further than Jess and Elvis did. But she'd expected him to at least be a *little* conflicted. But nope. Elvis was a rat through and through.

No. Worse than a rat. A flea on a rat. An amoeba on a flea on a rat. Like that Pink Lady with the red hair had said in *Grease*—it was the only part of the movie she liked when Kim had made her watch it about a billion years ago. Kim, of course, loved *Grease*. Jess knew Kim would have put on a leather jacket and danced around at a carnival for Teddy in a hot minute if he'd asked her.

But Jess hoped her best friend was done with all of that. At least their side of the cafeteria was just as full as the stupid bear cave across the yellow line. And Jess bet the numbers would turn even more in their favor as people realized what a butt Teddy was.

"Hey, Jess—look at the freshmen." Kim nudged her. "I thought I noticed something weird earlier. They're all wearing red accessories. Do you know why?"

The freshmen were filing into the cafeteria, last to lunch as always, a mass of people with red in their hair. Some had ribbons in their ponytails, others had headbands on. One guy who looked too huge to be a freshman had a red bandana tied around his neck.

"No idea." Jess shrugged, watching the freshmen join them in the hot lunch line or take seats on their side of the cafeteria. Not a single one crossed over to Teddy's side. "Did Olivia say anything about red headgear?"

"She doesn't tell me anything. Except that I need faster reaction times if I'm going to contribute meaningfully in the outfield."

"Sounds like Olivia," Jess said. "Come on. Let's go eat."

The door to the outside was almost exactly in the middle of the cafeteria. It was already propped open, and Jess swore she could feel the sunshine flowing toward her as she neared it, and smell springtime in the air. Spring smelled like freshly cut grass and freedom. But as they got closer, Jess realized all was not well. She saw it coming in slow motion, like people talked about watching a car crash. As Jess and Kim neared the door to the outside, Elvis and Teddy neared the door from their side of the cafeteria.

Jess was pretty sure it was the closest Kim and Teddy had been to each other since the breakup.

"Stop it right there." Elvis held a hand up in front of his

face. Jess had an absurd vision of her little sister's dance recital, an army of little girls in hot pink sequins doing vaguely coordinated hand gestures to "Stop! In the Name of Love." Elvis, still wearing his teddy bear ears, looked almost as ridiculous.

"Excuse me?" Jess asked.

Teddy, the coward, peeled off behind Elvis and power walked away from the door. Jess turned to Kim, to give her a *Can you believe this guy?* look, but Kim was already gone. Vanished.

"Look down at your feet," Elvis said.

Jess did. Her toes were right up against the yellow line in the middle of the cafeteria.

"Clearly, the door to the outside is on *our* side of the cafeteria." Elvis gestured to the door that was, in fact, very clearly right over the yellow line on the Team Teddy side of the room.

"You've got to be kidding me." Jess rolled her eyes. "You guys don't get the whole outside."

"I'm not saying we get the whole outside. Just that we get the door to it. You're welcome to go outside if you can figure out a way to get there."

"We can't go out another door, and you know that," Jess protested. "It's the only exit we're allowed to use that doesn't count as leaving the building."

"Then I guess you're in a bit of a pickle." Elvis shrugged.

"This isn't fair!" Jess protested.

"Wasn't fair when you took the hot food line. You've deprived an awful lot of innocent people of their Tater Tots. But that's life, I guess."

Jess seethed as Elvis took a step toward the outside, closing his eyes and tilting his face toward the sun.

"Mmm," he said. "Smells like spring."

"You did this on purpose," she spat. "You know how much I love eating outside. I was *just* talking about it!"

"How could I have done this on purpose when *you* claimed that side of the cafeteria?" he asked innocently.

The most annoying thing about all of this was that, in this specific instance, he was correct.

"This isn't over," she said.

"Oh no, Jessica," he replied. *Jessica.* Elvis never called her by her full name. Except when he was standing on top of a cafeteria table, betraying her. He'd probably switched over to Jessica because he knew how much she hated it. She was a *Jess*, not a Jessica! "I would imagine this is only just beginning."

Jess wasn't sure if she imagined it, or if he almost sounded sad when he said it.

Not that she cared.

He'd taken away her outside lunch.

And he was going to pay for it.

CHAPTER TWENTY-THREE

MS. SOMERS
DAY THREE

This was their second emergency all-staff meeting in a week, and from the rumors that had circulated in the teachers' lounge at lunch, it was the first time William Henry Harrison High had ever had all-staffs on consecutive days. It was not how Ms. Somers preferred to spend her afternoons. Not that she had a fabulous evening planned. She'd hoped to catch up on some stuff around the house. Do a load of laundry. Vacuum while listening to Bach's Concerto for Two Violins in D Minor.

Even thinking about it made her feel depressed. This was what she looked forward to at the end of the day? Vacuuming and Bach?

(No disrespect to Bach, of course. It was one of her favorite concertos.)

"Hey." Coach Mendoza slid into the seat next to the one next to Ms. Somers's aisle seat, leaving one metal folding chair in between them.

"Still haven't gotten a pair of ears from Sophie Maeby?" she asked.

"Didn't think they matched my hair," Coach Mendoza teased. "Teddy's a good kid. And he knows I think that without me dressing up like a bear," he added, on a more serious note. "Besides, Sophie was all out. Again. But she's apparently making more for tomorrow."

"Excuse me."

Mr. Dykstra squeezed past Ms. Somers and settled into the chair between her and Coach Mendoza. She was disappointed to see Coach Mendoza lean back into his seat, away from her. Why did Mr. Dykstra have to sit *here*, of all places? But, she supposed, the chairs were filling up now, as Principal Manteghi strode to the front of the gym.

"Thank you for joining me on short notice." Principal Manteghi tapped the microphone for silence. She shuffled some papers in her hands and placed them on top of the podium. "And thank you to the maintenance team for setting up the chairs in the gym on such short notice. Again."

"This school is in a state of chaos!" Ms. Powell shot to her feet, arm thrust up into the air. "What are your plans to restore order to the halls?"

"Calm down, Powell!" Ms. Somers turned around to see Mr. Rizzo shouting from the back row. He was wearing a pair of teddy bear ears. They were spreading to the staff now, too? Sure, Mendoza had joked about getting some ears, but she hadn't seen any teachers actually wearing them before.

Would Ms. Somers be expected to take a side? She wouldn't. She couldn't. She didn't want to believe that either Kim or Teddy was at fault. Honestly, she didn't even really want to believe they'd actually broken up. "We've got a little thing in the teachers' lounge called Tension Tamer Tea, Powell. Heard of it? Sounds like somebody needs a strong cup!"

"I thought we agreed that this year, all-staffs would be a heckling-free zone!" Ms. Powell said.

"Who's heckling?" Mr. Rizzo looked around the back row like he was searching for hidden hecklers.

"I don't think the school is in a state of chaos," Coach Finn said pointedly from the row in front of Ms. Somers, "but don't you think these teddy bear ears are a step too far?"

"A step too far? A *step too far*?" Mr. Rizzo repeated. "Since when is a headband a step too far?"

"When it hurts other students," Coach Finn said.

"I agree with Coach Finn," Ms. Johansson said. She was also in the row ahead of Ms. Somers. Ms. Johansson had her computer open like she was taking notes, but it looked like she was shopping for boots online. "I mean, I don't know if it's hurting anybody, but the ears are a distraction. Never mind that they're supporting Teddy, when we all know the breakup was his fault."

"It was Kim's fault," Ms. Powell said.

"If we can get a subpoena for Teddy Lin's DMs like I keep asking, then we can finally have conclusive proof that it was his fault," Ms. Johansson said. "We need to see those DMs. The International Olympic Committee needs to see those DMs. This isn't just about William Henry Harrison High anymore. It's about America!"

Mr. Rizzo started to hum the opening bars of "The Star-Spangled Banner." Principal Manteghi silenced him with a very effective look.

"We are not here to discuss the breakup of two of our students," Principal Manteghi reminded everyone. Although it seemed like that was exactly what they were doing.

"There's nothing in the Student Code of Conduct that expressly forbids animal ears," Mr. Rizzo said. "Honestly, if we start legislating animal ears, we may be preventing a student from expressing themselves in the future. Like, remember that cape boy? What was his name?"

"Ari Silver," Coach Mendoza said. "Kid wore a cape every day for four years," he explained to Ms. Somers in an undertone, leaning forward in front of Mr. Dykstra. "He graduated last year—before you got here."

"Like a superhero cape?" Ms. Somers asked.

"Like a wizard cape," Coach Mendoza answered.

"Yeah! Like the cape boy!" Mr. Rizzo snapped his fingers in recognition. "What if some kid wants to dress like an animal every day, and we're taking that future child's liberty away from them? It's crucial for teens to be able to manifest their individuality at this stage in their development!"

"You just want an excuse to wear a costume," Ms. Johansson said dismissively. "Anything that'll let you lord your Halloween costume contest win over the rest of us."

"This has nothing to do with that!" Mr. Rizzo protested. "I was a *taco* for Halloween. A taco is nothing like a bear!"

"Focus, please!" Principal Manteghi tapped on the microphone.

Ms. Somers hadn't realized feelings about the fact that

Mr. Rizzo had won the faculty costume contest for the fifth year in a row ran so deeply. But it had been an extremely impressive taco. If Ms. Johansson had thought she'd beat out a taco with her fairy costume, she had been kidding herself. The kids were way too old to care about fairies anymore.

Although maybe the cape boy would have voted for it.

"If I *was* going to be a bear, let me tell you, I wouldn't just be wearing ears," Mr. Rizzo continued, ignoring Principal Manteghi's exhortations to focus. "I'd be so bearlike that somebody would call Animal Control again."

"Did they end up getting all the snakes?" Ms. Johansson asked. "This is exactly why we shouldn't let students wear the ears. We're supporting a snake criminal."

"There were no snakes," Coach Mendoza said. "Some freshman girl heard a rumor, got scared, and called Animal Control."

"See? This is what I mean!" Ms. Powell said. "Total chaos!"

"Maybe there wouldn't be so much chaos if *some people* weren't trying to give every Teddy Bear in sight a demerit for some fabricated reason," Mr. Rizzo responded. "I've had Teddy Bears in and out of my classroom all day, complaining that they're being targeted by certain members of the staff."

"I can assure you every demerit I've ever given was for entirely sound reasons," Ms. Powell claimed. "Like disruption of the educational process!"

"Powell, I'm not even talking about you!" Mr. Rizzo threw up his hands in exasperation. "Everyone knows you're Team Teddy."

"If we can focus for a minute here, I'd like to discuss the fact that my educational process is *actually* being disrupted."

Ms. Somers squinted toward the front of the room, trying to figure out who was speaking way up in the first row. She wished she hadn't left her distance glasses in the car. "You freshman teachers have it easy—they're all on the same side. All of the juniors were crazy today. They pushed their desks to opposite sides of the rooms, refused to do any small group work with someone who wasn't on their 'team,' and turned in essays about why they were Team Teddy or Team Kim instead of the document-based question they were supposed to be answering on Expansion and the Jacksonian Era. Also, I believe there may have been some intentional farting for comedic effect."

"I thought the Fart Bandit had been apprehended!" Ms. Johansson shrieked. "Wasn't it a freshman? Is it spreading to the junior class? Does the Fart Bandit have disciples now?!"

"I can promise you this—the Fart Bandit is a member of Team Kim," Ms. Powell pronounced solemnly.

"FOCUS!" Feedback squealed out of Principal Manteghi's microphone. Ms. Somers clapped her hands over her ears.

Coach Finn raised her hand, waited to be called on, and said, calmly, "I think the ears are making Kim feel bad, and that's why we need to shut them down."

"But what about Teddy?" Coach Mendoza asked. "Isn't it nice for him to get a little support from his friends and teammates?"

"Especially considering the way he was savagely attacked earlier last week?" Ms. Powell asked shrilly.

"Calm down, Powell, you're making it sound like someone jumped him in the parking lot," Coach Finn said.

"Emotional damage leaves lasting wounds!" Ms. Powell retorted.

"Clearly," Ms. Johansson said in a way that made Ms. Somers think she wasn't talking about Teddy.

"People are wearing red ribbons in their hair to support Kim," Coach Mendoza said.

"They've also drained the art room of all the red paint," Mr. Buckley, the art teacher, said. "There's not a drop left!"

"Ribbons, ears, it's all the same thing," Coach Mendoza said. "The kids just want to support their friends."

"It's not the same thing," Mr. Rizzo scoffed. "The ears are a statement. The ribbons are *lazy*."

"It's hard to tell the kids apart when they all look like bears," Mr. Dykstra added.

Mr. Dykstra was notorious for being unable to learn his students' names well into the second semester. Ms. Somers had an absurd vision of him addressing them all as Bear. She let out a giggle, then quickly stifled it.

"Since there is nothing in the handbook preventing the wearing of animal ears *or* hair ribbons or headbands, I will let the students proceed," Principal Manteghi said.

"But—"

"While keeping a close eye on the situation, making sure to monitor it for any future escalation," Principal Manteghi concluded, cutting off Ms. Powell's protest. Ms. Powell sank to her seat, a disgruntled look on her face.

"Can you believe this Tom and Kelly nonsense?" Mr. Dykstra asked Ms. Somers in an undertone while Principal Manteghi shuffled some papers up at the podium.

"I don't understand why people are getting all bent out of shape about some breakup."

"Kim and Teddy," Ms. Somers corrected him, trying to keep a straight face.

"Tom and Kelly, they've been causin' problems from the get-go," Coach Mendoza said from the other side of Mr. Dykstra, his voice a gruff approximation of Mr. Dykstra's low tones.

Ms. Somers turned her face away so he wouldn't see her laugh.

"Sounds like it," Mr. Dykstra agreed. "Maybe give 'em both in-school suspension. Give 'em a minute to think about why they've got everyone running around dressed up like circus animals."

"It's Kim Landis-Lilley and Teddy Lin," Ms. Somers said. "I'm pretty sure you teach them."

"Oh, Kim and Teddy," Mr. Dykstra said, realization dawning. "We're still talking about that? I thought they broke up on Monday?"

Ms. Somers couldn't believe it had only been two days.

"Thank you for voicing your concerns," Principal Manteghi said, "but this meeting was not called to discuss animal ears. I'd like to introduce you to our newest staff member, Chris Guzman." A man Ms. Somers didn't recognize stood up from the first row, turned around, smiled, and waved at all the teachers. "Mr. Guzman will be covering for Señora Parrilla during her maternity leave, effective immediately."

"Immediately?" someone in the front row asked—probably someone from the Spanish department.

"Yes," Principal Manteghi confirmed. "Everything's fine, but Señora Parrilla will be on bed rest for the duration of her pregnancy."

Ms. Somers hoped Señora Parrilla would be okay. And she hoped Mr. Guzman would be okay, too, thrown headfirst into what was undoubtedly the weirdest episode in William Henry Harrison High history.

Ms. Johansson raised her hand.

"Who's taking over as Prom Committee advisor?" she asked.

"That would also be Mr. Guzman," Principal Manteghi said.

Mr. Dykstra snorted something through his mustache that sounded an awful lot like "sucker."

"And a big thank-you to Ms. Somers, for filling up our last prom chaperone spot," Principal Manteghi said, and Ms. Somers blushed as everyone looked at her and gave her a halfhearted round of applause.

"So you're going to the prom, Somers." Coach Mendoza leaned behind Mr. Dykstra to talk to her. "What made you sign up?"

"Someone told me it would be fun," she whispered back, then quickly looked forward so Principal Manteghi wouldn't glare at her for talking during the meeting.

"It will be. This is my fourth prom—I'll make sure we get good assignments. If we're lucky, we'll get stationed right on the dance floor."

"On the dance floor?" Would that mean they'd be dancing . . . together? Ms. Somers had a vision of herself swaying in the gym under the disco ball, wrapped up in Coach Mendoza's strong arms.

Ridiculous. She was being ridiculous. Ms. Somers was *chaperoning* the prom, not *attending* it.

"Oh, yeah. Our very presence is meant to discourage any kind of inappropriate dancing. Since teachers are such trolls."

Coach Mendoza, with a dimple that revealed itself in his left cheek when he smiled, was nothing like a troll.

"Rizzo got removed from dance floor duty last year after he did too many coffee grinders, so I think you'll be in luck," Coach Mendoza said. "I think that second dance floor spot has your name on it, Somers."

"You're both suckers," Mr. Dykstra said. Ms. Somers jumped—she'd forgotten Mr. Dykstra was sitting between them. "I wouldn't touch that prom with a ten-foot pole. It'll be all dancing bears and nonsense."

"I'm sure all of this Kim-and-Teddy stuff will be over by then," Ms. Somers murmured. It would be. Wouldn't it? She couldn't imagine it stretching over the next couple weeks and into May.

"That's why I get my chaperone credits during the chess tournament in January," Mr. Dykstra continued, like Ms. Somers hadn't said anything. "Those kids are zero percent nonsense."

"Nothing worse than nonsense," Coach Mendoza agreed. He winked at Ms. Somers behind Mr. Dykstra's back.

Ms. Somers wondered if maybe her life had been missing a certain amount of nonsense.

CHAPTER TWENTY-FOUR

NICO OSTERMAN
DAY FOUR

Nico always did his best crying in the shower.

He was pretty sure he was the first person to use the shower in the locker room at William Henry Harrison High since the early nineties, at least. Maybe longer. A stream of rust-colored water had shot out of the showerhead for several minutes before it ran clear. But when you needed to cry, like, *really* cry, sometimes you had to make do with what you had.

"Nico?" A voice floated through the empty locker room, echoing as it bounced off the tiles. Nico wished it was Sophie, coming to rescue him, braving the seriously gnarly sweaty-sock stench of the boys' locker room to tell him she'd made a mistake, that of course she didn't mean it, and that the days they'd been apart had been the worst of her life.

Nico held his breath, hoping he'd hear Sophie say that she loved him, and that they'd be together forever.

But Sophie's voice wasn't that low. Not even when she'd had that horrible cold in December and her voice had gone all deep and raspy. She'd told him not to kiss her; she'd said she didn't want to get him sick. But he'd kissed her anyway. Because that's what love was. Needing to kiss someone so badly that you'd happily take on their disgusting, drippy-nosed, hacking-cough cold. And now, that love was gone. Nico sobbed, unable to believe he'd really lost everything.

"Nico? Are you okay?"

Nico heard squeaky shoes approach him, and then stop. He cracked an eye open to see, of all people, Teddy Lin in a William Henry Harrison High T-shirt and gym shorts, paused at the threshold of the showers.

"Whoa," Teddy said.

Teddy stared at Nico. Nico stared at Teddy. Nico was mostly confused about why Sophie had dumped him, but he was pretty sure that Teddy Lin was the author of his misfortune. She'd started acting super weird when Nico told her Teddy was moving to Firenze. And then she'd made bear ears for the entire school. If that wasn't a declaration of love, Nico didn't know what was. And he had once arranged pepperonis into the shape of a heart on a DiGiorno pizza, so yeah. Nico knew a thing or two about love.

"Are you sure you should be in there, Nico?" Teddy asked eventually. "I don't think that water is safe."

"There's nothing this water can do to me that Sophie hasn't already done," Nico whimpered.

"Pretty sure Sophie hasn't given you tetanus." Teddy narrowed his eyes at the rusty showerhead.

"I'll be fine. I'm taking precautions. That's why I'm wearing all my clothes." Nico gestured to his waterlogged track pants. "Please. Just . . . go," Nico whispered, squeezing his eyes shut, unable to look at his rival any longer.

"Coach Mendoza marked you absent," Teddy said.

"I am absent." Nico's eyes snapped open. "Absent from happiness!"

"I'll just—I'll just let him know you're in here, okay?" Teddy hesitated on the threshold to the shower area. "Or maybe you can come out? Dry off a little bit? I'll get you a towel, and we can talk about why you're, um . . . . showering?"

Teddy Lin was *nice*. Nico wanted to hate Teddy for destroying his happiness, but as he watched Teddy looking at him with concern, he couldn't. Teddy had no obligation to lure Nico out of the shower. They'd never even had a conversation before. If their situations were reversed, Nico was pretty sure he wouldn't be here, coaxing Teddy Lin out of the shower.

Then again, Nico spent most of his PE periods faking medical emergencies and hanging out with Nurse O'Leary, who was totally cool.

"I need to be in here right now," Nico said firmly. He wasn't ready to talk about his feelings. Not with anyone, and certainly not with Teddy Lin, no matter how nice he was. "Now, if you respect my rights as an autonomous individual, please leave me alone to cry in watery peace."

"Um . . . okay."

Nico closed his eyes. When he opened them again, Teddy was gone.

It was true that Nico did his best crying in the shower. But he also did his best thinking in the shower. And as yet another tear mingled with the still-kinda-rusty shower water, Nico thought it might be time to stop crying and start thinking.

Usually, Nico liked to do his thinking in the form of a word cloud, or a color story. But he was too distraught for his usual creativity. His word cloud would only say *Sophie, sad, tears, crying, heartbreak,* and that wasn't particularly helpful. Nor was a color story of blue, blue, and more blue. No, what Nico needed now, even though Ms. Thurber would never believe it, was science.

It was true Nico had mostly slept his way through environmental science this year. But somewhere deep in the recesses of his brain, buried along with other stuff from middle school, like the plot of *Animal Farm,* was the scientific method.

Step one: Make an observation.

Done. Nico had observed that Sophie had dumped him. It was pretty hard to miss.

Step two: Form a question.

Why had Sophie dumped him? There was no other question. How could they go from blissfully happy to *over* within a matter of minutes?

Step three: Form a hypothesis.

Sophie had left him for Teddy Lin. It was the only thing that Nico could see clearly through his fog of pain and grief.

Step four: Conduct an experiment.

An experiment . . . Nico turned the water hotter, so hot that it turned his skin pink. What kind of experiment could he conduct? Hmm . . . If Sophie had broken up with Nico *because* of Teddy, then if Nico *removed* Teddy from the situation . . . she'd come back to Nico?

Nico turned the water to freezing cold, trying to calm himself down. That sounded like he was planning to *murder* Teddy Lin! And he wasn't, of course. Nico was a vegan. He wouldn't murder anything. Certainly not a guy who'd been nice enough to try to get him out of this rusty shower.

True, Teddy would remove himself from the situation when he moved to Firenze this summer. But Nico couldn't wait that long. Being away from Sophie hurt too much. No, he needed to remove Teddy now. And he would do that . . . by sending Teddy back to where he'd been before.

Kim! Yes! Of course! As inspiration struck, Nico turned off the shower. His track pants dripped onto the tiled floor as he realized that *of course* the way to *remove* Teddy from the situation was to *return* him to Kim. Kim and Teddy belonged together, just like Nico and Sophie did. And Nico would get them back together, no matter what it took. And then, Sophie would be his again.

Nico's shoes squeaked as he walked back into the main locker room, little eddies of water trailing him as he went. Just as he approached the first bank of lockers, the other guys in his PE class streamed into the locker room from the gym.

"Why are you wet, freak?" Corey Brooks shouted as he walked into the locker room, pulling his gym shirt over his head as he made his way to his locker.

"Why not?" Nico shrugged.

"Hey, Aquaman." Teddy Lin held up his fist for a pound as he walked by. Nico pounded his fist excitedly. He was gonna be like . . . like Teddy Lin's fairy godbrother. Pulling everything together for a magical series of circumstances that would bring Teddy and Kim back together. Put all four of them back on the course of true love. Even if the course of true love was never real smooth.

Hmm. That sounded good. Nico felt like he should maybe write that down.

"What's up with all those bear ears, anyway?" Corey yelled from his locker. "It's weird that Sophie's making them. Why's your girlfriend so obsessed with Lin?"

"She's not my girlfriend . . . right now," Nico said. Because it was true. But it wouldn't be true for long. He smiled brightly at Teddy, who just looked confused. "The ears are her way of supporting Teddy. And he definitely deserves support."

Teddy smiled back, but still looked confused.

"Where have you been, Corey?" Elvis Rodriguez asked as he pulled off his gym shoes. "Teddy Bears wear ears. Team Kim wears red. Everybody knows this."

"I've got better things to do with my time than pay attention to whatever you losers are doing. And nobody was talking to you, Smell-vis!" Corey shot back.

"Smell-vis is not an acceptable nickname!" Elvis cried, jumping to his feet. "I will answer to E-Rod or nothing! And there's no reason to resort to name-calling just because someone can't handle a little baseball glove smacky-smack."

"Dude, I wouldn't brag about that if I were you," Corey said. "It was lame, even for you."

"What happened with the baseball gloves?" somebody called from another set of lockers.

"Nothing, okay?" Corey answered shrilly. "Nothing!"

"Osterman!" Coach Mendoza barked from the locker room door. "Why are you wet?"

"I'm wet with brilliance, Coach!" Nico replied. His experiment would work. He knew it. Before they knew what had happened, Kim and Teddy would be back together, and so would Nico and Sophie.

"I don't even want to know what that means." Coach Mendoza shook his head wearily. "Get some dry clothes out of the Lost and Found, okay?"

The only pair of sweatpants in the Lost and Found was about six inches too short and the only T-shirt in there was ripe with the stench of somebody else's BO, but Nico didn't care.

All he could smell was hope.

And hope smelled like Sun-Ripened Raspberry body spray.

Hope smelled like Sophie.

CHAPTER TWENTY-FIVE

SOPHIE MAEBY
DAY FOUR

"So," Mr. Guzman said from his seat on top of Señora Parrilla's desk, drumming his hands on the edge of the desk. "Did you guys pick a prom theme before Señora Parrilla left on her maternity leave?"

The eight seniors on Prom Committee shifted uncomfortably in their seats. On her side of the room, Sophie exchanged glances with the three Teddy Bears sitting next to her. She wouldn't even look in the direction of Wendy Phan or any of those other deluded Team Kim people. It looked like the freshmen weren't the only ones wearing red anymore. Stupid Corey Brooks had a red sweatband pushing back his thick, curly hair. What a traitor. You'd think the fact that he was on the baseball team would mean he'd be loyal to Teddy—like Josiah Watkins, who was currently sitting on Sophie's left, proudly wearing his ears—but if this whole experience had taught Sophie anything, it was that loyalty was in short supply.

That's why Teddy was such a treasure. And if these Team Kim-bots couldn't see that, then there was no helping them.

Well. Once Sophie's mass order of Team Teddy T-shirts arrived from OverniteTShirtz.com, those red accessories would really look like amateur hour.

"Anyone? Anyone? Bueller?" Mr. Guzman joked.

"Um," Sophie said eventually, breaking the silence that hung in the room. "We'd been talking about Under the Sea?"

"More like Under the Gym," Wendy grumbled.

"I think you mean *inside* the gym," Sophie snapped. "Prom's not in the basement. Sounds like somebody needs a refresher on prepositions."

"Whoa, whoa, whoa." Mr. Guzman held up his hands. "Let's keep it calm, guys. Look. I know the gym isn't anybody's first choice of prom venue. Principal Manteghi told me that we just don't have the budget for anything else this year. And I get it. It sucks. It really does." Sophie almost felt bad for him. Mr. Guzman had no idea what he was walking into here. The issues in Prom Committee ran way deeper than the fact they were going to have prom in the gym. Who cared about the location? "But I'm sure we can think of an amazing theme that will transform the space."

"I don't want to do Under the Sea anymore," Wendy said.

"Me neither," Sophie shot back.

"Great! We agree!" Mr. Guzman said.

"No we don't," Wendy and Sophie said in sync.

"Whoa," Corey said. "Jinx. You owe me a Coke."

"That's not how jinx works!" Sophie said, exasperated.

"Sure it is. You guys said the exact same thing at the exact same time."

"That only works if you're part of the jinx . . . You know what? Forget it." Sophie tossed her curls out of her eyes. Corey was not worth her time.

"So what are some new ideas? We've gotta hammer down a theme today." Mr. Guzman drummed the desk again. Sophie had a feeling that this would become very annoying, very quickly. "We've only got a couple weeks till prom. Principal Manteghi, uh, *reminded* me that the theme's usually been picked way before now."

Quiet descended upon the room again. Sophie wanted to do something that would support Teddy. Prom was definitely going to be hard for him. He and Kim had been such a total lock for king and queen, and now, he probably didn't even know who he was going to go with.

(He was going to go with Sophie. Teddy didn't know this yet, but Sophie did. She just had to think of a really excellent prom-posal. Once she pulled everything together, she'd pop the question.)

"Bears," Noelle Bonolis blurted out from next to Sophie. Sophie shot her a look. Maybe Sophie had been hitting the pro-Teddy rhetoric a little too hard.

"You want to theme the prom *Bears*." Acid dripped from every one of Wendy's words.

"Yes. Bears." Sophie may have thought Noelle had lost it, but she couldn't admit that in front of Team Kim. So she was doubling down on bears. Was this what she had wanted? Of course not. Sophie, if she had thought about it, would have proposed One Night in Venice, or something like that. Something super romantic and Italian, to help Teddy get ready for his new life. Something that would make Teddy look at Sophie with love in his eyes, like she was glowing Under the Tuscan Sun.

"Bears. Um, okay?" Mr. Guzman asked.

"Like the Chicago Bears?" Corey asked.

"Or like a teddy bear tea party?" Wendy couldn't contain her giggles. "My grandma will be really excited about it."

"No! Like neither of those things." Sophie sat up a little straighter in her chair. *Think, Sophie,* she admonished herself. *Think.* "The bear is a . . . majestic creature. Powerful. Fierce. Like . . . like a prom should be."

What was she even saying? She wanted a powerful, fierce prom? None of this made any sense!

"I like the words you're using," Mr. Guzman said encouragingly. Wow, he was nice. Good thing he was teaching seniors. The freshmen would have eaten him alive. Freshmen—timid in the hallways, a disaster in the classroom. Full of contradictions. "But maybe you can help me visualize it a little bit. Show us what you see, Sophie."

"Um. Okay." What *did* she see? "We draw our inspiration from the bear's habitat." Yes! This was a thing! "The majestic brown bear, at home in the great forests of North America, prowling through pine-covered woods."

This could work. Maybe? Sophie felt like it was starting to come together in her mind.

"Picture . . . beautiful pine trees surrounding the gym. Lights twinkling from the ceiling like stars in the night sky. A small pond fed from a babbling brook, like the little waterfall the seniors made last year when the prom theme was A Night in the Tropics."

"A dude in a bear suit crawling around under the basketball hoop," Josiah muttered under his breath. Sophie shot him a look. There was no room for insubordination on Team Teddy!

"If you want to stick a bunch of trees in the gym and dress up like a bear, fine by me," Wendy said. "But I'm not doing it."

"Nobody said you had to go to prom," Sophie said. "In fact, I believe prom would be greatly improved if you and everyone aligning themselves with the tragedy that is Team Kim stayed far, far away."

"Whoa, whoa, whoa." Sophie had the feeling that Mr. Guzman had no idea what he was in for. "Anyone is welcome at prom. Provided that they're a senior."

"Forget the bears," Wendy said. "Who's ready for an idea that's *actually* good?"

Corey and Emma Gertz and Amelia Asaad raised their hands. Sophie rolled her eyes at them. It wasn't her fault that Noelle had stuck her with bears.

"Mr. Guzman is right," Wendy said. "Having prom in the gym sucks. But it's happening, and we have to deal with it. So I say we lean into it."

"You want our prom theme to be Smelly Gym Stank?" Sophie asked archly.

"No." Wendy Phan could be a champion glarer. Sophie had to actively remind herself not to quail in fear. "I think we should do Fifties Sock Hop. Something that makes *sense* in a gym. Diners and milkshakes and records. There's a lot of great stuff in the prom catalogue, and we could borrow a ton of stuff from the theater department. We can make it really unique and original. Make having prom in the gym a good thing."

Crap. That was actually a really cute idea. But Sophie was committed to the bear thing. There was no way she could back down now.

"And *Grease* is Kim's favorite movie," Emma Gertz said, flicking her red-beribboned ponytail.

"Emma!" Wendy scolded her.

"What?" Emma asked. "Is it a secret?"

Ugh. Sophie should have known this was more Team Kim nonsense! Forget leaning into the gym—this was propaganda, pure and simple.

"I cannot think of a more irrelevant factor in choosing a theme," Sophie said. "It's actually *offensive* that you'd even propose a fifties prom. Kim Landis-Lilley is not on Prom Committee."

"Neither is a *bear!*" Wendy said. "Or, for that matter, Teddy Lin!"

"Folks!" Mr. Guzman interrupted them. Sophie thought she detected a slight edge to his voice. "Let's keep it chill. Why don't we put it to a vote?"

Sophie knew exactly how this was going to go. Somehow, Mr. Guzman didn't.

"All those in favor of Bears?"

Sophie, Josiah, and Noelle raised their hands. Sophie coughed, and Madison looked up from whatever she was doing on her phone and raised her hand, too. What could be more important than making sure Teddy Lin got the prom he deserved?! Sophie would have to talk to Madison later.

"All those in favor of Fifties Sock Hop?"

Wendy, Corey, Amelia, and Emma raised their hands.

"So . . . looks like we have a tie," Mr. Guzman said.

"You could be the tiebreaker," Sophie jumped in. "Great shoes, by the way."

"Uh . . . thanks, Sophie." Mr. Guzman looked down at his dress shoes. "But I don't think that's fair. This is *your* prom. I want you guys to come up with something everybody's happy with."

Fat chance of that happening.

"Why don't we just have two proms?" Madison said without looking up from her phone as every head in the room swiveled toward her.

"Oh, uh, well, we don't have the budget for two separate venues—" Mr. Guzman started.

"We don't need that." Madison kept typing as she talked. "Just put a line down the middle of the gym. Like in the cafeteria. Two proms, one space. Boom. Problem solved."

What was Madison thinking? Or was she thinking more clearly than anyone? Sophie goggled at her. There was no way that could work . . . or could it?

"I don't think we need to do that," Mr. Guzman said. "Prom is about the whole class coming together. This seems a bit extreme—"

"I'm fine with it," Wendy said quickly.

"Me too," Sophie said just as quickly.

"This way, people can decide which prom they want to

go to," Wendy said. "I think it'll be pretty obvious which one is better."

"So do I," Sophie said.

"Well . . . this is *your* prom committee . . ." Mr. Guzman hemmed and hawed. "So I guess, uh, we'll put it to a vote? All those in favor of two proms?"

Every single hand in the room went up.

CHAPTER TWENTY-SIX

COREY BROOKS
DAY FIVE

Corey was looking good.

More importantly, he was smelling good. Corey took a deep whiff of his Axe Dark Temptation body spray. Usually he wore Phoenix, but today, he was going to be pure Temptation. The Temptation of Kim Landis-Lilley.

Corey leaned against Kim's locker and ran a hand through his hair. Some girl Corey didn't know sighed from across the hall, probably driven mad by longing. Maybe Dark Temptation was *too* powerful.

"Can I help you?"

Kim was now standing right in front of him. Corey straightened up a little. The cool thing about Kim was that she didn't know she was cool. Like, Corey was pretty sure she'd had that L.L.Bean backpack since seventh grade.

It was like how really, truly hot girls didn't know they were hot. Or didn't act like they were hot. Like, yeah, Sophie Maeby was hot, but how much of that was makeup, you know? Kim didn't even look like she wore makeup, and she was bonkers hot.

It was like Kim was Belle, and every other girl in their grade was one of those blond girls always following Gaston around. Corey had watched *Beauty and the Beast* with his niece over the weekend. Man, did Gaston get a raw deal. That Beast was a total, well . . . beast, and *Gaston* is somehow the villain? Not cool.

Corey had been thinking about asking Kim out even before those two idiots had attacked him out of nowhere, because, as he'd said, she was bonkers hot. But now, he was more determined than ever. He couldn't wait to see the look on Lin's face when he walked into the prom with Kim on his arm.

He hoped it stung as badly as a baseball glove smacked against an unprotected calf muscle.

"Hey, Kimmy." Corey smiled slowly, in a way that he knew, from personal experience, was totally devastating.

"Hi."

Hmm. She didn't appear to be melting at the sight of his devastating smile. Not ideal, but he could keep going.

"So I've got a very exciting update from yesterday's Prom Committee meeting." Corey leaned against Kim's locker with his arm up, the better to show off his biceps in his tight, bright red shirt, and really let that Dark Temptation waft its way down the hall.

Kim sneezed. Twice. Corey folded his arms across his chest. Maybe it was too much Dark Temptation?

"Oh. Um, okay," Kim said. "Well, I'm probably not going to prom, so . . ."

"I think you'll want to go to prom," Corey said, "when you hear what the theme is."

Corey paused for dramatic effect. He searched Kim's face for anticipation, but couldn't find any. Hmm. She was a tricky one.

"The theme is Fifties Sock Hop," he said. "Because I heard that somebody's favorite movie was *Grease*."

"I heard the theme was Bears." Jess Howard was now standing next to Kim. Corey frowned at her. None of this was going how he'd imagined it!

"The theme is also Bears. Kind of. But not really. Don't worry about the bears," Corey said soothingly. "Uh, Jess, can you give us a minute?"

"No," she said brusquely. "Homeroom bell's gonna ring any second. Thanks for the exciting update from Prom Committee. How 'bout you move so Kim can get into her locker?"

Corey slid over to the next locker as Kim opened hers and started pulling books out.

"Listen, Kimmy." Corey wouldn't let Jess stop him. He'd just pretend she wasn't there! "I wanted to talk to you about the prom because I want . . ." Here, he paused for dramatic effect. He couldn't wait to see the look on Kim's face! ". . . you to come with me."

There. He'd said it. How lucky was Kim?! Corey hadn't

planned on taking himself off the prom date market this early. He was going to wait for offers to come rolling in.

"Oh." Kim wasn't even looking at him! She was still getting books out of her locker? What was *wrong* with her?! Had she not noticed the red shirt he'd worn specifically because it was her favorite color? Could she not see the red ribbon he'd tied around his wrist *in support of her*? Should he pull the waistband of his boxers up above his jeans so she could see that they were red, too? Red and covered in hearts? He'd picked them out especially for today! "Thanks, Corey. That's really nice of you. But like I said, I'm not going, so . . . no."

"NO?!" Corey hadn't realized he had actually said "NO?!" out loud. He'd thought it had just been inside his head. But from the way everyone in the senior hall was looking at them, he'd definitely said it out loud.

"She said she doesn't want to go to the prom, genius." One of the weird art dudes was now standing on the other side of Kim. His jeans were covered in various dried paint splotches and his hands were dirty with what Corey seriously hoped was clay. If *this* clown thought he was going after Kim, he had another think coming. Kim would never go out with someone wearing a hideous red sweater with an ugly Santa stitched onto it. Who wore an ugly Christmas sweater when it wasn't Christmas? "Prom's a meaningless construct, right, Kim?"

"I don't have a *problem* with prom, Toby," Kim said. "I'm just . . ."

"Not going," Jess finished for her. "Don't you guys have your own lockers to be at?"

"Don't *you*?" Corey shot back.

"Forget prom, Kim," the guy who was apparently named Toby said. "Let me buy you a pizza."

"I'll buy you two pizzas!" Corey blurted out. What was happening to him? Why was he so off his game?

"Guys, she doesn't even like pizza." Marcus Dickson, from the track and field team, was now holding up two enormous bags of candy, nearly obscuring the Bulls logo on his red jersey. "M&M, Kimberly?" he offered, shaking the bags at her.

The bell rang—five minutes to get to homeroom.

"Thanks, everyone." Kim shut her locker and clicked the lock into place, looking flustered. "But I've gotta—I've gotta get to class."

"Think about my offer!" Corey shouted after her.

"And mine!" Toby echoed.

"And mine!" Marcus shook his M&M's some more.

"You guys suck," Corey muttered as Kim disappeared down the hall. "And your red shirts are lame. Especially you, Santa."

"You *all* suck." Jess rolled her eyes. "Three words for y'all—never gonna happen."

She was wrong, Corey thought as he watched Jess follow Kim down the hall. It *would* happen. Corey wanted Kim even more than he'd wanted her before. And Corey always got what he wanted.

"M&M?" Marcus offered.

"Sure, I'll take some," the weird art guy said.

Corey shook his head. No M&M's for him. He had to stay lean.

He had a girl to win.

CHAPTER TWENTY-SEVEN

TOBY NEALE
DAY FIVE

There was something about Kim Landis-Lilley.

Toby didn't know how he'd never noticed it before. Maybe because he hadn't talked to her, really talked to her, since they'd been in ceramics together freshman year. Their potter's wheels had been next to each other, and Kim had chatted to him genially while she'd thrown terrible pot after terrible pot. He still remembered the half-collapsed teapot Kim had pulled out of the kiln as her final project, remembered how hard they'd laughed when she'd tried to distract Mr. Buckley from its misshapenness by covering the whole thing in enormous purple flowers.

They hadn't had a class together since. But because she was Kim, she always smiled and waved at him in the halls when they passed each other. And Toby had never thought he was romantically interested in her or anything like that, but when he'd heard that Kim and Teddy had broken up, he felt something within him stir. It was the same impulse he felt when got inspired by a new project. The need to create something where nothing had been before. Toby had dashed to the art room after school, covering canvas after canvas in abstract works inspired by red sweaters and doe-brown eyes ringed with molten gold. Kim Landis-Lilley was his *muse*.

Which was exactly why he needed to *create* for her! Toby staggered back against the lockers. What was he thinking, asking Kim out for pizza?! Kim didn't need pizza! She needed *art*.

It was all coming to him now. Ideas flew faster and faster. Toby tore his sketchbook out of his backpack and drew feverishly, not wanting to forget a thing. It would take him some time to gather his supplies, to block out his piece, to pull all of this together . . . but Toby knew it would be worth it.

Kim Landis-Lilley was his goddess. And that was exactly how he was going to immortalize her.

"Mr. Neale," Principal Manteghi said as she rounded the corner. "I believe you have approximately forty-five seconds to make it to homeroom without getting a demerit for tardiness. I just gave your classmate Mr. Rothbart one for loitering. Perhaps you'd like one as well?"

Toby sighed as he clutched his notebook to his chest.

None of these philistines appreciated the artistic process.

CHAPTER TWENTY-EIGHT

PRINCIPAL MANTEGHI
DAY FIVE

"Mr. Guzman," Principal Manteghi said as she walked into her office. Chris Guzman was already waiting in there for her. He rose to shake her hand. "Is now still a good time to check in?" she asked as she sat.

"Absolutely." Mr. Guzman smiled brilliantly, like the entire school wasn't in danger of imminent collapse. Principal Manteghi had spent the last twenty minutes listening to the volleyball coach complain that the season was ruined, because no one on Team Kim would spike a ball set by a Teddy Bear, and vice versa.

Focus. She could deal with the volleyball team later. Right now, she had to check in with Mr. Guzman.

"Great." Principal Manteghi tried to force herself to mirror Mr. Guzman's brilliant smile. It felt more like a grimace. "Just wanted to see how your first couple days have been, make sure Prom Committee got off to a good start . . ."

"Totally. We even nailed down the theme, like you asked."

"Great." Principal Manteghi sighed with relief. At least that was one thing she could check off her list. "Did they end up going with Under the Sea?"

"Uh . . . not exactly." Mr. Guzman shifted in his seat. Uh-oh. Not a good sign. In Principal Manteghi's experience, people either shifted in the seat across from her because they were about to tell her something they didn't want to, or because they had hemorrhoids. Principal Manteghi didn't want to wish hemorrhoids on Mr. Guzman, but that was exactly what she found herself doing. "They decided to take a really creative approach."

"Meaning . . . ?"

"There's actually going to be *two* prom themes."

Principal Manteghi stared at Mr. Guzman. He blinked nervously back at her.

"Two," she repeated.

"Yup." He nodded. "Two."

"We don't have the budget for two proms." Principal Manteghi was trying not to panic. "We barely have the budget for one."

"No, no, no!" Mr. Guzman rushed to assure her. "It's still just the one prom. Same venue, same budget, same everything. Just . . . two themes."

She raised her eyebrows at him.

"They're going to put a line down the middle and split the gym in half," he explained weakly.

Principal Manteghi could barely keep herself from dropping her head into her hands and emitting a primal scream.

"Does this have anything to do with Kim and Teddy?" she asked wearily.

"Uh, I don't think so?" Mr. Guzman screwed up his nose in confusion. "Are those the seniors that broke up?"

Principal Manteghi would have bet her entire teacher's pension that the two prom themes had *everything* to do with Kim and Teddy.

"Listen, it was the only thing everyone on Prom Committee could agree on," Mr. Guzman said. "Isn't it better that they have the prom they want? And I promise we'll stay within budget."

Maybe she should demand that they choose one theme. At the moment, she honestly felt like canceling prom altogether. But what kind of monster would that make her?

"At least there's a theme," Principal Manteghi said eventually. "Er—themes."

"Yeah." Mr. Guzman smiled again, like having two proms at the same time was absolutely normal and not a sign that her beloved school was collapsing in on itself like a dying star. "Anything else you need from me?"

"Just a reminder to update your school calendar. They're repaving the parking lot the first weekend in May and you'll need to remove your car promptly. There was a reminder email."

"Cool." Mr. Guzman grinned. "Thanks!"

Principal Manteghi missed the days when she still felt

like everything was cool. Two prom themes?! She'd be the laughingstock of the district.

She grabbed a fistful of Hershey's Kisses out of the glass jar on her desk, resigned herself to the fact that she'd be here way too late for a Friday afternoon, and got to work.

CHAPTER TWENTY-NINE

OLIVIA LANDIS-LILLEY
WEEK TWO, DAY ONE

The entire freshman class was wearing red.

Last week, there had been red here and there, a shirt or a pair of socks or whatever, but today, the random bits of red had exploded into full-on ocular assault.

"Did we miss an email or something?" Daisy asked as an army of red-clad freshmen streamed around them, hurrying down to lunch. The hallway before school had been red, and her morning classes had been red, but this felt like the first time she was really feeling the impact of all the red. So much red. Olivia had been too tired to process what was happening first thing on a Monday morning. Uncharacteristically, she'd slept in really late over the weekend, which had totally thrown off her schedule. But she hadn't expected the constant barrage of texts and Facebook messages and

Instagram notifications pinging into her phone all hours of the day and night, desperately asking how her sister was doing, asking if it was true that Kim had been invited into a secret society of dumped celebrities that Jennifer Aniston ran out of a villa on the north shore of Kauai, and could Kim introduce them to Selena Gomez. At first, Olivia had taken great pleasure in shutting down each and every one of these idiotic messages, but around 3:00 a.m. on Sunday, she'd gotten so annoyed she'd hidden her phone in the freezer. Mama Dawn had found it this morning when she'd gone in for a toaster waffle, but luckily hadn't asked any questions, only handed the phone back to Olivia with a raised eyebrow. If Mama K had found it, Olivia would have been in for a long discussion about responsible electronics care, and probably a lot of probing questions about whether or not she was being bullied on social media.

Which she wasn't. If anything, she was a victim of too *much* support, drowning in the tidal wave of emotion everyone inexplicably felt for Kim.

Olivia's eyes blurred as the red T-shirts and hoodies and pants swam in front of her, an endless sea of nature's most jarring color. She rubbed her face with her Mighty Flying Arrows softball sweatshirt, trying to clear her fuzzy head.

"Seriously," Daisy said. "Is there, like, a freshman listserv that we're not a part of?"

"There's a lot we're not a part of. And that is fine."

Not that she'd know if there was a listserv. Her olivia .landislilley@WHHHS.edu email had crashed due to the sheer volume in her inbox and she couldn't log on anymore. Olivia pulled out her lunch bag and slammed her locker shut, finding brief satisfaction in the noise. She couldn't believe all these people were wearing red because of Kim. How had the Kim worship spread so far and so quickly?

Maybe Olivia should skip lunch and see if Coach Mendoza would let her beat the crap out of the punching bag in the weight room. That would probably feel even better than slamming a locker.

Gabe Koontz walked past Olivia, dressed like a bottle of ketchup.

"Was that . . ." Daisy trailed off, mouth open as her eyes followed the ketchup-Koontz down the stairs.

"Yup. Your eyes did not deceive you. That was Gabe Koontz, dressed as a condiment, all in support of my sister, the Red Queen of William Henry Harrison High."

What was *wrong* with everyone? None of these people even knew who Kim was, not really! Because if they'd known her, they'd have known her favorite color was purple. And Olivia couldn't fathom why they *cared*. Kim was a senior. Olivia was pretty confident that with the exception of Daisy, none of these freshmen had ever even talked to Kim. Why was one stupid breakup taking over everyone's lives? Was there really nothing more interesting going on at William Henry Harrison High?

"Olivia." Diamond Allen materialized in front of them, dressed in an improbably glamorous red jumpsuit with a delicate halter neck. "How *is* Kim?" she asked, all sympathy and solicitousness.

"She's fine," Olivia grunted as she power walked toward the stairs, hoping to escape to lunch.

"Fine? Really? That's not what I heard." Diamond didn't

take the hint and followed closely behind Olivia and Daisy, her platform sandals making little clomping sounds as she walked. "I mean, yes, of course, Kim is so brave, but the fact that she's debuting a one-woman show this weekend called *Linsane in the Membrane* makes me think she's struggling more than we see."

"What are you talking about?"

"Sorry, I should have said the full title," Diamond apologized. "It's called *Linsane in the Membrane: My Journey from Heartbreak to Healing.*"

Daisy guffawed. Olivia was too perplexed to even laugh at the absurdity of it all. There was no way Kim had written a one-woman show. Or that Kim would ever perform a one-woman show. Kim hadn't even done karaoke with Mama Dawn on their Carnival cruise, no matter how much Mama Dawn had begged. Even Olivia had caved eventually, but Kim had chosen to cheer from the safety of her seat with a virgin piña colada.

"Mr. Rizzo's letting her use the black box to perform," Diamond continued. "But this weekend is really only the beginning. They're actually filming Kim's show for a Netflix special."

"No one wants to see Kim on Netflix!" Olivia bellowed.

All of the freshmen massing at the bottom of the stairs, waiting to get into the lunchroom, turned to stare at Olivia.

"Wow, Olivia." Chloe Baker turned around to whisper at Olivia disapprovingly. "That was very harsh."

"She's your sister, dude," Diamond said. "Show a little compassion."

"What's holding up this line?" Gabe Koontz yelled, the

top of his ketchup bottle quivering with rage. "I heard there were Tater Tots today!"

Olivia curled her fists into balls, trying to calm down as conversation resumed around her and the freshmen slowly made their way into the cafeteria. She was so tired of people asking her about Kim. Tired of people talking about Kim. Tired of people expecting her to have some kind of response to Kim, and tired of people treating Olivia like she was some kind of heartless monster because she wasn't consumed by the tragedy of her sister's breakup. *Kim* wasn't even consumed with the tragedy of her own breakup! Olivia wished all of these red sycophants could have seen Kim last night, laughing it up in the kitchen with Mama K as the two of them made vegetarian lasagna, even though Olivia had asked Mama K repeatedly to take that dish out of the rotation, since it didn't have enough protein and the refined carbohydrates in the pasta weren't nutrient-dense. Kim certainly hadn't looked brokenhearted then. But Olivia knew if she tried to tell anyone that, no one would believe her, and they'd probably inform her that Kim had just become the country's youngest senator or something.

"Wanna get Tots?" Daisy asked gently.

"Sure." Olivia unclenched her fists.

Screw nutrient-dense. Olivia needed a Tot.

The way things were going, she was going to need a lot of Tots.

CHAPTER THIRTY

PHIL SPOONER
WEEK TWO, DAY ONE

"We are looking good, Spoony," Diamond Allen crooned with satisfaction as she surveyed the sea of red on their side of the cafeteria. "We are looking really good."

Phil didn't know about we. But Diamond certainly looked amazing. She looked like she should have been on a fashion runway, or maybe going to the Oscars, or something. Phil didn't even know what to call her outfit—it was pants that were somehow connected to the top, all made out of the same material—but it was incredible. Phil found himself mesmerized by the small gold necklace hanging against the elegant indentations of her collarbone, by the poetic curve of her shoulder against her top's delicate strap.

Who knew a shoulder could be poetic?

"I thought it would just be the freshmen," Diamond continued. Phil tore his gaze away from her shoulder, not wanting to look creepy. "But it's not. It's everyone on our side. Even the seniors! Did you see, Spoony? Corey Brooks? Wendy Phan? Jess Howard? We even got Jess Howard! That's, like, as close to Kim as you can get!"

Phil had seen Jess Howard. But for the first time this year, he couldn't have said anything about her. He didn't remember if she'd been wearing red, magenta, or any other color of the rainbow. He couldn't even be sure she hadn't been dressed as a ketchup bottle, like Gabe Koontz, who was trying to sit comfortably in his bulky costume. All he could see was Diamond, her eyes sparkling with excitement. He loved the way her voice sounded like a song, the way she came up with the funniest stuff in improv class like she wasn't even trying, and the way she laughed with her whole mouth wide open, so he could see every single one of her brilliantly white teeth.

Get a grip, Phil! he scolded himself. There was no way Diamond saw him the same way he saw her. After all, Diamond had a face that could launch a thousand ships, and Phil barely had a face. But just being next to her, hearing every one of her spectacularly enunciated words, was enough for him. It was more than enough.

It was more than he had ever dreamed.

"Hey, Spoony." A couple of sophomore girls stopped by their table. *Sophomores? Talking to Phil? Sophomores who knew his name?!* Phil was reaching unprecedented heights. The Phil Spooner of a couple months ago would never have dreamed that he'd be here, eating lunch with people, with *Diamond Allen*, and talking to *sophomores* who *knew his name*. "We heard you saw Teddy Lin chop down all the trees in Kim's backyard. They, like, totally squashed all the patio furniture when they fell. Is that true?"

"Um." Phil looked at the expectant faces of the sophomores, hanging on his every word. He looked at the ketchup bottle that was Gabe Koontz; at Chloe Baker, practically trembling with fear at the prospect of rogue trees squashing patio furniture; and at Diamond, beautiful, brilliant Diamond, leaning toward him, desperate to hear what he had to say. They were all desperate to hear what he had to say. Their attention made Phil feel like he was flying, but flying like Orville Wright, in a rudimentary airplane with no roof that might send him tumbling from the skies at any moment. "Yes?"

"I knew it!" the sophomores shrieked. "Oh my God," one of them said. "Apparently one of the trees was this, like, very rare maple that had been growing since, like, Abraham Lincoln was born. The tree was basically a historic landmark."

"Teddy Lin *murdered* those trees," Chloe pronounced solemnly as the sophomores left. "The police should have arrested him when I called about the snakes. They could have prevented tree murder."

Phil pulled the napkin out of his lunch bag and dabbed at the sweat beading on his brow. He had never set out to smear Teddy Lin. But here he was, painting Teddy as some kind of vigilante lumberjack with a vendetta against patio furniture. Never mind the fact that most of Team Kim was still talking about the fact that Teddy Lin had gotten the Olympics canceled.

"I can't believe Olivia didn't mention this when I talked to her earlier," Diamond mused. "Man, she is so shady."

"You were talking to Olivia?" Phil dabbed harder, like maybe if he dabbed hard enough, the sweat would recede back into his forehead. Was this it? The end? If anyone was going to catch Phil in his web of lies, a web that had started so innocuously and had spun further and further out of control, it was going to be Olivia. Maybe Olivia even knew the *real* reason Kim and Teddy had broken up. Maybe it had nothing to do with Instagram. Phil folded his napkin, trying to find a dry corner that wasn't drenched with his sweat.

"Mm-hmm," Diamond said. "And she said nothing about the trees. And she acted like she didn't even know about Kim's one-woman show this weekend."

"Oh, right." Phil had forgotten about Kim's nonexistent one-woman show. Had he made that up? Or had someone else said it? He couldn't even remember anymore!

"That girl has her head so far inside her softball glove, she wouldn't even notice if Teddy Lin set her house on fire." Diamond shrugged. "This is why Kim needs us, Spoony. She needs to see we're on her side."

Phil had a bad feeling that by this time tomorrow, everyone would be saying that Teddy Lin had set Kim's house on fire. Maybe Phil should start a good rumor about Teddy that would balance out all the terrible ones he'd accidentally found himself embroiled in? Or maybe he should say absolutely nothing.

"I just hope Kim can relax on the cruise she's going on this summer," Diamond said. "Apparently, the governor is paying for it, just as an acknowledgment of all she's gone through."

Phil nearly spat out his fruit punch.

CHAPTER THIRTY-ONE

NICO OSTERMAN
WEEK TWO, DAY TWO

"Have a heart!" Nico called, waving his red felt hearts as students zipped around the cafeteria, careful not to cross the yellow line. Nico, of course, was straddling the yellow line, his plastic baggie of felt hearts resting on a small folding table he'd liberated from the back of Ms. Somers's room. "Join the HeartBeats! Let's get Kim and Teddy back together! Do you believe in love?" he asked a random freshman girl who scuttled nervously by him in a red dress with red tights, the red ribbon in her ponytail trailing behind her. "Come on. Don't you believe in love?"

"Nico," Sophie hissed. She was standing before him, hands on her hips, teddy bear ears in her curly hair, still as beautiful as ever. Annoyed, but still beautiful. "Why are you handing out lumpy red circles?"

"These aren't lumpy red circles." He clutched one to his chest, affronted. "They're *hearts*."

"Okay. Why are you handing out 'hearts'?" she air-quoted.

"Because this isn't right." Nico drew himself up to his full six-foot-two height. "You are sowing discord and division where there should be harmony and unity."

"Have you been reading your mom's Word-of-the-Day calendar again?" Sophie crossed her arms in front of the TEAM TEDDY logo on her blue T-shirt.

"No!" He had, in fact, been reading his mom's Word-of-the-Day calendar again. Yesterday had been *harmony*. Today was *unity*. That would make even the most cynical skeptic believe in signs!

"Can you please get back on the right side of the line and stop embarrassing me?"

"I'm not embarrassing you! This has nothing to do with you!" It had everything to do with her. But Sophie didn't need to know that. "And I don't believe in the line anymore."

"Um, hello, Nico. Look at the line." Sophie pointed. "It's right there."

"I don't believe in the line as a *metaphor*!"

"What even are these?" Sophie pulled a felt heart out of his baggie.

"I told you. They're hearts."

"But what do they *mean*?"

"They *mean* that anyone wearing them is a member of the HeartBeats, a group dedicated to getting Kim and Teddy back together, no matter what. To getting things back to the way they should be."

179

"You're being ridiculous."

"Is it ridiculous to believe in *love*?" Nico cried. "You don't just throw away something that's good—something that's *great*—because of Italy! Love is stronger than Italy!"

A guy wearing red sweatpants and a red headband walked by and gave Nico some serious side-eye. Nico halfheartedly held a heart out toward him. He ignored it.

"You're being really disrespectful," Sophie said.

"To *what*?"

"To Italy, for one. To me, for another. You're making a mockery of everything I've done with the Teddy Bears. Like, how does this even work?" She slapped the felt heart in her hand onto her chest. It immediately fell to the floor. Sophie didn't bother to pick it up, which Nico thought was, ironically, extremely disrespectful. "You can't even wear these hearts. You need, like, a pin or something."

"Maybe you don't wear it," Nico muttered. He may not have totally thought this through. "Maybe you just hold it or something."

"But most importantly," Sophie continued like he hadn't said anything, "you're being really disrespectful to Kim and Teddy. It was *their* decision to break up, and we have to respect that."

"Since when did Teddy Lin's feelings become 'most importantly'?" Nico air-quoted right back at her. "You don't even know him."

"I know everything I need to know! Teddy!" Sophie cried as the man himself walked into the cafeteria, Elvis Rodriguez at his side. "Save me a seat outside, okay?" she shouted at Teddy as he walked toward them.

"Um . . . okay," Teddy said.

"Teddy!" Nico cried. "Remember when you and Kim were peanut butter and jelly at the Halloween dance? Didn't that feel *right*?"

"It felt kind of itchy?" Teddy screwed up his nose in confusion.

"Come on, man," Elvis said. "Let's go sit."

"Shut this down, Nico," Sophie hissed through her grin.

"I'm shutting this UP," Nico said, and even though that didn't sound right, he knew what he meant.

It was only the beginning for the HeartBeats.

CHAPTER THIRTY-TWO

ELVIS RODRIGUEZ
WEEK TWO, DAY TWO

"This is weird, Elvis," Teddy said as they sat outside, taking the first bites of their lunches.

"What's weird?" Elvis said.

"Everything."

Elvis laughed, but not because it was particularly funny. Everything *was* weird. It all felt wrong, and off, like he'd gone from being a regular Spider-Man to Dark Spider-Man, with three sets of arms. Not that Elvis thought he was evil or anything. He scratched under the collar of his itchy TEAM TEDDY T-shirt, wishing he'd washed it before pulling it on. Or that he'd just worn a Chicago Bears jersey like Josiah and his boyfriend had. They looked a lot more comfortable than Elvis felt.

As he watched Teddy chew his sandwich despondently—who knew a chew could be so despondent?—he knew he'd done the right thing, supporting his friend. Scratchy or not, pulling on the TEAM TEDDY shirt had been the right choice. But that didn't mean he didn't miss Jess any less. When she'd been talking in history yesterday about the whitewashing of World War I and how her great-great-grandfather was in the Ninety-Third Infantry, he missed her brilliance so badly it was like a visceral ache. And when she dropped her book in the hallway a couple paces in front of him this morning, he didn't recognize the cover, and Elvis realized that for the first time in years, he didn't know what Jess was reading. How could he not know what Jess was reading? It was as wrong and terrible as if he'd forgotten her name.

At least the sun felt nice.

CHAPTER THIRTY-THREE

JESS HOWARD
WEEK TWO, DAY THREE

Jess, in general, didn't really believe that things could go too far. Well, she didn't believe that good things could go too far. Certainly, if you put even one toe over the line and onto the side of darkness, you'd gone too far. Ask Anakin Skywalker how flirting with the dark side had gone for him—or better yet, ask the younglings at the Jedi Temple on Coruscant. But if you were on the right side of history, there was no way you could go too far. And Jess was doing the right thing. Supporting Kim was absolutely the right thing. Even if wearing red leggings and her mom's Wisconsin sweatshirt from her old Alpha Kappa Alpha days felt like all kinds of wrong. The reds didn't even match.

On her way out of school, Jess saw a tiny girl—had to be a freshman—wearing all red, sobbing on the phone as she complained that Ms. Powell had taken away their desks and made everyone on Team Kim stand throughout class. Which was way over the line—there was no way a teacher would do that. But then she heard that Mr. Dykstra had given everyone wearing teddy bear ears in his fifth-period class extra homework, which also made no sense—Jess wasn't even totally sure that Mr. Dykstra knew who Kim and Teddy were, and he hadn't given her class any extra work.

This was what this whole week had been like. All anyone could talk about was Kim and Teddy, and what side had done what to whom. At this point, the volleyball team's implosion had become legendary, and the current rumor was that the school had canceled the volleyball program altogether. French Club was facing disciplinary action after they'd ripped the French flag in half, separating the Team Kim red from the Team Teddy blue, and retreated to opposite sides of Madame Bisset's classroom to build barricades and belt out hastily rewritten selections from *Les Miz*. If you believed the rumors, Principal Manteghi hadn't been able to extricate them all, and sometimes you could steal hear the plaintive tune of "Bring Kim Home" or "Do You Hear Teddy Lin Sing?" if you wandered too close to the language arts hall. Jess hadn't heard them, but she was never over there.

"It was, like, totally bizarre," Noelle Bonolis said loudly as she and Madison Charles cut in front of Jess, their dumb teddy bear ears obstructing her view. She couldn't believe all those Teddy Bears had matching T-shirts now, too. Didn't Sophie Maeby have anything better to do with her time? "Coach Mendoza and Coach Finn got in a fistfight in the teachers' lounge. All because of Kim and Teddy."

Jess snorted. No way. Absolutely no way.

"I don't think Coach Mendoza would hit a girl," Madison said doubtfully.

"He had to," Noelle insisted. "It was self-defense. Coach Finn came at him with all this Krav Maga. Apparently she used to date this guy who was in the Israel Defense Forces. He personally trained her, and now she's lethal."

"No way."

"Way. She kicked the table in half, and then Coach Mendoza had to defend himself using a broken-off table leg. Luckily, he's, like, awesome with a baseball bat. He was able to fight her off, but it was close. And the table is totally destroyed."

"Wow. I—oh my God."

Jess stopped as she saw what Madison was talking about. Two guys from the maintenance team were wheeling a dolly containing a broken wooden table. Could that be the table from the teachers' lounge? Was it at all possible that any of this was true?!

Maybe things had, in fact, gone too far.

CHAPTER THIRTY-FOUR

KIM LANDIS-LILLEY
WEEK TWO, DAY FOUR

Everyone was staring at Kim as she walked into school.

Unfortunately, people staring at Kim had become way too common these past weeks. At least it was almost Friday. Kim didn't even care that she was still grounded into oblivion and would be spending the whole weekend doing nothing but homework and helping Mama K in the garden, just like she had last weekend. She just wanted to get out of school, away from a place where people talked *about* her instead of talking *to* her.

At home, the primary conversation remained, "How could you have skipped school, Kim? We're so disappointed in you." Sure, it was punctuated by Mama K complimenting how hard Kim had worked to pull up her history grade after turning her paper in late, or Mama Dawn winking as she silently handed over a butterscotch dip she'd driven home from the Dairy Star, but Kim hated that she'd disappointed them. Kim hated disappointing anyone. She even felt bad for letting Olivia down when she'd barked, "Kim, did you finish the almond milk? You know I need it to make my overnight oats." But both her moms' crushing disappointment and Olivia's need for proats—protein oats—were infinitely preferable to hearing vague whispers about herself.

Kim kept her head down and tried not to be bothered by the gossiping Teddy Bears or the stares of students wearing red—why were *they* staring? Weren't they supposed to be on her side? And what was up with the red, anyway? Why red? Kim had asked Olivia, since she was pretty sure it had started with the freshmen, but Olivia had only shrugged in response. Kim's favorite color was purple.

She pulled out her phone, trying to distract herself. But there it was again—the email from the limo company reminding her that the remaining balance was due on the limo she'd put a deposit down on. What was she going to do? Cancel it and lose her deposit? Or spend the whole night driving around in a limo with Jess? She couldn't imagine going to prom. Not after she and Teddy had made so many plans, not after they'd been looking forward to prom for the past four years. It would hurt too much.

Yeah, maybe she'd just ask Jess if she wanted to take a limo to the movies.

"Kim!" Jess charged through the crowd, fighting the students streaming into the building as she rushed down the hallway, her backpack bouncing as she ran toward Kim. "Have you been to your locker yet?"

"No. Why?" she asked curiously.

"There something you're gonna want to see. Well, not that you'll *want* to see, but that you'll definitely see…" Jess trailed off, then forcefully exhaled. "I wanted to prepare you, but I'm realizing that there's no way to prepare you."

"Prepare me for what?" Kim started picking up speed, power walking so fast she was almost jogging, wondering what Jess could possibly be talking about.

"For… this."

Kim skidded to a stop. There had formerly been a blank stretch of white wall before the turn into the senior hallway. But now, that wall was covered with an absolutely enormous mural.

"Is that… me?" Kim gasped. In the center of the painting, a figure with long brown hair, wearing a William Henry Harrison High softball uniform, stood daintily on top of a seashell. It looked like her, but an infinitely more beautiful version of her. The Kim in the painting was Kim on her best possible day, filtered by the most flattering Snapchat filter imaginable.

"Guess Botticelli didn't get the memo that Elvis and I broke up," Jess grumbled.

Kim dragged her eyes away from seashell Kim and saw two angels on the left side of the painting: an angel Jess with her arms wrapped around an angel Elvis. On the other side of the painting, Olivia, also in her softball uniform, held up a track jacket for Kim. Olivia, Kim had a feeling, was not going to be too pleased about this.

Was *Kim* pleased about this? She didn't even know! She felt like she should have been embarrassed that everyone was staring at her and whispering about her, embarrassed that there was a way prettier version of her floating around on a clamshell outside the senior hall. But if Kim was being honest with herself, she'd have to admit that she was immensely flattered.

"*The Birth of Kim-us.*" Jess guffawed. "Oh, man. I just noticed the title. This is *nuts*. Manteghi is gonna flip."

"How did someone even do this?" Kim murmured. There had been nothing on the wall yesterday. It seemed impossible that someone had created the entire mural in one night, never mind the fact that the mysterious artist had somehow broken into the school after hours. "Nobody could paint something this fast."

"It's not painted," Jess said. "Come closer. See? It's all been, like, photoshopped. This is a really giant poster."

"Huh." Now that she knew, Kim could clearly see that the poster was hanging off the wall, and the brushstrokes had been created digitally. That didn't make it any less impressive. If anything, she was almost *more* impressed that it had been done digitally. Kim's only experience with Photoshop had been watching Mama K try to put a smile onto Olivia's glowering face for the Christmas card a couple years ago, and that had failed spectacularly. But *how* wasn't even the most important question. "*Why* would someone do this?" Kim murmured even more quietly. It had been weird enough that Corey had asked her to prom, and Toby had wanted to get her pizza, and Marcus had gotten her M&M's, but now *this*? This was . . . a lot. Not a *bad* a lot, but just . . . a lot.

"Manteghi's gonna flip," Jess repeated, "and those Teddy Bears are gonna *freak*. One in particular. Is Angel Elvis wearing a diaper? Maybe this is some kind of artistic commentary on the fact that he's a giant baby."

Kim didn't care what the Teddy Bears thought. But she found she *did* still care what Teddy thought. What would he think when he saw giant-seashell-Kim? Would someone create a giant mural of Teddy on the opposite wall?

Actually ... Kim stilled for a moment. Had people been asking Teddy to the prom, too? Probably. They must have been. And every time she'd seen him recently, he was practically attached at the hip to Sophie Maeby, queen of the Teddy Bears. They must be going to prom together, Kim thought glumly. He'd replaced Kim already.

"Well, Kim, looks like you've got a secret admirer with some serious Photoshop skills," Jess said as she slung an arm around Kim. "Or maybe not so secret. It has to be Toby, right? I don't think anybody else could do this."

Toby Neale. Of course. Kim should have thought of him immediately—he was basically the Banksy of William Henry Harrison High. They hadn't really spoken since their ceramics class freshman year, but it was hard to forget about someone who stickered the school with tiny cacti.

"Toby's not my secret admirer. This was some kind of Team Kim protest art."

"No way," Jess scoffed. "Look at your face. This isn't, like, a giant mural of Big Brother in Oceania. This is a love letter."

A love letter. Kim had been with Teddy for so long, the idea of someone else liking her was so bizarre and foreign she didn't even know how to process it. When Toby had asked her about pizza the other day, had he been *asking her out*?! Kim hadn't even realized. She certainly wasn't ready to date anyone else! Even if Teddy was. Part of Kim wanted to roll into the cafeteria with Nico Osterman on her arm—just to see how Sophie and Teddy liked *that*. But deep down, she knew she wouldn't. She wasn't ready. And she didn't know if she'd ever be.

The bell for homeroom rang. Absolutely no one moved.

"Seniors!" Principal Manteghi's voice boomed over the crowd. "That was the bell for homeroom. Is everyone here looking for demerits? Dustin, that's one for loitering. Does anyone else—oh."

Kim realized that Principal Manteghi's route from the front door to her office must not have taken her past the senior hallway. Kim turned to see Principal Manteghi standing behind her, her mouth in a perfectly round O of disbelief.

"Kim," Principal Manteghi said weakly. "Did you have anything to do with this?"

"No, Principal Manteghi." Kim had very neat handwriting, but she couldn't draw anything more elaborate than a series of straight lines. And she was even worse at Photoshop than Mama K was.

"Do you have any information about who might have done this?"

"No, Principal Manteghi."

Principal Manteghi sighed.

"If anyone has any information about the vandalism of the senior hallway, please report to me immediately," Principal Manteghi announced. "Otherwise, proceed to homeroom, or the entire senior class will receive four demerits for loitering, tardiness, and disruption to the academic process. Dustin Rothbart, I saw that look. That's two."

Kim didn't know about the academic process, but as Jess pulled her down the hallway, she was certainly feeling disrupted.

What would Teddy think when he saw this?

CHAPTER THIRTY-FIVE

NICO OSTERMAN
WEEK TWO, DAY FOUR

Nico was late. Like, really late. Like, he had to check in at the front desk and get a pass late.

What the . . . There was a giant softball lady on a clam on the wall. Was that . . . Kim?! Nico leaned closer. It certainly looked like her. What was this thing? It looked sort of familiar. Nico pulled out his phone.

"Clam lady," he googled. "Lady on a clam," he tried. "Lady on a shell." Yes! That was it! *The Birth of Venus*, by Sandro Botticelli, circa 1486. Uffizi Gallery, Florence. Florence . . . That sounded familiar. Nico clicked on the Wikipedia page for Florence.

Firenze! Florence was *Firenze!* Where Teddy was moving! Nico staggered back a bit, thrown by the force of what he had uncovered. Nico wasn't being disrespectful to Teddy, like Sophie had so cruelly suggested. He was *helping* Teddy. Because clearly, Teddy had made this giant poster thing to get Kim back. Maybe Teddy wanted Kim to move to Firenze with him! Maybe they'd go to, like, Firenze College together! Yes! Nico had been right all along. The HeartBeats were what Teddy *really* wanted, not the Teddy Bears. And now, Nico had eight-foot-tall proof that he was right, and that the HeartBeats were the team *everyone* should be on.

Nico was going to need a lot more felt hearts.

CHAPTER THIRTY-SIX

SOPHIE MAEBY
WEEK TWO, DAY FIVE

"You know Teddy did it for Kim, right?" Sophie froze in her trek down the hallway as she heard the grating voice of some random girl. They must have been talking about yesterday's poster. It was all anyone was talking about. "Isn't it, like, the most romantic thing ever?"

"How do you know Teddy did it?" another random girl asked suspiciously.

Exactly, Random Girl #2, Sophie thought.

"Oh, it's, like, totally obvious," Random Girl #1 said. "This senior named Nico Osterman explained it to me."

If Sophie had been drinking something, she would have spat it out in shock. Instead, she inhaled sharply, then exhaled forcefully, trying to stay calm. *Nico.* She wouldn't have been surprised if her blood was literally boiling.

"You know how Teddy broke up with Kim because he's moving to Firenze?" Random Girl #1 continued.

"Uh-huh."

"Well, the poster was an ode to a painting that was *made* in Firenze. It's his way of telling Kim that he wants to be together, no matter the distance that separates them. That their love is stronger than anything. And that, like, maybe she should move there, too."

"Ohhh." Random Girl #2 nodded. "That totally makes sense. Wow. That *is* really romantic."

"Then why wasn't Teddy in the picture?" Sophie snapped.

"Huh?" Random Girl #1 said as the two of them turned to look at her. "Are you talking to us?"

"Yes, I'm talking to you!" Sophie sighed with exasperation. "If this was some big declaration of love, wouldn't Teddy be *in* the painting? Wait a minute." Sophie noticed two horrible red lumps safety-pinned to the fronts of their sweatshirts. "What exactly are those supposed to be?"

"Our hearts?" Random Girl #2 asked. "We're HeartBeats. We believe Teddy and Kim should get back together."

"What?! That's just—just—that doesn't even look like a heart!" Sophie bellowed.

"It's, like, a metaphor," Random Girl #1 said.

"No, it's not!" Sophie cried. "That has nothing to do with a metaphor!"

"Chill, okay?" Random Girl #2 said. "She said it's *like* a metaphor."

Sophie bit her tongue to keep from screaming. There was no *way* Nico's idiotic HeartBeats were gaining traction. Sophie wouldn't let that happen. She couldn't.

The Teddy Bears had to do something *big*.

And Sophie had the perfect idea.

She always knew that her mom's job as the superintendent's office manager would come in handy one day.

Today was that day.

CHAPTER THIRTY-SEVEN

TEDDY LIN
WEEK THREE, DAY ONE

This was the longest Teddy and Kim had gone without speaking since the day they'd met.

Teddy didn't know why he kept expecting her to reach out, but he did. Sure, *he* could have texted *her*, but since she was the one who had broken up with him, Teddy felt like if there was gonna be some kind of reconciliation, Kim should reach out first.

(Teddy was pretty sure Kim had broken up with him, anyway. Honestly, he still wasn't totally sure what had happened.)

But one week had passed, and then two, and not a word from Kim, which must have meant that they were absolutely, definitely, 100 percent over. Teddy sighed and leaned his head against the side of the car door.

"Come on, man," Elvis said, glancing over at Teddy from the driver's seat. "I bet things will have calmed down a lot over the weekend. Maybe everything will be back to normal today."

"*You're* still wearing the ears. And the shirt. And are those bear paw slippers?" Teddy pointed an accusing finger at Elvis's fuzzy brown feet, complete with claws.

"I'm being supportive. If nobody else is wearing teddy bear stuff, I'll take it off and change into my baseball clothes. Everyone's gonna start freaking out about prom soon, and they'll forget about the breakup. Prom's almost here."

Teddy didn't have Elvis's faith that things would have calmed down this week. Whoever had put up that giant love letter to Kim was still out there, Teddy thought glumly. He couldn't do anything like that! He could barely draw a stick figure! Elvis had tried to convince Teddy that it was just Toby Neale doing another one of his weird street art things, but Teddy didn't buy it. That poster was a declaration of love. Teddy had spent the whole weekend going over every birthday, every anniversary, every Valentine's Day in his head. Kim had always *said* she didn't care about big, romantic, over-the-top gestures, but maybe she had just said that because she didn't want him to feel bad? Or it was some kind of test, and he should have known to do something anyway? Maybe Kim had dumped him because Teddy's idea of a gift was so far away from over-the-top, he was practically under-the-top.

He wondered if the mystery artist was going to take Kim to prom. Probably.

"Hmm . . . what's going on?" Elvis mused. Teddy looked

up to see an enormous traffic jam, an endless line of cars clogging the road that should have taken them to school.

"That's weird."

"Yeah." Elvis honked. A whole bunch of cars honked back.

"I'm gonna go check it out."

Before Elvis could say anything, Teddy had unbuckled his seat belt, exited the car, and was jogging toward the parking lot. He wove through the parked cars and cut over to the sidewalk, slowing as he came to see the entire parking lot cordoned off by caution tape. He could tell the asphalt was new—it was much darker than it used to be, and there was something almost shiny about it—but Teddy wasn't sure why that meant it was shut down. Had it not dried over the weekend?

He got closer to investigate, coming right up to the caution tape. There was a series of depressions in the fresh asphalt. What *was* that? Teddy squinted, the shapes finally coming together. It was an enormous heart in the center of the parking lot, and right in the middle of the heart, someone had written *WHHHS* ♥ *TL*.

TL. Teddy Lin, Teddy realized with a sinking feeling.

"Oh my God." Teddy jumped as he realized there were two girls standing next to him, odd red felt lumps safety-pinned to the straps of their backpacks. "Somebody turned the parking lot into a Teddy Bear valentine."

Elvis had been very, very wrong.

Things were definitely not calming down.

CHAPTER THIRTY-EIGHT

PRINCIPAL MANTEGHI
WEEK THREE, DAY ONE

"And this is the only camera angle we have?" Principal Manteghi crossed her arms, squinting at the small TV screen in the maintenance team's office.

"Yup," Mr. Ciccone replied. "You can see that it's a team of seven or eight figures, but because they're all in black, there's no distinguishing features."

There was one distinguishing feature. On top of their ski masks, each of the parking lot vandals wore a set of teddy bear ears. Not that their headgear helped her a whole lot. From the giant *TL* in the parking lot, she'd already deduced that this was a Team Teddy crime.

"Thank you for your help, Mr. Ciccone. I'll let you know how we proceed."

Of course, Principal Manteghi had no idea how to

proceed. She still hadn't interviewed the senior art students about *The Birth of Kim-us* poster. Or found anyone who might be responsible for SnakeGate. And now she had to round up the members of Team Teddy to find out who had ruined the parking lot. It took everything Principal Manteghi had not to crumple into a ball on the maintenance team's floor. Taking the poster down hadn't been a problem, but repaving the parking lot was going to be a cost Principal Manteghi knew the district did not have in the budget. When she thought about calling the superintendent and letting him know what had happened, all Principal Manteghi wanted to do was go back to bed.

Assuming he didn't already know about it. She was sure the giant heart in the parking lot was already all over the internet, but Principal Manteghi was willing to bet that the superintendent didn't spend a lot of time on her students' Instagram stories.

"Sure thing, Principal," Mr. Ciccone said. "We'll let you know if we see anything suspicious."

Principal Manteghi nodded. At least *The Birth of Kim-us* was gone, she reminded herself, and that was something.

It wasn't nearly enough.

But it was something.

MR. RIZZO
WEEK THREE, DAY ONE

"Do lunch duty this year, Rizzo," they said.

"You'll never have to stay after school to monitor detention again," they said.

"It'll be easy," they said.

Lord, what a fool this mortal had been.

KIM LANDIS-LILLEY
WEEK THREE, DAY ONE

Drawing in the wet pavement on the parking lot had been a pretty bold move on Team Teddy's part. Kim could practically feel the tension on the Team Kim side of the cafeteria. Not that Kim really cared about the giant heart in the parking lot. Well, she tried not to care. But when she thought about Sophie Maeby drawing a giant declaration of love in the asphalt, Kim couldn't deny the prickles of jealousy that shot through her. Had Teddy liked it? Sure, the heart had said *WHHHS ♥ TL*, but Kim felt like it might as well have read *SM ♥ TL*. Kim wished she had a better view, but as much as she tried to look over the yellow line, she couldn't find Teddy in the sea of bear ears and blue TEAM TEDDY T-shirts. It had started raining during second period, and the cafeteria was unusually packed today, as all of the Teddy Bears who usually ate outside were stuck in here.

Something whizzed over Kim's head. She looked up, startled, but it was gone before she could see what it was.

"I cannot believe those Teddy Bears," Jess grumbled. "Cannot believe it." Another something whizzed by, and another. Something small, and round, and kind of golden. "We have to stand up to them. We can't let them draw all over the school, walking around here in their ears and their matching T-shirts. They're acting like they own the place, and they don't. There's just as many of us as there are of them."

"Tater Tots!" Kim exclaimed. That's what they were, she realized now as one flew lower. It barely made it over the line, dropping softly to the ground.

"Yeah, Kim." Jess eyed her oddly. "They're serving Tots today."

"No, not these Tots. Those Tots." Kim pointed above her head, where, sure enough, a few more Tots were flying by.

"Huh?"

Jess looked up. Together, they watched the Tots streak across the cafeteria, like a golden-fried meteor shower. Who was throwing them? Someone on Team Kim, obviously. Nobody knew for sure where the first Tater Tot had come from. But as Kim looked around, she knew that they were traveling from the Team Kim side of the cafeteria to the Team Teddy side of the cafeteria.

An operatic shriek tore through the normal lunchtime chatter, followed quickly by a surprised shout from the table behind Kim.

"Diamond, that's one for screaming," Mr. Rizzo said from his post straddling the yellow line. "And, Dustin, that's one for shouting."

"But Mr. Rizzo!" Diamond Allen stood in protest—Kim remembered her from the fall play. "Chloe's been attacked!"

Diamond pointed at a very small freshman girl who shakily stood up, her red heart-patterned sweater covered in an enormous chocolate-brown splotch.

"Pudding cup," Jess muttered grimly.

"You don't think . . . ?" Kim suggested.

"I *do* think."

Kim and Jess had watched Elvis eat a chocolate pudding cup literally every single day at lunch for *years*. And Kim hadn't thought Elvis was the type to throw food, but a lot of people were doing things Kim never would have expected them to. That poor freshman. A flying pudding cup was probably fairly terrifying when wielded by a moderately successful third baseman well practiced in the art of throwing home.

"FOOD FIGHT!" the freshman guy dressed like a ketchup bottle yelled as he stood—Kim wasn't sure what his name was. All the seniors had just been calling him Ketchup.

"Koontz! No!" Mr. Rizzo yelled. "That's one. And this is absolutely not a food fight! And, Dustin? You're at two now. There's no reason you should be standing!"

But it was too late. Because even as Mr. Rizzo issued the demerit, Ketchup—Koontz—was hurling a fistful of Tater Tots across the line into Team Teddy territory.

Things devolved pretty quickly from there. A bunch of quick-thinking freshmen grabbed the ketchup bottles from the condiment bar, charged bravely up to the yellow line, and began squirting Team Teddy with abandon. The Teddy Bears retaliated with a battery of particularly hard apples. One caught Kim in the shoulder, and she was pretty sure it would leave a bruise. Team Kim had all the resources of the hot food line—the cafeteria workers had abandoned their posts, and Kim didn't blame them—but the Teddy Bears seemed to be pulling pudding cups out of thin air, launching chocolate grenades into a sea of devastation.

Food rained down from every corner of the cafeteria. Kim was so shocked, she couldn't even find cover; she just watched somewhat dispassionately as a ham sandwich smacked her in the chest, leaving a smear of bright yellow mustard on her shirt. The noise was deafening. Kim thought she could make out the sound of Mr. Rizzo issuing demerits left and right over the screams of battle, but no one seemed inclined to stop. Jess, for instance, was hurling green beans with astounding velocity as she yelled, most directed at Elvis. Maybe Kim should have encouraged her to try out for the softball team. Those beans were traveling pretty fast.

"ENOUGH!"

Kim was surprised to see Olivia standing on top of a table. Somehow, she had done what Mr. Rizzo couldn't—everyone stopped. Kim watched a piece of lettuce slide down Jess's forehead and hit the ground.

"Olivia, that's one for standing on the table," Mr. Rizzo said weakly, but Kim could tell his heart wasn't in it. "Dustin, get off the chair. You're at three."

"That's enough, okay?" Olivia said. "I'm sick of it. I'm sick of all of this. Team Teddy this and Team Kim that and *who cares?*"

Jess looked pissed. Was Kim pissed? She didn't know. Of course she wanted Olivia to be on her team, but that didn't necessarily mean she had to be part of Team Kim. Sometimes Kim didn't even know if she wanted to be part of Team Kim.

"I'm starting my own group," Olivia continued. "It's called AntiKaT. Anti-Kim-and-Teddy. Because guess what? I'm done with this. And I bet a lot of you are, too!" she cried. "Who's with me?"

Kim stood there, stunned, as the cafeteria waited in silence. Olivia was *anti*-her. That was a lot worse than merely being done with Team Kim.

A solitary slow clap filled the silent cafeteria. Kim turned to see Wendy, their pitcher, walking toward Olivia while clapping her hands. Wendy was anti-her? And then more claps came. Daisy, Olivia's best friend. And some other freshman guy—was his locker next to Olivia's, maybe? Kim thought his name might have been Evan. And then she looked across the line to the Team Teddy side, and there were people crossing from over there, too, clapping while coming to join Olivia.

"This table is an AntiKaT zone!" Olivia declared. "Join me! Step over the yellow line! Get some hot food! Eat outside! Do whatever you want! I don't care! This is the table of common sense! Of freedom! Of no more Kim and Teddy! No more Kim and Teddy!"

Pretty soon, the rest of the table took up the chant. There weren't that many of them, but there were enough that the shouts of "No more Kim and Teddy!" echoed throughout the cafeteria.

Each one broke Kim's heart a little bit.

CHAPTER FORTY-ONE

SOPHIE MAEBY
WEEK THREE, DAY ONE

The parking lot escapade had been her greatest triumph.

It was infinitely more indelible than that stupid picture of Kim on a clamshell. This was something that couldn't be scraped off the wall by Mr. Ciccone. No, the message in the parking lot let Teddy know exactly how much everyone loved him. Literally. Although . . . Teddy hadn't really reacted much to it. And whenever Sophie thought about her mom somehow finding out that Sophie had ruined the repaving job the school district had been saving up for, her stomach roiled with guilt and anxiety. But she stuffed that guilt way back down in the corner of her brain where she hid the things she didn't want to think about, like when she'd gone to Six Flags with Nico in September and they'd stayed until the very last second the park was open, laughing and talking and holding hands on all of the roller coasters.

Why was she even *thinking* about Nico? She shook her head briskly to clear it as she pushed open Mr. Guzman's door and walked into Prom Committee.

As a group, they didn't look good. Noelle and Madison had ketchup and mustard stains all over their sweaters. On the other side of the table, Emma and Amelia and Corey were covered in something that was, best-case scenario, chocolate. Corey had bits of something Sophie couldn't even identify stuck in his thick hair. Sophie knew she didn't look much better. She'd spent the whole afternoon trying to get all the food off of her, but nothing could cover up the ketchup and mustard stains on her clothes. Plus, she smelled like a hot dog.

Nico had eaten so many hot dogs at Six Flags. Hot dog after hot dog. And he'd never gotten sick, not even when he went on all those upside-down roller coasters.

No! No more Nico! What was going on today?! She'd barely thought about Nico for weeks, except with annoyance, and now here he was, invading her brain.

"We're still waiting on . . . Josiah and Wendy?" Mr. Guzman asked from his perch on top of his desk, reading something off his computer screen.

"We're not, um, totally sure where Wendy is," Amelia said, tightening the red ribbon in her ponytail. "But I'm sure she'll get here when she can."

"And Josiah . . . ?" Mr. Guzman prompted.

Sophie looked at Noelle. She shrugged. Madison, as always, was on her phone.

"I'm sure he'll be here soon. Sooner than Wendy," Sophie said, glaring at Amelia.

Amelia glared right back.

The door to the AP Spanish room swung open, and Josiah stepped through, a solemn look on his face. Something was off about him. Sophie narrowed her eyes, trying to figure out what was missing.

The ears! The ears were missing! Sophie pointed at the ears on her own head. Josiah ignored her, avoiding her gaze.

"Josiah," Sophie hissed as he slid into a seat near the door. "Where. Are. Your. Ears?!"

He didn't respond.

"Glad you could make it, J-Dog!" Mr. Guzman said as he tapped out a little drum pattern on his desk. "Let's just get started. We'll update Wendy when she gets here. You guys have done a great job pulling resources from the theater department, so it looks like we are all good to go with Bears and Fifties Sock Hop. There's just a couple details left to finalize, right?"

"No," Josiah said.

"No?" Mr. Guzman asked, as Sophie shrieked, "NO?!"

"I can't be a Teddy Bear anymore." Josiah shook his head. "This Team Teddy versus Team Kim stuff . . . it's wrong. And I don't want to be part of it."

"What do you mean, my man?" Mr. Guzman asked gently. "What's going on in here?" he asked, tapping his heart.

Sophie didn't know how he could be so gentle. She wanted to throttle Josiah. He was *abandoning* the Teddy Bears?! What if this was the first step in a mass exodus? The whole point of the Teddy Bears was that they needed the numbers!

"Kim and Teddy shouldn't have broken up. Things were better when they were together. Teddy was happier. And I bet Kim was, too."

"No he wasn't!" Sophie said in a weird, strangled kind of voice that didn't even sound like hers. Teddy was going to be happier with *her* than he'd ever been with Kim! And he'd realize it as they danced under the majestic pine trees at the prom, enjoying the picturesque habitat of the noble North American brown bear! "What *happened* to you, Josiah?"

"I have seen things these past few weeks," he answered. "I have seen things that have made me reconsider what love is. Things that have made me reconsider what it truly means to be a friend."

"Everybody's seen things!" Sophie cried, exasperated. "Oh, look! I see a pencil! A stapler! A pair of scissors! That doesn't mean I think we should throw our prom themes out like a bag of hot garbage!"

"Sophie," Mr. Guzman warned.

Sophie tried to take a deep breath. She felt like she'd forgotten how to breathe.

"I think we should dedicate our prom to helping Kim and Teddy get back together," Josiah said. "That's what real friends would do. Friends don't just take sides and throw pudding. They help their friends figure out what's really best for them, and they help make that happen. And that's why . . . I joined the HeartBeats."

Josiah unzipped his hoodie to reveal a lumpy red felt heart safety-pinned to the front of his William Henry Harrison High baseball shirt. Sophie screamed, but no sound came out, only air. Madison patted her back absentmindedly.

"Thanks for sharing, Josiah," Mr. Guzman said. "Sorry if I'm not following—didn't get quite enough coffee today—but how does this relate to prom?"

"We can't do Fifties Sock Hop," Josiah said. "Or Bears."

"But . . . but . . . Bears!" Noelle protested.

"We're not theming the prom Let's Get Teddy and Kim Back Together," Emma said. "That's ridiculous."

"It's no more ridiculous than theming the prom Kim's Favorite Movie or Teddy's Favorite Animal. Although, FYI, Sophie," Josiah added, "pretty sure Teddy's favorite animal isn't a bear. I think it's a sloth."

The bear was the *symbol of a movement*. It wasn't about favorite animals! But Sophie was feeling so disheartened, she didn't even have the energy to explain that to him.

"Dude, I already bought a leather jacket for the Fifties Sock Hop," Corey said. "Unless you want to theme the prom Leather Jackets, I'm sticking with Sock Hop."

"We're not changing the theme," Emma said. "We're keeping Fifties Sock Hop."

"And we're keeping Bears," Noelle said, jutting out her chin defiantly.

"Fine." Josiah crossed his arms. "Then I want a third theme."

"A . . . third theme?" Mr. Guzman asked nervously. "How would that even . . . would we split the gym into thirds? I might need a math teacher," he muttered.

"What even is your theme?" Sophie narrowed her eyes at Josiah, that traitor.

"Perfect Catch."

Josiah looked at them all expectantly.

"Like a fish?" Noelle asked eventually. Sophie hadn't known Noelle was so into animals.

"No," Josiah said. "Like a *baseball*. Or a softball. Teddy and Kim both love playing. It's a romantic love-and-baseball-themed prom. We'll do the whole floor up like a diamond. Cover the walls with softballs, except the red stitching makes the shape of a heart. And by the end of the night, Kim and Teddy will realize they're each other's Perfect Catches."

That was actually kind of cute . . . if it wasn't against everything Sophie and all the Teddy Bears stood for! If Teddy and Kim were supposed to be together, they wouldn't have broken up. Period.

How could idiotic Nico and his poorly constructed felt hearts have conned Josiah Watkins into joining the HeartBeats? Who was next? Chris Foster, almost definitely. And how far would it spread from there? Through track and field and student council and Model UN and who knew where else? Sophie felt like this meant bad things were coming. Very, very bad things.

"Stop this Prom Committee!" Wendy banged the door open with such force, even Madison looked up from her phone.

"Wendy, great to have you," Mr. Guzman said.

"We can't do Bears and Fifties Sock Hop anymore," Wendy continued, like she hadn't even heard Mr. Guzman.

"Oh yes we can!" Noelle said. "Why is everybody always trying to cancel Bears?"

"Wendy?" Amelia asked, aghast. "Seriously? What's happening right now? Are you joking?"

"Thank you," Josiah said. "Another voice for harmony and unity."

"No. I'm done with harmony and unity." Wendy dropped into her seat. "I'm done with Kim and Teddy. I'm done with all of it!"

"This feels like a lot of negativity, but I'm glad you feel comfortable expressing yourself," Mr. Guzman said.

"If you're done with all of it, how about you leave?" Sophie had finally found her voice again! Wendy seemed to bring out her most antagonistic self.

"No way. I need to create a safe space at prom."

"For whom?" Sophie asked incredulously.

"For me and the rest of the AntiKaTs."

AntiKaTs? Really? Now Sophie knew Wendy had lost it.

"AntiKaTs?" Mr. Guzman asked. Someone obviously didn't have lunch duty.

"Mr. Guzman, the AntiKaTs are a fringe group whose interests we don't need to consider for prom," Sophie explained. "Just like the HeartBeats."

"Now wait a minute—" Josiah started.

"Don't lump us in with those losers!" Wendy interrupted, pointing at Josiah.

"I'm so confused," Emma said as she cradled her head in her hands.

"I can't even believe you right now. Fifties Sock Hop was *your idea*." Amelia turned to Wendy with betrayal in her eyes. "What theme are you even suggesting?"

"Nihilism," Wendy answered.

"Nile-what?" Corey asked.

"Is that a kind of fish?" Noelle asked.

"Noelle!" Sophie exclaimed. "Not everything is a fish! What is going on with you today?"

"I think I have low levels of DHA," Noelle murmured. "That's fish oil, right?"

"So what does that mean? And can I wear a leather jacket to it?" Corey asked.

"Corey!" Emma admonished him. "Not everything is about your stupid leather jacket."

"Whoa, whoa, whoa," Mr. Guzman said. "Let's keep it kind."

Everyone ignored him.

"Nihilism is the philosophical belief that life is without any objective meaning or purpose," Josiah explained. "Basically, it means that nothing matters."

"Exactly." Wendy nodded. "Nothing matters. Not Kim, not Teddy, not any of us. We are small and the universe is indifferent. We're nothing but specks of sand in comparison to the enormity of the cosmos."

"One measly little food fight and suddenly life has lost all meaning?" Sophie asked archly. "Mr. Guzman, permission to remove Wendy Phan from Prom Committee on grounds of . . . um . . . I don't know . . . killing the mood."

"You can't impeach anyone from Prom Committee, Sophie," Mr. Guzman admonished her.

"What would this Nihilism prom even look like?" Amelia asked.

"I don't know. Black balloons?" Wendy shrugged.

"So I *could* wear my leather jacket," Corey said. "It's black."

"It doesn't really matter how we decorate it," Wendy said. "And that's the whole point."

"*It doesn't matter,*" Emma repeated. "How can we give a

quarter of our prom space to someone who thinks it *doesn't matter*?"

"Every opinion matters," Josiah said quickly. Sophie narrowed her eyes at him. He was just trying to make sure he got his Perfect Catch theme pushed through, too, that stinker. "Even the opinion that it doesn't matter."

"Prom Committee isn't supposed to be harder than school," Noelle said. "This is making my head hurt."

"Let's just split the prom into four," Josiah suggested. "It'll be easier than dividing it into three. And that way every part of the senior class will have the prom they want."

"Split the prom into four," Mr. Guzman repeated.

"Yeah." Josiah nodded. "Use, I don't know, tape or something, to split it into four quadrants. Bears, Fifties Sock Hop, Perfect Catch, and Nihilism. People choose what quadrant they want to go to. It'll be just like two proms . . . except it's four."

"Four proms," Mr. Guzman said.

"Why not?" Wendy shrugged again. "As long as my AntiKaTs have a space, I'm happy. Four proms."

"Okay." Mr. Guzman took a deep breath, furrowing his brow. "All in favor of four proms?"

"Absolutely not." Emma folded her arms, like there was no way she could be incited to put this to a vote. "It's not fair, Mr. Guzman. Sock Hop isn't giving up an inch of its half."

"And neither is Bears!" Sophie piped up, spurred into action by Emma's confidence. Why *should* they give up any space just because these two traitors picked an unfortunate day to defect?

"Let's think about this logically, Mr. Guzman," Josiah said calmly. "What would *really* be unfair is sticking to an arbitrary delineation of space that would now, effectively, exclude half the senior class from what is supposed to be a celebration of the *entire* senior class. The only *fair* thing to do is to split the gym into four quadrants and make sure everyone gets what they need." .

"Yeah. What Josiah said," Wendy agreed.

"Don't do it, Mr. Guzman," Sophie pleaded.

"You know it's the right thing to do, Mr. Guzman," Josiah coaxed.

"You promised we could have half!" Amelia protested. "Don't break your promise."

"Circumstances change," Josiah countered. "Four proms. It's the only way."

"And it's not like you have any better ideas," Wendy said.

"Enough!"

Finally, they had broken through Mr. Guzman's chill. He blinked nervously from his perch atop the desk, almost like he'd surprised himself by raising his voice.

"It's four proms," Mr. Guzman said, "or no prom at all. All in favor of four proms?"

Unfair. So unfair. Sophie glowered at Josiah as she raised her hand, but it's not like she had a choice. She'd rather have a quarter of a prom than no prom at all.

She'd just have to make Bears the best quadrant.

Although she had a feeling that might be easier said than done.

CHAPTER FORTY-TWO

DAISY DIAZ
WEEK THREE, DAY TWO

Daisy's mom had said getting the button maker was a waste of money. That's why Daisy had gotten it delivered to Olivia's house and then hidden it in her locker at school for most of the year, trying to avoid another lecture from her mom about buying stuff she didn't need online. But look at Daisy now: Here she was, making buttons. Mom didn't know *everything*.

"Thanks for letting us use the art room, Mr. Buckley," Daisy said as she popped another button into existence. Man, this thing was satisfying.

"Absa-tootly, Daisy." Mr. Buckley grinned from behind his desk. Daisy tried not to stare at the small piece of lettuce stuck in the gap between his two front teeth. "Art is art, no matter what form it takes. And if art happens at William

Henry Harrison High, I'd like it to happen here in the art room."

"And not on the wall outside the senior hallway?" Daisy asked.

Mr. Buckley coughed.

"Well." He coughed again. "You can't deny that it was the work of a very talented artist. Even if it was in an unconventional location. Street art is art, too, you know."

Daisy looked around the room. There were a couple senior guys sketching at the table near the window. The only one she knew was Toby, who was always getting in trouble for putting weird art up all over the school. Daisy thought she saw the tips of his ears turning pink. Maybe *he* was the mysterious artist behind *The Birth of Kim-us*. It made sense. Man, Kim was so lucky. Daisy had never even had a boyfriend. And she'd definitely never had any guy make a giant, beautiful mural of her on a seashell, like a sporty little mermaid.

"I thought we agreed to never talk about that monstrosity," Olivia grumbled as she arranged the AntiKaT buttons in a straight line.

"Olivi-aaaah." Daisy sighed. "You look extremely *you* in that poster. In the best possible way."

"I don't look like . . . I don't look like Kim," she said softly.

Daisy put down the button maker and reached across the table to grab Olivia's hand. Olivia had never said anything like this before, but Daisy wondered how long Olivia had been thinking it. Kim looked like a Disney princess, that was true. But Olivia looked like an Amazon princess, and that was way better. Who would want to be Snow White when they could be Wonder Woman?

"You look like *you*," Daisy said. "And that's the best thing you can look like. And you can't tell me you're not happy that the mystery artist perfectly captured the definition in your triceps."

"Well . . ." A smile tugged at the corner of Olivia's lips.

"That's exactly what I thought." Satisfied, Daisy popped in another button. "I'm jealous. I wish someone would hang up a big picture of me! I'd love a giant *Daisy with a Pearl Earring* decorating the freshman hall."

Olivia snorted.

"Thanks for the buttons," Olivia said. "I'm gonna start getting them out there."

"What, now?" Daisy asked. "Are you sure you want to bring these buttons to softball practice? Isn't that kind of . . . I don't know, inflammatory?"

"Wendy stood up with us." Something in Olivia's face hardened. "You saw her. She's all in on AntiKaT. And there might be more now, too. Maybe I'll even stop by the baseball diamond on my way and see if anyone else from Team Teddy wants in?"

"Brave." Daisy picked up one of the buttons and pinned it onto her hoodie, admiring the cute little cat face she'd drawn, and the red circle with the line through it bifurcating the cat and the letters *KaT*. Maybe Daisy had a future in marketing, or graphic design, like Olivia's Mama Dawn. This AntiKaT was so iconic, it was basically the McDonald's golden arches. "They'll all lose their minds if Kim Landis-Lilley's little sister broaches the Team Teddy stronghold."

"Just because I'm related to Kim doesn't mean I'm Team Kim." Olivia scooped all of the buttons Daisy had made into her Adidas bag. "I'm Team AntiKaT, and proud of it. I'm gonna head to practice—I'm already later than I've ever been. Coach Finn's probably worried something happened to me. You sure you don't mind making the rest of these by yourself?"

"Sure I don't mind. I'm hanging with Mr. Buckley. Right, Mr. Buckley?"

"What's that?" Mr. Buckley looked up from whatever he was doing, a glob of orange paint in his left eyebrow.

"Don't worry about it." Daisy laughed. "See ya, Olivi-aaaah."

"See ya." Olivia grinned as she adjusted the AntiKaT button on the front of her warm-up jacket. It was nice to see Olivia smiling again, Daisy thought as Olivia jogged out of the room, her bag bouncing against her side. Maybe this AntiKaT thing was a good idea after all. In general, Daisy didn't really like to be anti things, unless those things were objectively horrible, like racism or murder, but sometimes supporting your best friend meant you had to be anti-something every now and again.

Daisy popped out another button. She was definitely going to make enough for all those senior art guys at the table by the window.

And maybe see if Toby took commissions.

CHAPTER FORTY-THREE

TOBY NEALE
WEEK THREE, DAY THREE

The whole point of Toby's art was that it didn't last. It couldn't. It was ephemeral, like most things in life. That was what Toby liked about street art. Or, uh, inside wall art. What he didn't like was the fact that people saw graffiti where you wanted them to see art.

The weirdest part was that nobody seemed to figure out that he was responsible for *The Birth of Kim-us*. Well, he was pretty sure that Mr. Buckley knew. But Principal Manteghi had never questioned him about it. Maybe she would eventually—she seemed pretty overwhelmed at the moment, with the parking lot and the food fight and everything. But for now, Toby was a free man. And it was great not to be suspended, but it wasn't so great that Kim didn't seem to realize that he'd made the poster.

Did she even like it? Toby had tried to watch her looking at her likeness, but it was hard to judge her facial expressions. She seemed to like it . . . but she hadn't said anything to him about it. If she even knew it was him! After all, Kim was only familiar with his ceramics work. Who knew if she ever saw his other works of street art in the hallways? And even then, all of that had been vastly different from this one.

Hmm . . . maybe he should make Kim a ceramic. No, no, he was much better with InDesign than with clay—he should stick to his strengths. Maybe he just needed to make Kim another piece. Something that focused more exclusively on her. Something that showed her just how luminous he thought she was.

"Toby?"

"Huh?" Toby blinked up at Ms. Thurber. He'd forgotten he was in environmental science.

"Toby, that's one for not focusing. And, Dustin, I see you looking out the window as well. Also one for not focusing."

He nodded. It wasn't his first demerit for that, and it wouldn't be the last. What none of his teachers seemed to realize, though—except for Mr. Buckley—was that Toby was *always* focused.

Just not necessarily on what they *wanted* him to focus on.

Toby flipped to a clean page in his environmental notebook and began to sketch.

CHAPTER FORTY-FOUR

PHIL SPOONER
WEEK THREE, DAY FOUR

All things considered, life was pretty good for Phil Spooner. He loved having people to eat lunch with. He loved having people say hi to him as he walked down the hall, a friendly chorus of "Spoons!" and "Spoony!" following him everywhere he went. He'd even had to resurrect his Instagram account, after discovering, much to his surprise, that @The_Philver_Spoon suddenly had almost a hundred followers. This morning, for lack of anything better to do, he'd posted his Brown Sugar Cinnamon Pop-Tart. @TheREALDiamondAllen had commented "lol spoony ur so random laugh-cry-emoji-laugh-cry-emoji-laugh-cry-emoji." The Pop-Tart already had thirty likes. In comparison, his first National Air and Space Museum post had two likes: from @airandspacemuseum and @MoreREALfollowerz4U.

On the one hand, Phil was outraged that a processed toaster pastry had garnered more acclaim than a building that housed some of the nation's greatest aeronautical treasures, but on the other hand, it was nice to be liked.

Phil was finally starting to see the appeal of this whole social media thing.

"Spoony, Spoony, my sweet lil' baby Spoons," Diamond crooned as she swirled her fork through her mashed potatoes. "What are we going to do?"

"Um . . . for lunch?" Phil asked, looking around the lunch table and out at the cafeteria. There were fewer people at their table now that Evan Loomis had gone to join Olivia and the AntiKaTs and Chloe Baker, of all people, had departed for the HeartBeats.

"Lunch is meatloaf and mashed potatoes, Spoony. I'm talking about Team Kim. We are in crisis."

They were in *crisis*?! Phil hadn't even realized! How could they be in a crisis he hadn't even noticed? He was a terrible member of Team Kim.

"What's the crisis?" Gabe Koontz asked, holding his slice of meatloaf in his hand as he chomped on it like a sandwich. Sometime earlier this week, Phil had stopped being surprised that he ate lunch with an anthropomorphic ketchup bottle every day. Now, Gabe's costume was just part of the daily fabric of life.

"Dude! Fork? Hello?" Diamond admonished him. Gabe shrugged. "God, you're dense." Diamond rolled her eyes at Phil. Phil rolled 'em right along with her, although apparently he was just as dense as Gabe. "Team Kim has suffered

a major, major loss, Gabe. Our numbers are low. Dangerously low. And these two new factions are growing by
the day."

"Who cares? It's a bunch of felt hearts and little cat
buttons."

"Gabe!" Diamond shrieked. "It's way more than that! An
ideological war is won on the strength of its symbols, and
currently, in that department, we're getting our butts
kicked."

An ideological war is won on the strength of its symbols. Wow.
Diamond Allen was a genius.

"The way things are going," Diamond said darkly, "by
the end of the week there might not even be a Team Kim
anymore."

"No!" Phil cried, the word torn from his throat with pure
anguish. "There *has* to be a Team Kim."

And there did. Diamond and Gabe Koontz and all the
rest of them had no idea how badly he needed this. Without
Team Kim, there was no Spoony. And where would he be
then? Back to eating lunch alone. No more people stopping
him in the hallway to talk about Kim and Teddy. No more
Instagram followers. No more Diamond at his side, her
laughter so loud it made his ears ring with joy. He wouldn't
lose her. He couldn't lose any of this.

"I like your fire, Spoony," Diamond said approvingly. Phil
swore he could see fire in her own eyes, like the incandescent
moment a match turned to flame.

She wanted fire? He'd give her fire.

"We need to do something that lets the Teddy Bears,

and the AntiKaTs, and the HeartBeats, and everyone else know that we're still strong. That we're still a force to be reckoned with. That Team Kim is everywhere!" Phil pounded his fist on the table for emphasis, adrenaline surging through him. "We'll do something that will lift Kim's spirits. Something that lets her know that we're all still on her side."

"We're not, though," Gabe pointed out. "I mean, not even all the freshmen are Team Kim anymore. A bunch of 'em went AntiKaT, and there's even a couple HeartBeats."

"Don't even mention the name Chloe Baker right now." Diamond held up her hand in front of Gabe's face. "Don't you dare. I cannot with that right now. Spoony, I need *you*," she said.

She needed him. Diamond Allen *needed* him.

"So, Spoony, what should we do?" Diamond asked. "What's something Kim really loves? Something that we could do to help lift her spirits?"

Phil had not thought this through. All he'd wanted was to keep everything going, to keep Diamond looking at him with fire in her eyes, but now, of course, he had to say something. As Diamond looked at him expectantly, Phil cast his eyes wildly around the cafeteria. What was a thing Kim might like? The silence drew on longer and longer. Diamond was going to get suspicious. She'd figure out that Phil didn't know anything about Kim Landis-Lilley. Maybe she'd figure out that Phil didn't even know why, exactly, they'd broken up! Panicking, Phil looked from table to table, searching for something, anything, to say.

Focus, Phil, he thought. He closed his eyes, centering

himself, like Mr. Rizzo had taught them to do before beginning a scene. What did he know about Kim? Not much. He used to sit at a table where he could see Jess Howard eat lunch every day, but he hadn't been looking at Kim then, just at Jess, peeling her daily clementine.

"Oranges," Phil blurted out as he opened his eyes, the clementine all he was able to think of.

"Oranges?" Diamond asked.

"Yes. Uh, oranges." Here Phil was, yet again, improv-ing with reckless abandon. Why, Mr. Rizzo? Why had he chosen to instruct his students in this most dangerous pastime? "Kim has all these wonderful, happy childhood memories . . ."

"Of oranges?" Gabe Koontz furrowed his brow.

"Of her grandmother's orange tree farm in Florida!" Phil said desperately. "Kim spent every summer there as a child, harvesting oranges, learning the ways of the seeds . . . and the pulp . . . and the juice . . ."

"Huh," Diamond said. "Those Landis-Lilleys are a real interesting family."

"Indeed." Phil was nodding so vigorously he feared he'd do himself a minor injury. "It's a fascinating field, oranges."

"So we should . . . bring her some oranges?" Gabe asked.

"Yes," Phil said decisively

"Cool," Gabe said. "My parents can probably get us a deal. They run the grocery store," he explained to Phil, as though Phil hadn't realized who owned Koontz Market. "Come by after school and I'll hook you up with some produce."

"Great work, Spoony." Diamond nodded at him. "Team Kim couldn't do it without you."

Phil smiled at her weakly. Of course Team Kim couldn't do it without him. There wouldn't even *be* a Team Kim without him.

And Phil was starting to worry that maybe that wasn't such a good thing.

CHAPTER FORTY-FIVE

MS. SOMERS

WEEK THREE, DAY FOUR

Ms. Somers couldn't believe it was almost time for the Spring Concert.

This was going to be the crowning achievement of her first year of teaching, and her seniors were the jewel in the middle of that crown. She couldn't wait for all of their parents to hear how much they'd improved this year and to enjoy all they'd accomplished. Happily, Ms. Somers hummed a bit of Bach to herself as the fifth-period bell rang and she shut the door to her classroom.

Something . . . was wrong. As Ms. Somers surveyed her classroom, she realized all of her seniors had mixed themselves up. There were violins in with the violas and violas with the cellos and one bass standing in the back corner of the room, like he wasn't even part of the orchestra anymore.

"Seniors," Ms. Somers chided them, trying to make her voice as stern as possible. "I'm not sure if this is some kind of practical joke, but please return to your assigned seats."

"I'm so sorry, Ms. Somers," Sophie Maeby said, and she really *did* sound sorry, "but we can't sit with these deluded wannabes."

"*Deluded* isn't a nice word, Sophie. That's one. And, Dustin, I see you nodding along. That's also one."

As Ms. Somers issued her first-ever demerits, she wasn't sure who was more shocked—her, Sophie, or Dustin Rothbart.

"I promise you, Ms. Somers, we're doing this for the good of the orchestra," Josiah Watkins said from over in what used to be the cello section, where he was now the lone cello standing with a bunch of violins. "We'll be *more* in harmony this way. I can't play with Teddy Bears or Team Kim or the AntiKaTs anymore."

"We don't want to play with you HeartBeats anymore, either!" Amelia Asaad cried from her first-chair violin seat, surrounded by a mixed-up muddle of first and second violins on that side of the classroom.

"It'll be okay, Ms. Somers," Sophie said. "I'm sure we can all still hear one another totally fine."

"Lawrence can't hear everyone!" Ms. Somers gestured to Lawrence Goulet, standing stubbornly in the corner by her desk with his bass. "Lawrence, what are you even doing back there?"

"I'm standing in my truth."

"Ms. Somers, do not even bother," Sophie said.

"Sophie," Ms. Somers warned. "Could you please stand in your truth with the other basses, Lawrence?"

"No, I cannot," he said. "Because I am the only person at this school brave enough to admit what's really going on!"

"And what's really going on is . . ." Ms. Somers prompted.

"This whole thing is a conspiracy!" Lawrence shouted. "Kim and Teddy *never even existed*!"

Ms. Somers wasn't totally sure what to say to that. She knew for a fact that Kim and Teddy existed. She had seen them both, on multiple occasions, all year long. Ms. Somers wasn't even sure what HeartBeats and AntiKaTs were— this was some information that would have been useful to include in an email—but she did know, at the very least, that Kim and Teddy were real.

"Just leave him in the corner, Ms. Somers," Sophie begged. "Or he'll try to convert you into a Truther."

Ms. Somers stared at her disorganized orchestra, wondering what she should do. Give it a try? Force them to move?

"Everyone needs to return to their assigned seats," she announced. "Or it will be four demerits and an automatic detention for the entire class."

"We thought you might say that," Josiah said seriously. "But we're not going to move. We've decided, as a group, to accept the detention."

In *this* they were united, but they couldn't handle standing next to one another for one measly class period?

"We're, like, so sorry, Ms. Somers," Sophie said. "But we just can't."

"But I bet we'll still sound fine," Amelia said. "Ready, everyone? One, two, one two three . . ."

Amelia lifted her bow and conducted the orchestra into the opening measures of Bach's "Sleeper's Wake." It did not, in fact, sound fine. Everyone's rhythm was slightly off, which made the entire debacle sound out of tune, especially when punctuated by random outbursts of bass from Lawrence Goulet, who clearly could not hear anyone from over in the corner.

Ms. Somers had no doubt that this was going to be the worst Spring Concert William Henry Harrison High had ever seen. Or heard. Maybe she should hand out earplugs with the programs.

She wondered if she was the only teacher having this many problems in this post-Kim-and-Teddy universe.

CHAPTER FORTY-SIX

NICO OSTERMAN
WEEK THREE, DAY FIVE

"According to last night's reading, what's one effect that ingesting microbeads has on aquatic organisms? Hmm . . . let's see . . . Nico?" Ms. Thurber sounded surprised when she called on him.

"Ms. Thurber, have you ever been in love?" he asked, his hand stretched proudly into the air.

"Not an appropriate question, Nico. That's one. And Dustin? Laughing is disrespectful. That's one, too."

Nico had a feeling he wouldn't be getting Ms. Thurber to join the HeartBeats, then. But he *needed* to get a teacher. The Teddy Bears had Mr. Rizzo and Ms. Powell. Team Kim had Ms. Johansson and Coach Finn, and maybe even Mr. Dykstra, although Nico was pretty sure Mr. Dykstra couldn't remember who was in his own classes. Nico needed a real powerhouse of a teacher. Someone who would really get the HeartBeats the respect they deserved.

Wait a minute. Forget teachers—Nico didn't need a teacher.

He needed Principal Manteghi.

CHAPTER FORTY-SEVEN

PRINCIPAL MANTEGHI

WEEK THREE, DAY FIVE

Principal Manteghi was behind.

Woefully behind, on absolutely everything. How was it already Friday? Principal Manteghi wasn't sure if she was grateful for the weekend or terrified of leaving school when there was still so much to be done. Three weeks of Team Kim and Team Teddy had wrought more destruction than she would have thought possible.

Focus, Manteghi. She needed to focus. She pulled out a fresh yellow legal pad and a mechanical pencil. When Principal Manteghi needed to focus, she made lists. Lists relaxed her. They soothed her. And so she began:

1. Find SnakeGate culprit—zero leads
    (maybe Toby Neale?)

2. Find *Birth of Kim-us* culprit—question senior art students (could also be Toby Neale?)

3. Find parking lot culprit—question Teddy Lin, Sophie Maeby, Elvis Rodriguez, and other high-ranking Teddy Bears

4. Break news of parking lot vandalism to Superintendent Harwood (find out if it's bad that I decided to resume normal parking anyway)

5. Devise appropriate punishment for all-school food fight (cancel prom? Too harsh? Does that only punish seniors?)

Making this list was not, in fact, soothing. How could she punish the entire school for the food fight without punishing innocent students who may have been caught in the crosshairs? Mr. Rizzo had no idea who had started it, and Principal Manteghi wasn't going to hold her breath waiting for a student to come forward.

Maybe she *should* just cancel the prom. But that only really punished the seniors. Although, really, none of this would ever have happened if it hadn't been for two seniors . . . Why couldn't Kim and Teddy have broken up after graduation, like a normal senior couple?

"Hey, Principal Manteghi!" Mr. Guzman popped his head into her office.

"What?! Oh—hello, Mr. Guzman," she greeted him, startled.

"Just wanted to give you a quick update," he said. "It's four proms now, not two. Okay, great, thanks so much, bye!"

"Four proms?! Wait—what?! Mr. Guzman!"

But he was already gone, his head disappearing out of her office as abruptly as it had appeared. *Four* proms?! This was ludicrous! Maybe she *should* cancel it.

"Principal!" Lois from the front desk bustled into her office, covered in Post-it notes. A large coffee stain decorated the front of her blouse.

"Lois!" Principal Manteghi was shocked at the normally neat Lois's disheveled appearance. "Are you all right?"

"The parents, Principal Manteghi," Lois sputtered. "The parents."

Principal Manteghi's heart sank. She should have known this was coming.

"Chloe Baker's mother wants to know why Ms. Powell is preventing members of Team Kim from sitting during class," Lois plucked a Post-it off her shoulder and read. She picked another one off her arm. "This one—can't quite make out my handwriting—wants to know if you're aware that Mr. Dykstra has been assigning supplemental essays to anyone wearing teddy bear ears. This one . . ." She retrieved a Post-it note from her elbow. "Evan Loomis's mother is complaining that Ms. Johansson has forced all AntiKaTs to complete additional homework *and* to meditate on the destructive forces of negative thinking, which, she feels, has no place in a math curriculum. Valid point, honestly.

I'm sure there's one about the HeartBeats somewhere, but I can't quite find it at the moment." Lois shuffled through the stack of Post-its stuck to the top of her notebook.

"Are these teachers actually doing this?" the principal asked incredulously. She couldn't believe that her staff would be so biased, so cruel! She didn't want to believe it.

"I couldn't say, Principal." Lois shook her head. "I'm only reporting the calls as they come in."

The calls. It couldn't just be the phone lines that were flooded. Almost trembling with trepidation, Principal Manteghi refreshed her email inbox. Her eyes danced over the flood of angry, all-caps subject lines flooding her inbox.

SUBJ: POWELL HAS LOST IT!
SUBJ: TEAM KIM PERSECUTION
SUBJ: JUSTICE FOR TEDDY
SUBJ: IS THIS SCHOOL UNSAFE FOR MY DAUGHTER?!?!
SUBJ: PLEASE LISTEN TO THE HEARTBEATS!!!
SUBJ: TRANSFERRING IMMEDIATELY
SUBJ: FOOD FIGHT IS HATE CRIME AGAINST STUDENTS WITH FOOD ALLERGIES!!!!!!
SUBJ: NUDE ART IN SCHOOLS?!

Nude art?! Principal Manteghi hadn't been a fan of *The Birth of Kim-us*, but it certainly wasn't nude! These rumors were spiraling out of control. Principal Manteghi owed it to the school—and to herself—to set the record straight.

"I think it's time, Lois," Principal Manteghi said grimly.

"Oh no, Principal." The color drained from Lois's face. "I know things are bad, but I didn't think they were *that* bad."

"Desperate times call for desperate measures." Principal Manteghi swallowed hard.

"Call in the PTA."

CHAPTER FORTY-EIGHT

KIM LANDIS-LILLEY
WEEK FOUR, DAY ONE

If Kim's parents had any idea how far everything had gone, they probably would have insisted on homeschooling her for the last couple weeks of senior year. Kim hated keeping things from her moms. She'd never outright *lied* to them, but she also hadn't exactly told them there had been a giant poster of her standing on a clamshell, either.

Or that there was now a giant rendering of her face where the clamshell version of her had been.

Somehow, none of that had come up over the weekend. It was so much easier to live in denial when she wasn't at school. Kim sighed and pushed past the crowd that had gathered around the new poster to get to her locker. It wasn't that the poster wasn't good. She looked beautiful in it, again, way more beautiful than in real life, but this time, she didn't really want to see it.

She was tired of people staring at her face—both her real face and her giant painted-on-the-wall face. Kim missed the days of chatting by her locker with Teddy, days when he'd bring her an egg-and-cheese breakfast sandwich "just because" and she knew that meant it would be a great day, because they'd started it off together.

Kim didn't want to miss him. But she did.

The opening strains of "Grease Is the Word" filled the senior hall. Kim looked up to see Corey Brooks in a leather jacket with his hair slicked black, strutting toward her locker. He pulled out a sign from behind his back and held it up. It said *PROM?*

Normally, Kim would have explained to him gently, but firmly, that her original no meant no, and that she was not interested in going to the prom. Sure, a couple months ago, Kim couldn't wait to go to prom. But now? No way. She wasn't going. Not with Corey, and not with anyone. And while normally she would have said that, today, she just wasn't in the mood. This was way too much for a Monday.

Kim grabbed her books and left. Corey could dance his way on over to somebody else.

CHAPTER FORTY-NINE

ELVIS RODRIGUEZ
WEEK FOUR, DAY ONE

"What's up with the leather jacket?" Elvis asked Corey Brooks as Corey stalked down the hall.

"It's your mom's, E-Rod!" Corey shot back.

Hmm. There was a lot to unpack there. First of all, Elvis's mom already had a leather jacket. Well, technically, it was brown suede, and technically, it was fake, but that was still basically a leather jacket. And second . . .

"Did you hear that?" Elvis marveled, pulling Teddy to a stop as he clutched his arm.

"Hear what?" Teddy asked.

"He called me E-Rod!" Elvis cheered. "Sure, when Corey says it, it somehow sounds like an insult, but he did it! He called me E-Rod!" Elvis was still hanging on to Teddy's arm, shaking it back and forth with joy. "This is it, man! This is my moment! Sure, everything else is kind of a garbage fire, but this is my beam of light! Things are finally turning around!"

"A garbage fire?" Teddy asked.

"Come on, Teddy. This hasn't exactly been the senior spring of our dreams. I literally spent the weekend putting out fires."

"Literally?" Teddy raised a skeptical eyebrow.

Fine, Elvis had been putting out figurative fires. He'd spent the whole weekend trying to squash a rumor that Teddy had burned Kim's house down, and trying to keep Teddy from finding out about it. It was so unfair. If you believed the rumors—which Elvis didn't—Kim had spent the weekend on Jennifer Aniston's private island, getting life coaching from Oprah, while Elvis was busy trying to defend his best friend from being reviled as a snake-releasing, Olympics-ruining arsonist. Why did Team Kim get all the good rumors? The Teddy Bears may have had the merch, but the PR machine behind Team Kim was unstoppable.

"Not literally," Elvis muttered. He reached under his teddy bear ears to scratch his head. "Like, you don't know this because you don't wear the ears, but the nubbins at the base of this headband are digging into my head, man. I think they're making me go bald, too." Elvis pushed the base of the ears aside. "Does it look like my hair is thinning down there?"

Elvis's dad claimed he shaved his head on purpose because he wanted to look like Albert Pujols, from the Angels, but Elvis wasn't buying it. His dad had never supported an LA team in his *life*. No, Elvis was confident his dad shaved his head because he was bald, and that was *not* how Elvis wanted things to go down. Elvis wouldn't ever say it out loud, but his thick, shiny hair was his pride and glory.

He was confident that was how he'd snared Jess.

"No, Elvis, you're definitely not balding." Teddy pulled Elvis back to reality, and away from dangerous thoughts, like how Jess used to absentmindedly pat his hair when they'd sit next to each other while she read. Elvis couldn't go down that road. No, that way madness lay, or whatever it was that King Lear had said in the fall play. "You can also take the ears off if they're bothering you. I'm not wearing any."

"You don't *need* to wear them. You *are* Teddy. I'm wearing them because I'm supporting you."

"And I appreciate that. But I promise I can feel supported without you wearing a headband. Or the bear slippers. Or the T-shirt. You've been wearing that thing every day for weeks."

"I wash it," Elvis said defensively. And he did. Maybe not as often as he should, but he did. "Wait a minute. There's something weird on my locker." An odd red color had appeared where no red color should be.

"Is it another giant picture of Kim's face? Because that's all today needs," Teddy muttered.

"No, it's . . . ribbons." Elvis reached out his hand to stroke the shiny surface. His entire locker had been wrapped in Team Kim's signature red ribbons. "How did they do this?" he asked. "They must have opened . . . But how could anyone . . . ? Of course," he said as realization dawned.

"Does Jess know your combination?"

"That she does," Elvis replied grimly. He spun his lock around and then pulled the door open, only to discover that all of the contents of his locker had *also* been wrapped in red ribbons. "Well, that is just . . . fantastic." Elvis pulled out his math book and attempted to pry it open. "Anybody have scissors?" he shouted down the senior hall. No one responded. "See what I mean?" Elvis gestured to the beribboned contents of his locker. "Everything's a garbage fire."

"It's not a garbage fire. It's . . . festive."

Elvis studied his best friend critically, unable to tell if Teddy's optimism was genuine or just willful ignorance. Elvis was over everything. He missed Jess. And he knew, from the way Teddy's gaze had lingered on the latest Kim poster, that Teddy missed Kim, too. Elvis was just a lonely dummy wearing animal ears with a locker full of ribbons.

Again: Not how he wanted to spend the end of senior year.

"I'll get us some scissors," Teddy said. "It looks like they hit my locker, too."

"Why are you being so chill about this?" Elvis demanded as Teddy retreated down the hall to the nearest classroom. "What do we do now, Teddy? Retaliate?"

"No, man," Teddy called over his shoulder. "That way madness lies."

Whoever played King Lear in the fall play must have really nailed that line.

Elvis sighed and began untying his books.

CHAPTER FIFTY

OLIVIA LANDIS-LILLEY

WEEK FOUR, DAY ONE

Olivia's least favorite artist was back at it again.

At least this time she wasn't *in* the picture. Olivia didn't care *what* Daisy said; that had *not* been a good picture of her. Next to the luminescent Princess Kim, Olivia had looked like a troll holding a warm-up jacket. In real life, Olivia knew she looked like a troll next to Princess Kim, but she'd rather not have that blown up and magnified on the wall of her high school, thanks so much. So at least this time, Kim was luminous all on her own, her giant face looming beatifically over the senior hall.

"Kim with a Pearl Earring," Daisy read off the wall as she appeared by Olivia's shoulder. "Hey! That was my idea! That guy totally copied me!"

"What guy?"

"That senior art guy with the man bun!" Daisy said. "I *knew* he was listening to us talk!"

"Daisy Diaz!" Principal Manteghi boomed. Daisy and Olivia jumped. How long had she been standing behind them? "Do you have any information on the identity of the serial vandal who's graffitied the senior hall?"

"Um...no?" Daisy said timidly, exchanging worried glances with Olivia.

"Fine." Principal Manteghi sighed with exasperation. "Senior. Man bun. Exactly as I suspected," she muttered. "I'll do it myself."

"Did I just totally rat Toby out?" Daisy asked Olivia.

"Kind of. Maybe. But you didn't mean to!" Olivia reassured her. "And Principal Manteghi would have figured it out eventually. It seems obvious that it was Toby. I don't know why she hasn't busted him yet. Covering the school with weird stuff is his whole jam."

"I guess." Daisy chewed on her lip.

Privately, Olivia felt that the sooner this guy was stopped, the better. Someone posting up giant versions of her sister's face everywhere was just plain embarrassing. It was almost as embarrassing as all the people who had texted Olivia this weekend to ask her how they could stream Kim's TED talk. Olivia had deleted every single social media app, but the texts still came rolling in. This time, her phone had ended up in the freezer on Saturday.

"Maybe we should start putting little AntiKaTs everywhere," Daisy suggested. "Like Banksy. Or Toby Neale."

"No, thanks." Olivia shook her head. The last thing she wanted to do was anything that could get her in trouble.

William Henry Harrison High softball was currently hanging together by a thread, and not to brag, but Olivia knew that she was the thread keeping them together. She couldn't afford to be benched for disciplinary reasons. During their last couple practices, it had felt like she was the only one alive out there. She tugged on the end of one of her tight French braids absentmindedly, worrying about the game this afternoon. They weren't playing like a team, and even the best player couldn't win a game single-handedly.

Maybe Olivia shouldn't have started the AntiKaTs. Because the Team Kim girls weren't talking to the AntiKaTs, and Wendy was pretending everyone on Team Kim didn't exist, and then Molly Santos had decided to join the Teddy Bears because she wanted to ask out Teddy, and then the rest of the outfield declared for the HeartBeats . . . It was a mess. Olivia had wanted all of this nonsense to *stop*, but by founding the AntiKaTs, she'd only made it all worse.

The bell rang, jerking Olivia out of her gloomy thoughts.

"Come on." Daisy nudged her. "Up, up, and away to homeroom."

Olivia climbed the stairs, two at a time, trying to do some glute toning on her way up. There was an odd citrus smell in the stairway. Even more oddly, the smell intensified as they climbed the stairs, until they reached the freshman hall, which smelled so much like citrus, Olivia's eyes started to water.

"What *is* that smell?" Daisy asked.

"Oranges," Diamond Allen answered as she walked by them, a five-pound bag of oranges nestled in her arms.

Olivia didn't even want to know.

CHAPTER FIFTY-ONE

JESS HOWARD
WEEK FOUR, DAY TWO

"Jessica! Jessica Howard!"

Jess recognized the voice immediately, but she wasn't used to hearing it sound quite so angry. She kicked an orange out of her way as she turned to face Elvis. Where were all of these oranges coming from? Ever since yesterday, more and more of them had appeared. Just a few minutes ago, Jess had to help Kim move a pile of oranges out of the way of Kim's locker so they could get it open. It would have been a great time to have Force powers, so Jess could have lifted them all out of the way, like Rey had with the rocks on the mineral planet of Crait. Instead, she'd had to use her hands, and now little bits of the peel were all up under her nails. Jess had a feeling she was going to smell like her grandma's favorite air freshener all day.

"Did you or did you not pay my little brother to *shave my head* while I was sleeping?" Elvis demanded.

Kim shot Jess a look so incendiary Jess could feel it scorching her ears. Kim was not usually prone to incendiary looks, so maybe that's why this one felt extra smoky.

"I don't see any shaved head here," Jess said.

Elvis whipped around and pulled up his hair in the back. Sure enough, hidden under his hair, there was a tiny shaved square, exposing the base of Elvis's skull. Manny must not have gotten very far.

"This was low, even for you, Jessica. You know I'm scared of going bald!"

"You're scared of going bald?" Kim asked. "Elvis, you have a *ton* of hair."

"For now!" Elvis cried. "Who knows what the future will hold? Certainly not a full, luxurious head of hair, if this one has anything to say about it!" Elvis jerked his thumb at Jess. "How did you even orchestrate this? Were you hanging out outside the middle school, waiting for Manny with a ten-dollar bill so you could lure him into a life of crime? Because that's creepy, Jess. That's really creepy."

"I didn't pay Manny ten dollars." Jess had no idea whether Manny had ratted her out or not. She wasn't sure how much information to reveal. But she could truthfully say she didn't pay Manny ten dollars.

She'd given him a king-size Snickers instead.

"You know what maybe hurts the most? Your plan was *stupid*," Elvis hissed. "I woke up when I heard the electric razor, Jessica! Obviously! What were you thinking?"

Huh. Jess *hadn't* been thinking. She should have specified

that Manny use shaving cream and a razor. Although seeing how mad Elvis was about losing one little tiny square of hair...Jess found herself feeling kind of relieved that Manny hadn't been able to shave his brother further.

"This was just mean," Elvis continued. "Especially so close to prom. How would you like it if I paid Imani to come in and shave *you*?"

Jess patted her curls protectively. The thought of her little sister wielding a razor for any type of reason was terrifying. Imani had the hand-eye coordination of a fish.

"I hope Jess had nothing to do with this," Kim said meaningfully, "but if she *did*, I'm sure she's very sorry."

"Hypothetically. If I had something to do with it. Which I'm not saying I did."

"You took things too far, Jessica," Elvis said. "This goes way beyond Team Kim and Team Teddy stuff. Like the locker with the ribbons? Very funny. And whatever these oranges mean, I'm sure that's very funny, too—"

"I don't know what the oranges are," Jess interrupted him. "We had nothing to do with that."

"But hair, Jessica? Hair is *not* funny. Hair is *personal*."

Maybe she had taken it too far. She'd thought it would be funny, but now, seeing how mad Elvis was, she was having a hard time remembering what, exactly, was going to be so funny about it.

"I don't even understand why you did it," Elvis continued. "Do you hate me that much?"

"I don't hate you—"

"You *must* to attack me like this! Is this all because I wouldn't let you eat outside? Seriously? It's not even that nice outside! It's a couple of picnic tables next to a parking lot."

"It was more the principle of the... Never mind," Jess mumbled.

"Do not come after my hair again, Jessica!" Elvis called as he marched back down the senior hall, narrowly avoiding bumping in to Lawrence Goulet and his *KIM AND TEDDY NEVER EXISTED* conspiracy sign. "Or you will *not* like what happens!"

It was the longest conversation they'd had since they'd broken up.

"Please tell me you did not do what he said you did," Kim said.

"His head isn't shaved. So, ergo, no, I must not have done anything."

"Jess!" Kim exclaimed. "Don't give me that double-talk, lawyerly answer. What were you *thinking?*"

Truth was, she hadn't been thinking. But instead, she said, "You know, just Team Kim versus Team Teddy stuff."

"This had *nothing* to do with Team Kim, so don't pretend it did. This was just about you and Elvis. And again, I ask: Why?"

"I dunno, I guess... maybe there's still part of me that's mad he chose Teddy over me," Jess admitted.

"But that's exactly what you did when you picked me!" Kim protested.

"It's different."

"It is exactly the same, Jess, and you know it. Please promise me you won't shave anybody else."

"I won't. But technically, I didn't—"

"Just promise."

"I promise. Okay?" Jess said. "I promise."

Kim was still looking worriedly down the hall in the direction Elvis had gone, like she was perhaps fearful of some kind of retribution. But Elvis wouldn't do anything— Jess was sure of it. He'd never be coordinated enough to pull anything together. And he was too much of a people-pleaser to do anything that would truly upset anyone, even a member of Team Kim. But Kim was still looking down the hallway with worry in her eyes, even though the only person there was Lawrence Goulet and his stupid sign.

"Hey there—Lawrence, my man?" Jess waved in his face as he passed. "Kim is literally right here."

"That's what they want you to think," he replied, sailing past Kim like she didn't exist.

It was small consolation, but at least Jess could take comfort in the fact that she wasn't the biggest fool at William Henry Harrison High.

CHAPTER FIFTY-TWO

LAWRENCE GOULET
WEEK FOUR, DAY TWO

These people were blind. Blind to the truth! Why couldn't they see what was right in front of them? Clearly, this entire Kim-and-Teddy fiction had been cooked up by the administration as a distraction. As a distraction from *what*, he wasn't totally sure, but he was going to figure it out.

Lawrence had a feeling that it had something to do with the superintendent. Thanks to some intensive online research, Lawrence had been able to find the minutes for the Board of Ed meeting where the superintendent had proposed repaving all the parking lots. He'd been awfully insistent. Too insistent. Something was rotten here, and the administration was using Kim and Teddy to throw them all off the scent. But what were they covering up? He needed information. He needed access. He needed—

"Lawrence." Ms. Thurber glared at him. "I'm not going to tell you again. You need to put that sign away during class. You're already at one."

"But the people deserve to know the truth!" he cried.

"That's two. And, Dustin? It's not funny. You're at one."

"Lawrence, I'm literally sitting *right here*," a male voice said from behind Lawrence. It was probably the puppet the administration wanted them to believe was "Teddy Lin," but Lawrence knew better. No such person had ever existed, or ever would exist. "You know I'm real, man. I've sat three rows behind you this entire year."

Lawrence wouldn't engage with this pawn of the administration. Who knew what his agenda was? Maybe they were paying him off. Maybe they were funneling Tater Tots directly to him. Lawrence also had a lot of theories about what the school did with their leftover Tater Tots, but that was an issue for another day.

"Teddy, I appreciate your frustration," Ms. Thurber said, "but let's return to the text. Now, if we look at paragraph three, what evidence can we find to support the first argument?"

Blind. They were all blind.

Standing in your truth was lonely sometimes.

CHAPTER FIFTY-THREE

MR. RIZZO
WEEK FOUR, DAY THREE

Principal Manteghi had denied Mr. Rizzo's request to transfer off of lunch duty. Detention, bus duty, *anything* would have been better than this. Mr. Rizzo clenched his travel coffee mug protectively, eyes darting warily from side to side as he scanned the perimeter for miscreants and flying edible projectiles. No more open coffee mugs for him. Not since a Tot had splashed in there during the Great Food Fight, ruining his coffee and soaking his favorite Bonobos shirt, the Riviera Short Sleeve with the pineapple print, with horrible brown sludge.

The stain had *not* come out.

After his initial request had been denied, Mr. Rizzo had made a second request for backup in the cafeteria, but Principal Manteghi had denied that as well, citing the fact that they were understaffed. Understaffed! As if Mr. Rizzo didn't know that! He'd been at this school for eight years, since he'd bounced out of college with his theater degree and his teaching certification. And who was always first to volunteer when they needed another chaperone? Mr. Rizzo! Who had turned William Henry Harrison High's sad drama program into a sensation that rivaled any school in the district? Mr. Rizzo! Who stayed after school so his students had a place to run lines even on days they didn't have rehearsal, even when someone would much rather have been at home, watching *Golden Girls* in his sweatpants? Mr. Rizzo!

Principal Manteghi was a good principal—she was certainly far better than her predecessor. But Mr. Rizzo felt she could have appreciated him just a little bit more.

Coach Mendoza nodded grimly at Mr. Rizzo from across the cafeteria, his arms folded menacingly, as if he was just daring someone to throw a pudding cup and see what happened. Although Principal Manteghi had denied his request, Mr. Rizzo had noticed that since the food fight, various members of the PE team just happened to be crossing through the cafeteria more and more often, which he greatly appreciated. PE and arts had to have each other's backs, or those core curriculum teachers would run roughshod all over them.

There hadn't been any further incidents in the cafeteria since the Great Food Fight, and it appeared almost as though a newfound status quo had been reached. The dividing line between Team Kim and the Teddy Bears remained strong as ever, only now there were bastions of AntiKaTs and HeartBeats staking out their own tables on both sides.

But even though things had been relatively calm, Mr. Rizzo knew he couldn't relax. Once you'd been squirted with an industrial ketchup bottle by a freshman, perhaps you could never relax again. Mr. Rizzo took another sip of his coffee, hoping that the caffeine would make him feel more alert, instead of making him flinch at any sudden noises, like it usually did.

Suddenly, a chord progression started playing through the speakers in the cafeteria that were supposed to be used for announcements only. Thunder rumbled. Every student quieted as their heads turned toward the speakers, like animals on the Serengeti sniffing an upcoming storm. Oh no. Oh no, no, no. Mr. Rizzo would recognize those opening bars anywhere. He and a few other male members of the faculty had performed this very song at the Staff Back-to-School Karaoke Night to a full standing ovation. Coach Mendoza, who had, in fact, been part of that very same performance, locked eyes with Mr. Rizzo from across the cafeteria.

"Nobody start dancing!" Coach Mendoza barked. "If anyone even attempts to *Magic Mike* in this cafeteria, you will be suspended faster than you can say Channing Tatum. Dustin Rothbart? That's one for bopping your head in time with the music."

And just as the Weather Girls reached the chorus and sang, "It's raining men" for the first time, the sprinklers on the Team Kim side of the cafeteria opened up, dousing everyone in the vicinity, Mr. Rizzo included, with an ice-cold shower.

The screaming started immediately. It was so loud that it

almost drowned out the music. It certainly drowned out Coach Mendoza as he started running toward the Team Kim side, shouting at everyone to remain calm. But no one was quite as loud as Jess Howard.

"ELVIS RODRIGUEZ!" she bellowed as she charged toward the Teddy Bear side. "I AM GOING TO MURDER YOU!"

"Rizzo!" Coach Mendoza shouted. "Restrain her if you have to!"

Yeah, right. Mr. Rizzo wasn't getting involved in any kind of physical altercation between students. And if Elvis Rodriguez was responsible for this impromptu shower, Mr. Rizzo was definitely more on Jess's side, teddy bear ears to the contrary.

"I'm not doing anything!" Elvis shot back. Mr. Rizzo looked over at Elvis, peeking around from behind Coach Mendoza. "I'm just standing here!"

"Stop hiding behind Coach Mendoza and let me murder you!" Jess yelled.

"Murder is expressly forbidden by the Student Code of Conduct!" Mr. Rizzo said, but it was hard to maintain authority when wet. Also, he was pretty sure that the Student Code of Conduct didn't actually mention murder.

"I know this was you!" Jess said. "This weird song choice has you written all over it!"

"It's not a weird song choice, it's thematic! Not that I had anything to do with it!"

If Mr. Rizzo's hair hadn't been completely ruined, never mind the fact that his shirt was dry clean only, or the fact that he'd have to send yet *another* unfortunate email to

Principal Manteghi, he could almost have enjoyed the drama of it all. As abruptly as they'd started, both the music and the sprinklers shut off, but the damage had been done. Everyone on Team Kim—and a few HeartBeats who had been caught in the crosshairs—was well and truly soaked.

"Jessica, please return to your seat," Coach Mendoza said. "Everyone, return to your seats!" he added, louder. "We'll retrieve towels from the locker rooms for those of you who were hit by the sprinklers. Everyone just remain calm and stay seated!"

Mr. Rizzo wondered if Coach Mendoza had ever had theater training. He certainly projected well.

"Rizzo," Coach Mendoza said in an undertone. "Can you get Finn and the rest of PE to help you bring the towels in? And let Principal Manteghi know what happened?"

"On it." Mr. Rizzo felt bad leaving Coach Mendoza alone, but it seemed like he had it all under control, somehow able to keep Jess Howard and Elvis Rodriguez apart merely by standing between them.

As Mr. Rizzo passed by them on his way out of the cafeteria, he heard Elvis Rodriguez whisper, "Maybe this is just what happens, Jessica, when you attempt to shave a man."

Mr. Rizzo decided it was better not to ask too many questions about that.

CHAPTER FIFTY-FOUR

MS. SOMERS
WEEK FOUR, DAY THREE

The third-floor copy room was Ms. Somers's favorite place to cry.

Nobody ever came up here except for the freshman teachers, and if you timed it right, you were pretty much guaranteed to be alone. Plus, the gentle whirring of the giant printers drowned out any unpleasant sniffling noises. And the printers were warm, too, almost like they were alive. She rested her hand along the side of Third-Floor-Copy-Room-Printer-01A.

Someone knocked on the door of the third-floor copy room.

"Come in!" she called, which was ridiculous, since anyone could come in whenever they wanted to. It wasn't her room. Ms. Somers saw Coach Mendoza's face appear in the small glass window of the copy room door. She hastily ran her hands under her eyes, wiping away her tears. Sometimes never wearing mascara paid off. At least there wouldn't be any black streaks.

"Somebody spit in your rosin?" he asked, closing the door softly behind him.

"No," she replied, laughing. "Just a bad day. Well, a whole series of bad days."

No matter how many demerits she gave out, no one in her orchestra classes would sit where they were supposed to. Everyone sounded abysmal. And so many of the oranges piled outside of Kim Landis-Lilley's locker had rolled down the senior hallway and toward the orchestra room, where they'd been soundly squished, that the whole area surrounding Ms. Somers's room was disgustingly sticky.

"Let me guess. It had something to do with Teddy Bears and Team Kim and HeartBeats and AntiKaTs and who-knows-what-the-next-thing'll-be."

"Truthers."

"What's that?"

"Truthers are the next thing. Lawrence Goulet is saying the whole thing's a conspiracy. Kim and Teddy never even existed."

"Huh." Coach Mendoza chewed his lip contemplatively. "That's a new one. And a weird one. Haven't seen that. This Goulet kid must not take PE."

"Guess not." Ms. Somers laughed again. "How did you know I was having a Kim-and-Teddy problem?"

"Who isn't?" Coach Mendoza shrugged helplessly. "You heard about the sprinklers going off in the cafeteria today?" Ms. Somers nodded. Boy, she was glad she didn't have lunch duty. "I spent the whole lunch period giving towels to screaming kids. And all of my classes have been a mess for weeks. Nobody will work with anybody who isn't on their team."

"What did you do?"

"Made them do a series of body-weight challenges. Push-ups, sit-ups, planks, squats. Silently and individually. I promise you, nobody had fun." He grinned. "But then again, I have it pretty easy. I'm not trying to get them ready for a concert in a week. There's no End-of-the-Year Gym Presentation."

"You know about the concert?" she asked, surprised.

"Of course. Josiah—he's in the outfield—it's his last cello concert. I wouldn't miss it. And I wouldn't miss Ms. Somers's first Spring Concert, either."

Ms. Somers was touched. It was so nice of him to support his students' extracurricular activities. And the idea that maybe, just maybe, *she* had something to do with him coming to this specific concert . . . well, that touched her, too.

"You might want to miss this one," she said ruefully. "It's going to be a disaster."

"I'm sure it'll be better than you think. And even if it's not, you've already done the most important thing. You've gotten these kids excited about music in a new way."

"I haven't—I'm sure that's not—"

"Josiah listens to Bach before all of our games. I promise you, he didn't do that for the first three years he was on my team. That's all because of you."

Their eyes met, and Ms. Somers knew neither of them was thinking about Bach or Josiah Watkins anymore.

"Come on, Somers," Coach Mendoza coaxed. "Let's get out of here. I'm buying you a burger."

"Don't you have baseball practice?" she whispered, stepping toward him almost involuntarily.

"Technically? Yeah. But I'm canceling it. I think the guys could use a break from one another, anyway. They've already smacked one another with baseball gloves. Who knows what kind of violence they'll resort to next."

"Smacked one another?" Ms. Somers repeated. "I feel like I would have remembered reading about that in a disciplinary email."

"You would have ... if I'd reported it." Ms. Somers was scandalized, and a little delighted, that Coach Mendoza had so flagrantly violated the chains of disciplinary action clearly delineated in the Student Code of Conduct. "I'd rather have the guys work things out among themselves, if at all possible. I had a feeling sticking them all in detention wouldn't help anything. But look at it this way. As long as your students haven't started fencing with their bows yet, you're at least a step ahead of me." He smiled, revealing Ms. Somers's favorite dimple. "Come on. Let's get out of here before all the parents descend on the school for Manteghi's meeting. Let's go get burgers. Do you eat red meat?"

"I do," she answered.

"So ..."

"So ... okay," she said.

"Okay?" he asked.

"Yeah." She smiled. "Let's go get burgers."

CHAPTER FIFTY-FIVE

PRINCIPAL MANTEGHI
WEEK FOUR, DAY THREE

Principal Manteghi's least favorite aspect of a career in education could be summed up neatly in one word: parents.

And she knew she wasn't the only educator to feel this way. She'd heard it over and over again, at all the schools she'd worked at. In general, the parents at William Henry Harrison High were better than most. They were involved in their children's lives and invested in the school, but not so much that they made daily operations difficult.

But as Principal Manteghi looked out over the overstuffed auditorium, the mild-mannered parents she'd shaken hands with at Parents' Nights past had disappeared.

In their place was a mob.

"Attention!" Principal Manteghi tapped on the mic for quiet. "Attention, please, attention, William Henry Harrison

High parents! I know you have a lot of questions, and I'd like to get this meeting started as soon as possible."

"Of course we have questions!" Principal Manteghi squinted at a man in a tweed blazer standing up near the back of the auditorium. "And you'd better have a heck of a lot of answers!"

Principal Manteghi exchanged glances with Lois as the parents murmured angrily in response. As she had feared, this was not going to be easy.

"I'd like to know why a simple breakup has derailed the entire educational process!" a woman in the front row asked, her blunt-cut bob swinging around her cheeks. "Is the foundation here really so weak that one high school relationship sends the entire operation into chaos?"

Principal Manteghi had been asking herself the same question for weeks.

"This isn't a simple breakup." A tall African American man in a gray sweater stood up in the middle of the room. "If you knew the full extent of what Teddy's done to Kim, you wouldn't be calling it simple."

Jess Howard's father, Principal Manteghi realized. Of course he'd stand up to defend Kim . . . particularly since Kimberly Landis Senior had called Principal Manteghi to let her know that neither she nor her wife would be attending, and that she thought it was highly inappropriate that the principal had called a PTA meeting to discuss the relationship status of two of its students. Arnold Lin had sent her an email expressing almost exactly the same sentiment. And Principal Manteghi thought she had worded her PTA meeting email so carefully, too, trying to make sure that it wasn't all about Kim and Teddy! But it was. Everything was. No matter how outrageously things had spiraled out of control, or how futilely she tried to control the chaos, all roads led back to Kim and Teddy.

A small part of Principal Manteghi had hoped that maybe one or both sets of parents might change their minds, but as she cast her eyes around the auditorium, it became evident that neither the Landis-Lilleys nor the Lins were in attendance. Fantastic. Not that Principal Manteghi would have shuttled all of the issues that had plagued William Henry Harrison High since the breakup onto their shoulders, but still . . . it would have been nice if this mob of parents had someone else to look to for answers besides her.

"What Teddy's done to *Kim*?" The man in the tweed jacket stood up again. Principal Manteghi recognized him now— Sophie Maeby's father. Principal Manteghi gripped the podium for support. "I don't know what you've heard, Howard, but you need to check your ears. That Landis-Lilley girl is heartless. She eviscerated that poor boy!"

"Heartless? Sounds like someone's been breathing in a few too many exhaust fumes," Mr. Howard shot back.

"You want exhaust fumes? I'll give anyone who comes into Maeby Motors with Team Teddy bear ears a bump off the listed price. You could be driving off the lot in luxury today!"

"Nobody wants your rusted-out lemons, Maeby!"

"Excuse me?" Mr. Maeby bellowed. "These are luxury certified pre-owned vehicles! Certified, Howard!"

"Certified by whom?" Mr. Howard scoffed. "Show me the Carfax, Maeby!"

"If anyone on Team Kim is looking for a deal"—Gabe Koontz's mom jumped out of her seat, easily recognizable in her hunter-green Koontz Market polo—"we've got a special on bags of oranges down at Koontz Market! Swing on by for the freshest produce in town and the best way to show your loyalty!"

"No more oranges!" Principal Manteghi said into the microphone. There were already far too many citrus fruits rolling around the hallways, especially outside of Kim Landis-Lilley's locker. Principal Manteghi was afraid they'd rot before maintenance could get them all, or they'd discover a few desiccated oranges hidden in vents or stuffed in corners next fall.

"Half price!" Mrs. Koontz added quickly before sitting down again.

"Things may have gotten slightly out of hand," Principal Manteghi admitted. She was shocked no one had asked about today's incident with the sprinkler system. Maybe they hadn't heard about it yet.

Well, Principal Manteghi certainly wasn't about to bring it up.

"Slightly." The woman in the front row with the bob rolled her eyes.

"But we are here to defuse the situation, not to escalate things."

"And what are your plans to defuse the situation?" The woman with the bob stood up. "Dr. Phan," she introduced herself to the room. Wendy's mom. Right. "This school needs stricter measures. Outlaw teddy bear ears, red accessories, felt hearts, all of it. Maybe even suspend Kim and Teddy. Just take them out of the equation. Problem solved."

Suspend Kim and Teddy? The auditorium erupted into outrage. If Principal Manteghi was confident that Kim had put up the snake posters, or that Teddy had vandalized the parking lot, or either one of them had set off the sprinklers, she could have—and would have—suspended them in a heartbeat. But with absolutely no proof of any actual misconduct, she couldn't suspend them for breaking up. As much as Principal Manteghi would have loved order back in her halls, she couldn't do something that unfair.

"At William Henry Harrison High, we don't suspend students without a reason," Principal Manteghi said loudly into the mic as the auditorium quieted down.

"You don't seem to do much of anything at William Henry Harrison High," Dr. Phan said.

Principal Manteghi was grateful for the sympathetic look Lois shot her. It would have been nice if more of the staff had been here to support her.

"Now what do we have here?" The doors at the back of the auditorium swung open and Mr. Rizzo walked through. Blessedly, he'd removed his teddy bear ears, and he'd changed into dry clothes. Principal Manteghi thought she recognized the suit as one Nathan Detroit had worn in the recent William Henry Harrison High production of *Guys and Dolls*, but at least it wasn't entirely outlandish. "What is this, a parent meeting or a Comedy Central roast?"

A handful of parents laughed appreciatively. Principal Manteghi swore she could feel the tension in the room diffuse.

"May I?" Mr. Rizzo asked as he approached the mic. Principal Manteghi nodded wordlessly and stepped aside, grateful for the support. She would never, ever say a bad word about the drama department ever again.

"Wish we'd had a packed house like this for the spring musical!" Mr. Rizzo quipped as even more parents laughed. "Some of you missed quite the *Guys and Dolls*."

Even Wendy Phan's mom was nodding and smiling up at him. How was he doing this? Mr. Rizzo was magic!

"Now, I understand that some of you parents have been concerned by recent events here at William Henry Harrison High. I know how that old rumor mill can get going." He chuckled, and the rest of the auditorium chuckled, too, a low, warm rumble. "But I'd like to remind you that what we've really seen here is simply a series of different forms of artistic expression. Some misguided, perhaps, some misplaced, but at the end of the day, that's all this is: artistic expression."

The parents murmured thoughtfully as Principal Manteghi considered Mr. Rizzo's words. He wasn't *wrong*, exactly. The snake posters, the Kim art, the giant heart in the parking lot . . . Most of these acts of defiance had been misguided art projects. Even the musical accompaniment to the sprinklers could be seen as a type of performance art. Somehow, when Mr. Rizzo put it like that, it didn't seem so bad.

"What about the food fight?" a woman in the third row asked timidly.

"Reports of the food fight have been wildly exaggerated," Mr. Rizzo lied confidently. "We all know this school has been nut-free since '03, so no one was really in danger. And besides, what is food if not another medium, and what is a cafeteria if not another canvas?"

At that, a couple parents even applauded. Principal Manteghi had no idea why Mr. Rizzo was wasting his talents here. He should go into politics.

"I would like to commend Principal Manteghi for creating the kind of environment here at William Henry Harrison High where our students feel so comfortable expressing themselves. Not every principal could foster such a hotbed of artistic creativity."

Now the parents were applauding *her*? This meeting had gone from angry mob to appreciative audience in mere minutes. Principal Manteghi was stunned. Maybe things actually *would* be okay.

"Wanted to warn you," Mr. Rizzo said in an undertone, his hand covering the microphone as the parents continued to applaud. "Superintendent Harwood is waiting in your office. He knows about the parking lot."

Maybe things weren't so okay after all.

CHAPTER FIFTY-SIX

TEDDY LIN
WEEK FOUR, DAY THREE

"Practice is canceled today," Elvis read off the piece of paper taped to the dugout. "Please use your free time for cross-training."

"Any of you nerds want to join me in the weight room?" Corey Brooks asked. "I could use a spotter."

"Hard pass," Elvis muttered.

Teddy didn't even bother to answer. Since the Great Baseball Glove Smack-off, they were managing to be civil to Corey, for the sake of the team, but just barely. Teddy had heard a rumor that the whole Teddy-Kim-HeartBeats-AntiKaT situation had completely destroyed both the girls' and boys' lacrosse teams. Everyone knew volleyball had been disbanded early. But they couldn't—wouldn't—let that happen on the baseball team. Baseball was just too important.

In the distance, Teddy heard music. He looked toward the noise, straining his ears to try to figure out what it was. More music?

"Please tell me you're not about to set off the sprinklers on the field, too," Teddy told Elvis.

"I never said that was *me*."

Elvis and Teddy exchanged looks. Teddy didn't know *how* Elvis had done it, but he knew he'd done it. That sprinkler stunt was 100 percent Elvis's revenge on Jess for her attempted shaving.

"What is that?" Teddy asked, squinting across the baseball diamond.

"Some kind of nonsense. And my best guess is that it's for you, man," Josiah said to Teddy. "You know, there's one easy way to stop all of this. Why don't you just talk to Kim? Apologize? You guys can get back together, and everything will be the way it was before. When you were happy and we weren't all going insane."

"Josiah," Elvis warned. "No HeartBeats talk at practice."

"I'm just saying." Josiah held up his hands.

The music got louder. Teddy still couldn't figure out what song it was; something up-tempo and poppy, but what, exactly, he had no idea.

"They're not gonna get back together," Corey scoffed. "Not now, not since I asked Kim to prom. She knows she's got options. Better options."

"What did she say?" Teddy asked, knowing that he was

being way too intense for someone who was allegedly over his ex. Teddy could feel Elvis watching him, and tried to keep any kind of desperation off his face. "When you asked her to prom? What did she say?"

"Thirsty much, bro?" Corey laughed. "Anyway, I'm, uh, I'm working on it."

"That would be a no, then." Elvis patted Teddy on the back. "She said no. Not that you care. Because you don't. Right?"

"Right."

Teddy had a feeling that his *right* was the least convincing *right* of all time.

Was Josiah right? Should he just talk to Kim? Apologize for . . . whatever it was he'd done, exactly?

Teddy would have loved nothing more than to simply rewind and go back to the way things were before. But it felt like way too much had happened for that to be possible.

Or maybe he was just being a coward because he was afraid Kim didn't want to talk to *him*.

"And just as I predicted." Josiah pointed over the hill, where a group of students wearing William Henry Harrison High baseball shirts and teddy bear ears appeared, streaming down toward the baseball diamond. At the center of them all was Sophie Maeby, holding a megaphone. "Here comes the nonsense."

"Two! Four! Six! Eight!" Sophie cheered through the megaphone as the other Teddy Bears danced semi-coordinatedly around her. "Who's the bear who's really great?"

"Why is this happening?" Teddy muttered. Elvis patted him again.

"One! Three! Five! Seven! Who was sent here straight from heaven?"

"Dude," Corey Brooks said with disbelief, watching the cheer through his iPhone screen. "This is nuts. I'm putting this on YouTube."

"Oh Teddy, you're so fine, you're so fine you blow my mind, hey Teddy!" they all cheered. "Hey Teddy!"

Teddy could feel his entire body cringe.

"Oh Teddy, you're the bomb, tell me that you'll go to prom, hey Teddy!"

The Teddy Bears behind Sophie unfurled a giant banner that read, *Teddy, will you go to prom with me? Love, Sophie* ♥.

"Whoa," Corey said. "Forget the leather jacket. Maybe *this* is what I need to do for Kim."

"Corey," Elvis warned him.

"It's a free country, man," Corey shot back. "I can ask whoever I want to prom."

"Elvis," Teddy said desperately, "what do I *do*?"

Teddy knew he was probably more stressed than the situation deserved. But there was something about an army of anthropomorphic bears dancing its way toward him that he found deeply unsettling.

"I take it this means you *don't* want to go to prom with Sophie Maeby?" Elvis asked. Teddy glared at him. "Just checking," Elvis said quickly.

"I don't want to go to prom with anyone," Teddy said.

"You're absolutely right. You don't need to go to prom *with* anyone," Josiah said. "But you should still go. There's no reason to miss out on prom. I think you're really going to enjoy the theme."

"I thought there were four themes?" Corey asked.

"*Four* themes?" Elvis repeated.

"Yes. Technically, there are four themes," Josiah said. "But don't worry about that. Just promise me you'll go to the prom. Alone."

"Um . . ." Teddy looked back and forth from Josiah to Elvis. "Okay?"

"Great," Josiah said happily. "Just great. Don't worry about Sophie—I'll deal with her."

"Guess we're going to the prom, then," Elvis said as Josiah strode purposefully over to Sophie and the other Teddy Bears.

"Have fun, losers. I'm still gonna take Kim," Corey said.

"Sure you are." Elvis rolled his eyes.

Kim had done a lot that had surprised Teddy recently.

But he hoped, beyond all else, that she wouldn't do something quite as surprising as go to the prom with Corey Brooks.

CHAPTER FIFTY-SEVEN

KIM LANDIS-LILLEY
WEEK FOUR, DAY THREE

"You ready to go, Olivia?"

Kim dangled the car keys by their I LEFT MY ♥ IN SHIPSHEWANA keychain, a relic of a road trip that must have happened before Kim existed, or back when she was too young to remember. Kim loved it when Mama Dawn worked remotely and let Kim borrow her car to drive herself and Olivia to and from school; Jess had no idea how lucky she was to *always* have her own car.

"Olivia?"

Still no response as her little sister silently packed the rest of her softball gear and zipped up the top of her muddy Adidas bag. Kim sighed as she ground her heel into the dirt of the baseball diamond, shifting her weight impatiently. Why was Olivia giving *her* the silent treatment? If anyone should be giving anyone a silent treatment, Kim should be freezing out Olivia! Kim watched the little AntiKaT button on Olivia's sweatshirt glint in the sun. Olivia was lucky their moms didn't know what that meant. After Mama K had yelled at Principal Manteghi about the PTA meeting—Kim wasn't sure what was more embarrassing, the fact that there had been an entire PTA meeting about her breakup, or the fact that her mom had yelled at the principal—Mama K had called a Landis-Lilley family meeting. And after a somewhat confusing lecture on the sociology of relationships and their impact on adolescent development, Mama Dawn and Mama K had announced that they were Officially Staying Out of It, since they had complete confidence in Kim to navigate her own social life as a fully autonomous individual.

And then Mama K had called Teddy's parents to get them on board with her position of neutrality, and Kim almost exploded from mortification. Forget Principal Manteghi. That was definitely the most embarrassing thing. No contest.

Yeah, imagining what Mama K had said to Teddy's parents—Kim couldn't bring herself to listen in on the call—was even worse than Olivia's stupid AntiKaT button.

Anti-her. How could Olivia be anti-her? What had Kim done to Olivia that was so bad, anyway?

Nothing. Absolutely nothing. Kim could feel herself starting to fume as Olivia slung her softball bag over her shoulder and stalked toward the parking lot without so much as a backward glance in Kim's direction. Never mind the fact that Kim had been waiting patiently for Olivia to pack up her stuff long after everyone else had left. Never mind the fact that Kim had cheerfully shuttled her silent sister to school this morning. Never mind the fact that Kim had been tiptoeing around a surly Olivia for *weeks*, never complaining when Olivia used the last of the oatmeal to make her proats, even though Kim had wanted to make oatmeal chocolate chip cookies.

Kim dumped her backpack in the back seat, slammed the door, got into the driver's seat, and slammed that door, too.

Olivia raised her eyebrows imperceptibly but didn't look at Kim.

She. Was. Infuriating.

"You know what, Olivia?" Kim turned on the ignition, wishing the car had a bit more roar to the engine for emphasis. "If you have a problem with me, please just say it to my face instead of giving me the silent treatment like a baby."

"A baby," Olivia repeated. Words, finally! "Oh, *I'm* the baby?"

"Both literally and figuratively. You're certainly acting like a baby."

"I'm just trying to live my life. You're the one who's messing it all up with your . . . your . . . drama!" Olivia exploded. "Hey, wait a minute . . ." Olivia pressed her nose to the glass as she looked out the window, watching the turnoff to Emerson Road retreat in the distance. "Kim. You're going the wrong way. Kim. You missed the turn to go home. Kim. Kim. Where are you going?"

"We are going to the Dairy Star to have a serious conversation."

Olivia groaned in response and slumped in her seat.

"Can't you lecture me at home?"

"No. And I'm not lecturing you. We're having a conversation."

"You're too obsessed with the Dairy Star," Olivia complained. "Why do you have this preoccupation with having important conversations at a mediocre soft-serve shack?"

"It's not mediocre." Kim gripped the steering wheel, watching her knuckles turn white as she tried to calm down. "It's excellent and you know it."

"It's not even good ice-cream weather. And it's all sugar. There's no nutritional value. Coach Finn says the ideal post-workout snack should consist of complex carbohydrates and lean protein. Ice cream is none of those things."

"Calcium, little one." Kim turned calmly into the parking lot. Apparently white-knuckling the steering wheel was actually an effective relaxation technique. "Live a little, Olivia." Kim put the car in park. "One cone won't kill you."

For half a second, Kim thought Olivia might stay in the car. But Kim heard the crunch of gravel behind her as Olivia followed Kim to the window. Assuming her sister's order hadn't changed, Kim got a butterscotch dip and a small chocolate-and-vanilla swirl.

"You're so weird, Kim," Olivia muttered. "Who likes butterscotch that much?"

"I do. Thanks, Mrs. Schuster." Kim took the cones from Mrs. Schuster at the window and walked toward a picnic table, Olivia following sulkily behind. Kim took a bite of her ice cream as she sat, and all of a sudden, things didn't seem quite so bad.

"So why are you so anti-me?" Kim held out the swirl for Olivia, who took it, grudgingly.

"I'm not anti-*you*. I'm anti-you-and-Teddy."

"We broke up, Olivia. There is no more me-and-Teddy."

"There's more you-and-Teddy now than when you were together!" Olivia took an angry chomp off the top of her soft-serve. "That's all I hear, all day long. Kim-and-Teddy this. Kim-and-Teddy that. People asking *me* about it, constantly, as if I have any kind of opinion, which I most emphatically do not."

Kim considered this. She hadn't actually realized that people were harassing Olivia about the breakup. She'd assumed Olivia had been going through life undisturbed, setting records for mile run times and stretching her hamstrings and hanging out with Daisy, like she always had.

"I mean, do you have any idea how annoying that is?" Olivia continued. "People actually know who I am now, but it's not because of anything I've done. It's not because I'm, like, single-handedly carrying the varsity softball team, even though I'm only a freshman—and don't protest. You know it's true. Everybody's been a mess." Kim hadn't been about to protest. They *had* been a bit of a mess. Kim winced as she remembered some of the more humiliating plays from last week's game. "Nope." Olivia laughed darkly. "People know me only as Kim Landis-Lilley's little sister. Everything I've always aspired to be."

Huh. Kim had no idea—no idea!—that Olivia felt this way. If anything, Kim frequently felt like she couldn't measure up to *Olivia*. Olivia, Coach Finn's favorite. Olivia, who made everything look so easy, who played circles around everyone on the team—Kim included. Olivia, who was faster and stronger and just plain better than Kim could ever hope to be.

"But of course you don't know what that's like. Perfect Princess Kim, with her perfect Prince Boyfriend, and her perfect life. How do you have a good hair day *every* day? That's not natural, Kim! It's not! Have you ever even had a zit?!"

"I have *zits!*" Kim jutted her chin into Olivia's face. "I'm just good at covering them up! What do you think this is?"

"Get your face out of my face!" Olivia swatted her away.

"Then don't ask me about my zits!"

The two of them stared at each other, breathing heavily. They almost never fought. Olivia and Kim were much more likely to ignore each other if they didn't get along instead of hashing things out. Actually, the more Kim thought about it, she couldn't think of anyone she ever fought with. Not Teddy, not Jess, not her moms . . . Kim had always prided herself on her ability to get along with everyone. But now, she felt like it might be some kind of defect.

Maybe she never fought with anyone because she hadn't been saying what she needed to say.

"I'm not some kind of perfect princess, Olivia."

"I didn't say that," Olivia responded mulishly. "I think everyone *else* thinks you're some kind of perfect princess. *I* know you're not perfect. I've seen your gross feet."

"I don't have gross feet!"

"They're kind of gross."

"Fine. They're kind of gross." Kim accepted that. She had

the kind of feet that were vastly improved by socks. "And I don't think everyone thinks of you as *just* my little sister. Or if they do, it's just because I'm older. It's not because I'm particularly remarkable or anything. Pretty much every single sibling in our school is known as Whoever's little sibling. That's just part of being younger."

"Well. I don't like it."

"Well, sorry, dude. I was born first. There's nothing I can do about that." Kim bumped Olivia with her shoulder, and was rewarded with a small smile. "Besides, I'll be gone soon, and by this time next year, I bet nobody will even remember me. By then the school will be too busy building the Olivia Landis-Lilley Softball Trophy Case. Maybe they'll even build a statue of you out on the field."

"Shut up," Olivia said, but she was smiling.

"I will not shut up. Because you're just that good. You're incredible, Olivia. I'm so proud to be your teammate *and* your sister."

Kim looked at her little sister, and in that moment, she remembered waiting with Mama K in the hospital for Mama Dawn to give birth to Olivia, and how excited she was to have a sister. She remembered finally meeting the tiny, red, screaming bundle waving her fists in the air. Her little sister. Her stubborn, brave, infuriating, beautiful little sister.

"I love you, peanut," Kim said.

"There's no need to get sappy."

"Yeah, there is. I love you."

"I know," Olivia said gruffly. "I love you, too, you big weirdo. And just so you know . . ." Olivia cleared her throat. "The whole AntiKaT thing was never about being *against*

287

you, or Teddy, or even against the two of you being together. I just wanted all the craziness to stop."

"Me too, peanut," Kim said. "Me too."

Kim put her arm around her sister and pulled her close. Olivia hardly protested.

CHAPTER FIFTY-EIGHT

SOPHIE MAEBY
WEEK FOUR, DAY FOUR

Rejected by Josiah Watkins.

This was a new low.

Not that there was anything *wrong* with Josiah. He was objectively handsome, like the long-lost son of Idris Elba. He was athletic, musical, academically gifted . . . Basically, if Josiah Watkins had rejected her on his own behalf, Sophie would have gotten it. Well, she would have been confused, because Josiah and Chris were adorable together, so she couldn't really imagine a scenario in which she asked Josiah to prom, but if such a scenario existed, she would have gotten it. Josiah Watkins was most definitely out of her league. But the fact that Josiah rejected her *for* Teddy was patently humiliating. Sophie glowered at Josiah across the gym, where he was cutting giant baseballs out of construction paper.

After everything Sophie had done for Teddy! The teddy bear ears, the T-shirts, the ruined parking lot. She'd even ended up with a stupid Bears prom because of him! Sophie sighed as she tried to stick some fake pine needles on a branch made out of an old paper towel roll. Much like this sad tree she was making, her life was a hot mess.

"You know, Ms. Somers," Sophie said. "Love is a real B-word."

"I don't think she's paying attention." Mr. Rizzo gently took the tree branch out of Sophie's hands and affixed it to the cardboard trunk. Ms. Somers, painting bark onto another cardboard tree with Coach Mendoza, wasn't paying attention to anyone except Coach Mendoza.

If Sophie had been in a different kind of mood, she would have thought it was pretty cute. Ms. Somers was practically glowing, and somehow, today, her usually messy hair looked more artfully disheveled than straight-up disastrous. Even her khakis were almost fashionable.

"But yes, Sophie," Mr. Rizzo said, "love can be a real B-word."

Sophie nodded. It was nice of all the chaperones to come help them with the decorations. From the way things looked at the moment, Sophie had a feeling the prom would mostly look like a Symphony in Recyclables, but there was only so much you could do on a practically nonexistent budget.

"Looking great over here, gang!" Mr. Guzman said as he walked by, flashing them a thumbs-up. Again, on another day, his deluded enthusiasm might have been charming, but Sophie was not in the mood.

Sophie watched Josiah affix the construction paper baseball to the wall. Those stupid HeartBeats. Did they even *care* that Teddy was moving to Firenze? All they were trying to do was delay the inevitable! Well, the HeartBeats *had* been started by Nico, after all, and he was practically famous for his lack of foresight. The number of times Sophie had seen him sit down to eat soup without a spoon was truly shocking.

Not that Sophie's foresight had gotten her anywhere. Did she even want to be a Teddy Bear anymore? She contemplated heading over to join Wendy and the AntiKaTs in Nihilism, but there wasn't anyone over there. Maybe they'd leave their quadrant totally undecorated. That was probably the *most* nihilistic approach.

Sophie spotted a pair of very nice Tory Burch wedges walking right up to the edge of her tree.

"Sophie," Principal Manteghi said, disappointment radiating off every inch of her pantsuit-clad frame. "Please come with me."

CHAPTER FIFTY-NINE

NICO OSTERMAN
WEEK FOUR, DAY FOUR

The suit was Nico's dad's. It was so short that you could see the intricate patterns on both of his mismatched socks, and it was so big in the waist he'd had to belt it. Except he couldn't find a regular belt, so he'd threaded an old yellow belt from karate that he'd found in his closet through the belt loops. Nico hadn't taken a karate class since elementary school, but somehow, it still fit.

Normally, Nico avoided suits at all costs—which was why he didn't own one—but when you had to meet with the big cheese, you had to bring out the big guns.

Nico leapt out of the guest chair in the principal's office when he heard footsteps approach the door. But when he turned to see Principal Manteghi, she wasn't alone.

"Nico?" Sophie asked.

"Sophie?" Nico asked. She had a brown smudge on her cheek that Nico really hoped was paint, and her curly hair was piled haphazardly on top of her head, but she looked more beautiful than ever. Even if there was a sadness in her eyes that Nico didn't like.

"*You're* my afternoon appointment?" Principal Manteghi arched her eyebrows at Nico.

"Yes, sir," Nico stammered. "I mean, ma'am. I mean, your eminence." He smoothed his tie. Seeing Sophie show up here unexpectedly had thrown him off his game.

"Nico, would you mind waiting in the hallway while I talk to Sophie?" Principal Manteghi asked.

"This will only take a minute of your time, Your Grace." Nico ushered Principal Manteghi toward her chair. She sat, reluctantly, while Sophie hovered uncertainly in the doorway. "I'm here to ask for your support."

"I support all of my students."

"I mean your specific support. For the HeartBeats." Nico pulled the brochure out of his jacket and spread it across the principal's desk.

"What is that?" Sophie asked, advancing from the doorway.

"It's some informational paperwork on the HeartBeats," Nico said. He'd made it in the computer lab during his free period—using the color printer—and he thought it looked pretty snazzy. He'd printed out a ton of really cute pictures of Kim and Teddy he'd found on Facebook. After all this time, neither of them had taken down any of the pictures of the two of them together. That was basically another piece of evidence in itself! Nico made a mental note to add that to the brochure.

"This isn't informational paperwork," Sophie said. "It's a collage."

"It's a collage of *information*," Nico rebutted.

"I'm sorry, what am I looking at here?" Principal Manteghi asked.

"I think we can all agree that things here at William Henry Harrison High were better before Kim and Teddy broke up," Nico said. "The HeartBeats propose a return to those kinder, gentler times."

Sophie snorted. Nico shot her a look, and that's when he realized she wasn't wearing her ears. Sophie wasn't wearing her teddy bear ears! That had to mean something. That might mean *everything*.

"Think about it, Principal Manteghi," Nico said, but he was talking right to Sophie. "Wouldn't it be better if *everything* went back to the way it was before?"

Nico looked deep into Sophie's eyes. Sophie stared back. He would have given anything to know what she was thinking. Nico used to be able to read her like a book, but now, she was an inscrutable mystery. Like *Mrs. Dalloway*. Nico hadn't understood a word Virginia Woolf had written.

"As much as I appreciate the . . . effort that has gone into this collage," Principal Manteghi said, "I'm still not really sure what you're asking here, Nico."

"The HeartBeats would like your official patronage," Nico supplied promptly. "The Teddy Bears have Mr. Rizzo. Team Kim has Ms. Johansson. I heard the AntiKaTs recently got Mr. Dykstra. And since the HeartBeats are the team for reason and harmony, we thought there would be no better faculty representative than *you*, Principal Manteghi."

"While I appreciate the sentiment, Mr. Osterman, I cannot align myself with any partisan group."

"But that's the whole point of the HeartBeats! We want an end to partisan groups! Which is exactly why—"

"My answer is no, Nico," the principal said gently but finally, and Nico knew there would be no changing her mind. It was a blow, but maybe Sophie taking her ears off signaled the beginning of the end of partisanship anyway. Maybe he'd done it *without* Principal Manteghi! "Now, if you'll excuse us, I need to speak with Sophie. Privately."

"About the parking lot?" Nico asked. Sophie shot him a look that was so mean he could feel the tips of his ears beginning to smoke.

"Do you have information you'd like to share, Mr. Osterman?" Suddenly the principal was all seriousness.

"He doesn't!" Sophie squeaked with distress.

"No." Nico shrugged. "I just assumed you called her in to talk about the parking lot because she's the most likely culprit. Sophie's more of a Teddy Bear than Teddy Lin is. Or she used to be. She took off her ears. I don't know if you noticed."

But much to Nico's astonishment, it was *Sophie* who looked surprised. She reached her hands up to her hair.

"My ears," she muttered. "I must have forgotten . . . maybe I took them off . . . painting . . ."

"Sophie, I had a long conversation with Superintendent Harwood earlier. I know your mother knows him well." Nico watched Sophie blanch. Crap. He couldn't let her go down for this, even though she was almost definitely guilty. What should he do? Confess to a crime he didn't commit? If he took the blame, maybe she'd love him again!

"Repaving the parking lot is going to be enormously expensive," Principal Manteghi continued. "And that is money the school district does not have. Whoever vandalized the parking lot has done a serious disservice to the school, and to everyone who works so hard to make this a successful place. Your mother included, Sophie."

"I . . ." Sophie said, wild-eyed. "I . . . I . . ."

"Sophie couldn't have done it," Nico jumped in quickly, the only thought in his mind that he had to save Sophie. "She was with me."

"With you," Principal Manteghi repeated as Sophie's eyes met Nico's, her familiar brown gaze a tempest of confusion and hope. "I thought the two of you broke up."

Principal Manteghi knew that?! Weird. Maybe this school was keeping tabs on all of them. Just like the government!

"It was more of a . . . conscious uncoupling," Nico said. "At the time of the incident, Sophie was over at my place while we were discussing ethical disengagement in the age of social media. My mom can verify that she was there."

She would, too. Nico loved his mom, but she was a little scattered. Nico knew she wouldn't remember if Sophie or anyone else had been there, and she'd blithely agree to whatever Nico suggested.

"How very Gwyneth of you," Principal Manteghi said wryly. "So there's really nothing you'd like to say to me, Sophie?"

"I'd like to raise money to repave the parking lot. Not because I had anything to do with it," Sophie added quickly, even though Nico was pretty sure everyone in that office knew exactly who was behind the giant WHHHS ♥ TL. "But because I want to help. I'd definitely like to donate all the money from my teddy bear ears and the T-shirt sales. Seeing as it was a Teddy-related crime . . ."

"And look how successful Sophie was with all of her Teddy Bears merchandise!" Nico jumped in. "I'm sure she can fund-raise for the parking lot in no time."

"That's a very generous offer, Sophie," Principal Manteghi said, but Nico thought she sounded tired. He hoped Manteghi hadn't caught too much heat from the superintendent because of the parking lot.

"I've got some ideas," Sophie said. "Can I—"

A knock on the door interrupted Sophie's strategizing. Nico, Sophie, and Principal Manteghi swiveled their heads toward the sound.

"Howdy-doody." Mr. Buckley poked his head in through the door, showing off the gap in his teeth as he smiled. "I've got someone here who'd like to chat with you."

"That's fine, Mr. Buckley." Principal Manteghi stood. "Nico, Sophie—I suppose we're done here."

"Thank you, Principal Manteghi," Sophie said fervently as she backed toward the door. "I'll raise the money. Promise."

Principal Manteghi waved them away, and Sophie and Nico scooted past Mr. Buckley and Toby Neale. The office door shut behind them, and then it was just Sophie and Nico alone in the hallway.

Together again. Just like Nico had wanted all this time.

"Thank you, Nico," Sophie whispered. She reached out to grab his hand, and Nico admired her pale pink manicure—Essie's Romper Room, her signature color. So much had changed, but that, at least, was the same. "You didn't have to do that."

"I didn't do anything," Nico said, "but I'd *like* to do something."

"Nico—"

"Sophie. Please." He gathered her beautiful pink-nailed hands in his. "Won't you at least consider a conscious recoupling?"

Her ears were off. That had to mean something. Didn't it? Didn't it?! Everything Nico had done with the HeartBeats had been leading up to this moment. It had to work out. It had to.

"I don't love you anymore, Nico," Sophie said gently. "I did, once. And I appreciate you so much. As a person. And I appreciate the times we had together. But we can't get back together. I'm not the same Sophie I used to be."

"Is it Teddy Lin?" Nico asked. "Because I'm pretty sure he's getting back together with Kim—"

"It's not Teddy." Sophie squeezed his hands once, and then dropped them. "But it's also not you."

Of all the possibilities, this was the one Nico had never considered.

But here he was, alone, watching Sophie walk away.

Again.

CHAPTER SIXTY

TEDDY LIN

WEEK FOUR, DAY FIVE

"Hey, Teddy? Can I talk to you?"

Teddy tensed as he turned around to see Sophie Maeby standing alone in the hallway. He looked around, wondering if Teddy Bear cheerleaders were going to start tumbling out of the lockers and ask him to prom again.

"Uh, sure, Sophie." Teddy swallowed nervously as he closed his locker. "What's up?"

He never should have asked Josiah to go talk to her. He should have explained why he couldn't go to the prom with her himself, instead of hiding in the dugout like a coward. This was exactly the awkward interaction he deserved.

"I just wanted to let you know that I'm disbanding the Teddy Bears." Sophie twirled one curly lock of hair around and around with her index finger. Maybe she felt awkward, too. "And it's not because of anything you've done. Or because you didn't want to go to prom with me or whatever. Just to be clear."

"Okay, that's—"

"I still think you're awesome," she continued, "and I know you're going to be amazing in Florence."

"Florence?" Teddy repeated.

"Yeah. You know, Italy?" she prompted him.

Teddy still had no idea what she was talking about.

Maybe it was time to start clearing some things up.

"Sophie, I'm not going to Italy," he said.

"You're *not*?!"

Sophie looked as shocked as if Teddy had just told her he was secretly a cyborg.

"But—but I thought you were moving to Italy. And that was the whole reason you broke up with Kim!"

"No, I'm definitely not moving to Italy." Teddy didn't even want to know how that rumor had happened. What had people been saying about him? "And Kim broke up with *me*—I have no idea why."

He didn't even know why Kim broke up with him. And that was the real heart of the matter, wasn't it? Teddy hadn't just been hiding in the dugout from Sophie's prom-posal. He'd been hiding in the dugout from his *life*.

What had he been doing this whole semester? He'd just been letting things happen *around* him. Yeah, okay, maybe the conversation he'd tried to have with Kim hadn't exactly been successful, but then he'd just immediately given up? This was ridiculous. He was being ridiculous. He didn't even know where Kim was going to college! Kim had been the biggest part of his life for *years*, and after one unfortunate conversation, he now didn't know anything about her.

He had to talk to her. He had to at least *try*.

"Are you okay, Teddy?" Sophie asked. He'd forgotten she was standing there.

"Yeah—you know what? I *am* okay, Sophie. Or at least, I'm gonna try to be okay."

Teddy pulled his phone out of his pocket and began to type.

CHAPTER SIXTY-ONE

PHIL SPOONER
WEEK FOUR, DAY FIVE

The oranges were starting to rot.

The weirdest thing about this was that Phil didn't even know where the oranges *were*. The maintenance team had picked up all the loose ones that had been rolling around by Kim Landis-Lilley's locker, but up on the third floor, there was a distinct scent of rotting citrus.

"So you're coming to my anti-prom party?" Diamond asked him for the third time. "As in, yes? You'll definitely be there?"

"I'll try to swing by."

Or course he would be there. Phil couldn't believe he had prom night plans. Freshmen couldn't go to the prom unless they were invited by seniors, a policy Diamond had been very vocally against, hence her creation of the anti-prom.

Everyone was going to dress up and go to Diamond's house, and she'd made a special anti-prom playlist and had told him there was definitely enough room in the basement for them all to dance.

Phil was going to ask Diamond Allen to dance with him. A slow one. It might take him some time to work up the courage, but he would do it. After all, he was Spoony now. He could do anything.

"Excuse me? Diamond?" Phil turned, and the figures from his worst nightmares appeared on the third floor. Phil used to have nightmares about showing up to school and realizing he'd forgotten to wear pants, or about the clown from his baby cousin Eva's first birthday party, but recently, there had only been one nightmare.

And it was Jess Howard and Kim Landis-Lilley standing in front of him on the third floor.

"Diamond?" Kim asked again. Funny how the harbinger of Phil's demise had such a sweet and melodious voice. Phil clawed at his throat, desperate for air. Why wasn't there any air up here?! All he could breathe in was rotting citrus and his own fetid lies, and they were choking him! He was rotten, just like a Koontz Market orange left out in the hall for too long! All of his newfound Spoony confidence abandoned him, and once again, he was just boring old Phil Spooner. He was Cinderella after the stroke of midnight, left standing alone in the freshman hall clad only in rags and clutching an undoubtedly uncomfortable shoe.

"What is going on with you, Spoony?" Diamond asked.

"Phhrrraaaw," Phil croaked in response, unable to get any words out. What should he do? Start running? Head for home and never come back? His mom would probably homeschool him, if he asked. She'd always been very accommodating.

"You are Diamond Allen, right?" Kim asked for the third time, a little less sure of herself.

"Yeah, that's me," Diamond said, grinning.

"I thought so. I recognize you from the fall play. I'm Olivia's sister. Kim."

"I know who you are," Diamond said eagerly, like some celebrity had popped up to the third floor instead of Kim Landis-Lilley. "All the freshmen—all the *good* freshmen, anyway—we just want you to know that we support you one hundred and ten percent and we so admire everything you guys are doing."

"Um . . . thank you?" Kim said, exchanging glances with Jess Howard. "This might sound a little weird—sorry—but there's one question I have to ask."

"Did you tell everyone to bring in oranges?" Jess asked bluntly. "Because it's weird and it smells and Manteghi won't stop asking us about it."

"I *wish* I could take credit for that," Diamond said wistfully. Nope. Oh no. This was it. The end. Forget homeschool. That wouldn't be enough. Phil would have to change his name and move to another country, or the shame would follow him for the rest of his natural days. "But that was all—"

"A team effort!" Phil cut in desperately, beads of sweat dripping uncomfortably into his eyes. "A real Team Kim effort!"

"Spoony, what are you—?"

"Wait a minute," Jess Howard said. "It's the Sunchips guy!"

Phil didn't know how he had ever admired Jess Howard's elegant hands or her taste in reading materials. True, Phil hadn't found himself thinking about Jess in ages, or even seeking her out in the library. He'd found himself wrapped up in Diamond's brilliance and her incredible volume and her confidence. Phil had abandoned Jess as the crush of his youth. She was naught but the instrument of his destruction.

No. That wasn't fair. Phil was the author of his own destruction. The minute he'd started spinning his web of lies, there was only one way for all of this to end. Hubris, just like Mr. Rizzo had taught them. It was exactly what had taken down King Lear in the fall play, back when Diamond Allen had played the Fool.

Now, there was only one Fool, and his name was Phil Spooner.

"So if you—or whoever is bringing in the oranges—could stop, that would be so great." Kim smiled. Was she not even going to react to Jess's Sunchips comment? Was there some sort of patron saint of Idiot Freshmen watching out for Phil Spooner? "I've had more than enough conversations with Principal Manteghi this semester," Kim added conspiratorially.

"No worries," Diamond replied breezily, like Phil wasn't spontaneously combusting, like he wasn't about to turn into a pile of ash that would blow away with the slightest gust of wind when someone opened the door to the third-floor copy room. How was everyone else having this conversation so calmly?

Because everyone else wasn't a big fat liar whose pants were on fire, Phil thought darkly.

"We were just trying to support you," Diamond continued.

"And I definitely appreciate that," Kim said sincerely.

"Supported by an orange." Jess snorted. "Freshmen are so weird. No offense. See ya, Sunchips."

Jess and Kim turned and disappeared down the stairs, without asking any more questions, without poking holes in the stories Phil had spun that in no way lined up with reality. Just like that, they were gone.

It was a miracle, but it didn't matter. That was it. He couldn't live like this anymore. Sure, he'd maybe almost kind of gotten away with it, but how long could this go on for? Enough was enough. He was done.

"I don't know why Kim and Teddy broke up," Phil blurted out.

"Huh?"

"I don't know why they broke up. I never did. I made it up."

"Spoony?" The confusion and hurt in Diamond's eyes almost made him stop right there, but he'd started going down the path of truth and righteousness, and he couldn't turn back now.

"And I don't know what her favorite color is. And I'm pretty sure her grandma doesn't have an orange farm. I don't even know if she likes oranges. Actually, based on this conversation, I'm willing to bet she doesn't."

"What are you saying, Spoony?"

"I'm not Spoony." Phil sighed heavily. "I'm just Phil Spooner, liar."

Diamond looked at him, hard. "So you made it all up."

He nodded at her, shamefaced.

"Why?"

"I wanted to feel . . . important, I guess." He shrugged. "I wanted people to sit with at lunch."

"You could have sat with us anyway."

"Maybe." Phil never would have been able to sit at their table without being invited. He wouldn't have been brave enough. "I *did* hear Kim and Teddy break up, but I thought if I didn't know *why*, people wouldn't believe me. So I improv-ed."

"That is not how you improv, Spoony." Diamond looked like she was trying not to laugh. "But then again, you've *never* understood how to improv."

"I'm really sorry, Diamond. I'm sorry about everything. It just . . . it all just got out of control."

"It's okay, Spoony," she said gently as she reached out to touch his arm. "Maybe we all got a little out of control."

Diamond Allen, Phil realized, wasn't just loud and talented and beautiful and brilliant. She was also incredibly kind and generous and forgiving, and Phil could never, ever deserve her.

But at the very least, he could try.

"May I buy you an ice cream?" Phil asked grandly.

"You're so weird, Spoony." She rolled her eyes affectionately. "But yeah. Sure. You can buy me an ice cream."

It was a start.

PART

THREE:

RECONCILIATION

CHAPTER SIXTY-TWO

KIM LANDIS-LILLEY
WEEK FOUR, DAY FIVE

Kim had an incoming text from a poop emoji.

Jess, she thought, laughing to herself. Jess must have changed Teddy's name in her phone to a poop emoji. Teddy's name . . . Teddy's name! Kim's heart started to beat faster as she clutched her phone.

"Are you coming?" Jess asked.

"No!" Kim said, clutching the phone closer, like she was afraid Jess would look at it. Jess, Kim was confident, would *not* want her to even look at what the poop emoji had to say. "I forgot. I have to, um, check in with Coach Finn. Softball stuff."

"Okay. Do you want me to wait?"

"No!" Kim said again, too loudly. "I don't know how long

it'll take. I'll just—I'll get a ride from one of my moms. I'm sure someone can come pick me up."

"Suit yourself." Jess shrugged, readjusting her backpack. "See ya."

Once Jess had safely disappeared down the hall, Kim glanced down at her screen.

"Can we talk?" asked the poop emoji.

Could they talk? That wasn't a simple question, and it didn't have an easy answer.

On the one hand, Teddy had dumped *her*. He'd broken her heart, and she didn't know if she ever wanted to speak to him again. On the other hand, Kim wanted answers. *Why* had he done it? On the other other hand, the entire school—Jess in particular—would lose their collective minds if they knew Kim and Teddy were talking again. But on the other other other hand—that was way too many hands—Kim just plain missed him.

Eventually, she texted, "Meet me at the Dairy Star."

They'd talk.

CHAPTER SIXTY-THREE

TEDDY LIN
WEEK FOUR, DAY FIVE

Teddy had gotten some random Teddy Bear to drop him off at the Dairy Star after school. Perks of being the head of a team he wanted no real part of. But better than getting his usual ride from Elvis, who would have undoubtedly wanted to stay at the Dairy Star with Teddy, and that, Teddy could not do. He needed to be alone. Luckily, the Dairy Star was empty, apart from Teddy and the large butterscotch dip he'd bought for Kim. He clutched the cone in his hand, holding it out in front of him so it dripped onto the metal table.

He hoped she was coming. He wouldn't blame her if she didn't. But he hoped she would.

Everything had spiraled so far out of control. He should have talked to her a long time ago, back before school had become a war zone of Teddy Bears and Team Kim and

HeartBeats and AntiKaTs. Back when they had just been Kim-and-Teddy, and everything had been simpler.

Teddy watched a red Toyota Corolla he didn't recognize pull into the parking lot. Moments later, the passenger door opened, and Kim got out. It was just a car. It shouldn't have weirded him out so much. But seeing Kim driving around with someone he didn't know seemed like a symbol of everything he'd missed during the last four weeks. After a quick wave to whoever was driving, the car sped away, and Kim was alone in the parking lot.

With him.

"Hey." Teddy stood up quickly. Why was he so nervous? This was *Kim*. Kim, who had seen him dressed up like a bumblebee for Halloween in first grade. Kim, who had been there when he'd ripped his pants wide open on the playground in third grade. Kim, who hadn't laughed when he'd been so anxious to kiss her that their teeth knocked together in sixth grade. Kim had seen him at his worst and even then, she'd made him feel like he was at his best. She always had. "Thanks for coming."

"You know I'll do anything for a butterscotch dip."

"Butterscotch is for old people," he said automatically.

Kim smiled. "But I got you one anyway."

He held out the cone in front of him, and she took it.

"I'm sorry," Teddy said. "I shouldn't have—"

"Broken up with me?" she supplied.

"Broken up with *you*?!" Teddy asked, aghast. "What are you talking about? You broke up with *me*."

"No I didn't! You broke up with *me*!"

They looked at each other, and then burst out laughing. Teddy took a seat at the table, and Kim joined him.

"Listen," Teddy said, "I'm sorry if what I said that day in the gym came out wrong."

"I'm sorry I ran away without asking you what you meant." Kim swallowed nervously. "So, um . . . what did you mean?"

"I meant . . ." Teddy tried to think, really think, about what he wanted to say. He had to put this perfectly. "I meant that I love you, of course. And that of course you're one of the best parts of my whole life. I just wanted to make sure that we still have lives. Like, as separate people. As Kim and Teddy, not just as Kim-and-Teddy."

"That makes sense." Kim nodded. "But we do, you know. Just because we spend a lot of our time together doesn't mean that's all we do. We're two totally autonomous, fully functioning individuals who choose to spend their time together."

"Yeah. I think . . . I think I was getting freaked out about college. I *am* freaked out about college," he amended. "Everything's going to be so different. Not just for me and you, but for . . . well . . . absolutely everything."

"It's a lot."

"What if we go to different schools? What if we're really far away from each other? What if . . . Kim, sometimes *I* don't think I know how to be me without you."

"I don't want to be me without you," Kim said simply. "But I know that I can be if I have to be. I've been me without you for weeks. And it wasn't, like, the time of my life, but I was fine. I was still *me*. I was still Olivia's sister and my moms' daughter and Jess's best friend. I still played softball and did my homework and ate too many M&M's. And I'm sure you kept doing all the things that make you Teddy, too."

He nodded, looking down at his hands. Somehow Kim's rationality was making him feel self-conscious about the crazy mess that had been created in the wake of their breakup.

"Look, Teddy, I love you. Do I hope that it's me and you when we're eighty, sitting here eating butterscotch dips as actual old people? Yeah, I do."

Teddy laughed.

"I still won't eat butterscotch even when I'm eighty," he said.

"Fine. *I'll* be eating the butterscotch," Kim amended. "But if things change when we're in college, then they change. Let's just see how it goes. Wow." Kim shook her head, laughing. "I can't believe I'm being so Zen about this."

Teddy couldn't believe it, either. Kim, his Kim, with her five thousand planners and her perfectly scheduled life, wanted to just see what happened? These past couple weeks had changed a lot of things. But as Teddy watched Kim pick up her ice cream, he knew nothing had changed the way he felt about her.

Maybe, like Kim said, things would change next year. But for now, all Teddy wanted was to be by her side.

There was nowhere else he'd rather be.

"Okay," Teddy said.

"Okay what?"

"Okay, I want to be with you. And see what happens."

"Okay, then." Kim smiled. "So what do we do now?" she asked. "Do we tell everyone we're back together? Wait—just to be super clear—we *are* back together, right?"

"Yes," Teddy said firmly. But the idea of telling everyone . . . after the whole school had picked sides . . . made his stomach start doing backflips.

"Jess will lose it," Kim murmured.

"So will Elvis. And Sophie Maeby."

"Yeah, what's up with that, anyway?" Kim took a big bite of her ice cream. "I didn't even know you and Sophie knew each other."

"Honestly? I have no idea." Teddy shook his head. "All of a sudden one day she was just . . . there. With a billion teddy bear ears. Speaking Italian."

"She must have secretly been in love with you for years."

"Like that art guy? I heard Manteghi is making him create a ton of Mighty Flying Arrows posters as part of his punishment. But, you know, just with our school mascot, not with your face on it."

"Who, Toby?" Kim shrugged. "Nah, I think he was just seizing on a moment in the cultural zeitgeist. He's like the Andy Warhol of William Henry Harrison High, and I was just a can of Campbell's soup."

Teddy laughed.

"So what do we do, keep this a secret?"

"I guess?" Kim said.

"I don't want to keep it a secret. I want to go to the prom with you," Teddy said, impulsively, but as soon as he said it, he knew it was right.

"Prom? Are you serious? That's kind of the opposite of secret."

"I know," Teddy said. "But it's kind of a big deal. We've been talking about it for *years*."

"I've been telling everybody for weeks that I wouldn't go."

"Everybody?" Teddy asked. "Like Corey Brooks?"

"Yeah . . ."

"We shouldn't miss out on prom just because of Corey Brooks."

"What'll Jess say? Elvis? *Everybody?*"

"They'll say what they want." Teddy reached out to squeeze Kim's hand. "I just want to dance with you."

"Well . . . I guess I did put the deposit down on the limo already," Kim said.

"So that's a yes?"

"Yes, Teddy Lin," Kim said. "I'll go to prom with you."

Teddy knew he was grinning like a gooey idiot, but he didn't even care.

"Now there's only one question," Teddy said. "Which prom should we go to? I heard there's four different proms."

"All of them?" Kim suggested. "None of them? I don't know, Teddy. But we'll figure it out."

Kim interlaced her fingers with his, and everything felt right again.

They'd figure it out.

CHAPTER SIXTY-FOUR

SOPHIE MAEBY
PROM

"It's really hot in here." Noelle Bonolis's voice was barely intelligible, muffled as it was by the bear suit.

"Well, if it's hot in there, you shouldn't have suggested Bears!" Sophie snapped. "If we'd done A Night in Firenze like I'd wanted to, you could have been wearing a toga or something."

"I don't think they wear togas in Firenze."

"We would have gotten to the details later, okay?"

Even though she now knew Teddy wasn't moving to Florence, Sophie still stood by it as a valid prom theme. Certainly more valid than Bears. But if Sophie had learned anything about human nature over the past few weeks, it was that people—herself included—did not want to back down. Hence why Sophie was still stuck in a Bears-themed quadrant, despite the fact that she'd attempted to disband the Teddy Bears.

That hadn't been totally successful, either. Most people had flat-out refused when Sophie had told them the Teddy Bears were done, and absolutely no one had responded to her official disbandment Instastory. Almost everybody in the Bears quadrant was still wearing their ears. Well, Sophie was still wearing her ears, too, but that was just because she wanted to match the theme.

Sophie pulled a Kleenex out of her purse and dabbed at the sweat on her forehead, trying not to smudge her makeup. Even without a furry bear suit, it was hot in here. She looked anxiously around the Bear quadrant of the gym. Somehow, the fake pine trees were staying mostly upright, and after seven or so attempts, the twinkling lights really did look like stars in the night sky. The bear suit, borrowed from last year's William Henry Harrison High drama department production of *The Winter's Tale*, wasn't totally realistic, but at least it was dark enough in here that no one would notice. The best part of all was the backdrop affixed to the wall, provided by Toby Neale. Sophie was pretty sure it was part of some *Birth of Kim-us* punishment, but the majestic bear standing on top of a waterfall really did look nice.

Honestly, it looked as good as a prom themed Bears could possibly look, and Sophie would have to content herself with that. She cast anxious glances over toward the other quadrants. Nihilism, with its random black balloons and its *LIFE IS MEANINGLESS* banner, obviously looked ridiculous, but Fifties Sock Hop was unbelievably cute. She watched Amelia Asaad and Emma Gertz chatting in their poodle skirts underneath a giant record and next to a pink Cadillac. How did they afford that pink Cadillac? It was a cardboard cutout, but still—it looked awesome. And then over in Perfect Catch, everything was even worse—by which Sophie meant, of course, that it looked even better. The whole floor of that quadrant was a baseball diamond, and the walls were decorated with baseball cards depicting famous couples—including Kim and Teddy. Josiah wore his baseball uniform with a bow tie, which looked surprisingly cute, somehow, probably because the bow tie matched the red-and-white stripes on Chris's shirt. Now that every other long-term couple in the senior class had imploded, the two of them were probably a lock for prom kings.

Standing next to them, in a bright red jacket and black pants, was Nico. Her Nico.

Not her Nico anymore, Sophie scolded herself. As she watched his nose ring glinting in the light of the disco ball, Sophie didn't want him back, exactly, but she couldn't help but wonder what this had all been for. Teddy hadn't fallen for her. He'd totally rejected her prom-posal, and now, he wasn't even here. And even though he wasn't moving to Firenze, by this time next year, Teddy would probably have forgotten that Sophie even existed. And all she'd have were pictures of her teddy bear ears squishing her updo and the memories of the travesty of an event she'd created. Actually, people would probably remember her forever as the sad girl who insisted on a stupid prom theme, which wasn't exactly the kind of notoriety Sophie was interested in.

A prom themed *Bears*. It was too ridiculous for words. At least Sophie wasn't in the bear suit.

"Can I please change into my dress?" Noelle whimpered.

"Fine." Sophie sighed. What did it matter anymore? What did any of it matter? It's not like anyone thought Noelle was actually a bear.

Sophie should go hang out with Wendy in Nihilism. As she watched Noelle pull off her bear head, Sophie had never been more aware of the absurdity of life. She'd worked so hard, and for what?

For absolutely nothing.

A gasp rippled through the gym, and Sophie turned to see what it was.

Kim and Teddy stood in the doorway, holding hands.

Together.

Teddy and Kim were back together.

And if that wasn't proof that the universe was laughing at her, Sophie didn't know what was.

Stop it, Sophie, she scolded herself as she closed her eyes and took a deep breath. When she opened them again, she looked at Kim and Teddy. *Really* looked. And she couldn't deny that there was a certain . . . rightness to seeing the two of them together. Teddy Lin and Kim Landis-Lilley were supposed to be hand in hand, just like they had always been. And Sophie found that she didn't feel jealous of Kim in the way she thought she would. Like, she wanted what Kim had, but she didn't want *Teddy*. Not really. She just wanted someone to stand hand in hand with, and to feel the rightness of it all the way down to the tips of her toes.

It would have been nice if Nico had been that person. Like, if he'd turned out to be "the one" after all. But he wasn't, and Sophie knew now that it was better to be alone than to be with someone and not feel the rightness of it.

She never wanted to feel that way again.

CHAPTER SIXTY-FIVE

TEDDY LIN
PROM

"Is everyone staring at us?" Teddy whispered.

"Everyone's definitely staring at us." Kim squeezed his hand—once, twice. Teddy squeezed back, just once. Because that was their thing. The three squeezes. "But it's okay. They'll get used to it."

"Do you, um, do you wanna dance?" Teddy asked, unable to tear his eyes away from the dance floor. The music was still playing, but everyone had stopped dancing. Instead, there was just a sea of people staring at them.

"Sure," Kim said nervously.

There was nothing he could do about people staring. All he could do—all he wanted to do—was dance with Kim.

Teddy led Kim out onto the dance floor and started stepping from side to side, the only kind of dance move he ever attempted. But as he watched Kim start to smile, her arms flapping out at the side like an adorably uncoordinated chicken, Teddy let himself relax. This was just him and Kim, back together, dancing badly, but happy because they were with each other.

And that was all that mattered.

CHAPTER SIXTY-SIX

NICO OSTERMAN
PROM

"Nico, my man," Josiah Watkins marveled. "We did it. *You* did it."

Nico couldn't believe it. There they were, right in front of him, Kim and Teddy, back together.

Teddy led Kim out onto the dance floor, and they joined in the group of people who had mostly stopped dancing to stare at Teddy and Kim. Wow, neither one of them could dance. Like, *at all*.

It was actually kind of cute, in a spectacularly uncoordinated kind of way.

But even though they had no skills, Nico had never been happier to see two people bopping back and forth in the glow of the twinkle lights. Just as Nico had dreamed they would.

"We might actually have a shot of winning our last game now." Josiah clapped Nico on the back. "Order and harmony have been restored to the universe. Everything's finally going to be all right."

Was it, though? Nico accepted the congratulations of his fellow HeartBeats. He received their hugs one by one as various HeartBeats peeled off to the dance floor. He watched them dancing, joined by Teddy Bears and AntiKaTs and Team Kim, and it was truly the reunified version of William Henry Harrison High Nico had dreamed of, come to life.

But he was still alone.

"Congrats, Nico." She was standing behind him, but Nico knew it was Sophie before he even turned around. He would recognize the smell of her Sun-Ripened Raspberry body spray anywhere. "I guess the HeartBeats weren't so stupid after all."

"They were kind of stupid." Nico's breath caught in his throat as he turned to look at Sophie. Her dress reminded him of the night sky, small sequins twinkling against the dark blue fabric. Her curly hair was piled on top of her head, exposing the regal lines of her neck. His Sophie, more beautiful than he'd ever seen her before.

"I mean, yes, your felt hearts were stupid. But not the HeartBeats. It *worked*. Look at them. Kim and Teddy, back together."

Nico looked out on the dance floor, at Kim and Teddy dancing together like two giant chickens.

"I didn't do it for them, Soph. I did it for *you*. I did it for *us*."

"I already told you, Nico." She shook her head sadly.

"There is no more *us*. But . . . I'd like to dance, if you would? As friends? For old times' sake?"

"Sure, Sophie." Nico nodded, hoping she couldn't hear the sound of his heart breaking. "I'd love to dance. As friends."

As they walked onto the dance floor, the music changed to a slow song.

Nico gathered her into his arms, one last time.

CHAPTER SIXTY-SEVEN

MS. SOMERS
PROM

"And now, DJ Mr. Guzman is gonna kick it old-school."

Ms. Somers recognized the song immediately. As the kids coupled up, slow-dancing with their arms around each other's waists, it took everything she had not to sing "Dreaming of You" along with Selena. Ms. Somers had loved this song when she'd been in high school. She'd listened to it over and over again, thinking about the different guys she had crushes on, hoping that one of them might ask her to dance or something.

"You want to dance, Somers?"

Coach Mendoza stood in front of her, his hands jammed into the pockets of his gray dress pants, his black tie charmingly askew. Here he was, her unbelievably handsome *boyfriend*, better than any guy she'd had a crush on in high school.

"I'm sorry, were you not paying attention during our pre-prom chaperone meeting? Aren't you supposed to be chaperoning the dance floor in quadrants one and two?" she teased. "Quadrants three and four are *my* territory."

"I think we'll be able to keep a better eye on all the quadrants if we team up. I feel like there might be something shady going down in Sock Hop that you might need backup on." He held out his arms, and she walked into them.

"Oh, I see. You have no interest in dancing with me. This is purely a chaperone tactic." He was warm, and solid, and Ms. Somers couldn't help but rest her head on his chest.

"Obviously. Come on, Somers. Get your head in the game. Tonight, I'm a chaperone first. Boyfriend second."

Boyfriend. Ms. Somers thought she'd never heard anything quite so wonderful as Coach Mendoza calling himself her boyfriend. And she thought that she'd never felt anything quite so wonderful as Coach Mendoza's hand at the small of her back, steering her gently around the gym, from the Bear quadrant to the Baseball quadrant to the Fifties quadrant to the Nihilism quadrant. It was all so wonderful she completely forgot she was supposed to be on the lookout for any kind of unscrupulous dancing activity.

"Why, Somers and Mendoza," Mr. Rizzo said as he moonwalked past them in his powder-blue tux, abandoning his post by the punch bowl in quadrant four to check up on them. "I knew I shouldn't have been removed from dance floor duty. I've already busted three couples for dancing too close. And you two are the worst of them all! Do I have to give *you* a demerit for PDA?"

"Not right now," Coach Mendoza said. "I can wait."

Ms. Somers smiled up at him.

She hoped she wouldn't have to wait very long.

CHAPTER SIXTY-EIGHT

JESS HOWARD
PROM

He was waiting for her right where she knew he would be, where the northern woods of the Teddy Bear quadrant met the Fifties Sock Hop of the Team Kim quadrant. Jess walked right up to the masking tape line that divided them, remembering all the times she'd stepped up to the yellow line in the cafeteria, remembering how she'd vowed to destroy Elvis Rodriguez.

Now, she was glad she hadn't.

She only wished she hadn't destroyed a very small part of his hair.

"Hey," Elvis said.

"Hey." Jess nodded. Elvis did look awfully cute in his tux with his hair slicked back. He almost never wore his hair slicked back like that, except if he was going to a dance or to church on Christmas Eve or Easter or something. Jess had forgotten how much she loved the way his hair looked like that.

It also conveniently covered his bald patch.

"DJ Mr. Guzman is sure spinning some ancient tracks tonight," she joked, not sure why she was suddenly nervous.

"I can tolerate a lot of things, Jess," Elvis said seriously. "But I cannot tolerate any disrespect to Selena."

"Anything for Selenas," Jess said, and winked.

Elvis grinned so widely that Jess couldn't help but smile back. She was surprised to find that she was glad she'd come to the prom, even though she hadn't really wanted to come, certainly hadn't been planning on coming, and had initially been harboring very dark and murderous thoughts against her best friend when she'd walked into the gym.

Man, Kim could be real cagey when she wanted to be. She'd insisted Jess come to the prom despite Jess's many protestations, but had spun a whole web of convoluted lies about why they couldn't come together, and then Jess had walked in to see Kim and Teddy. Together. Holding hands.

Jess had a *lot* of questions for Kim. But right now, looking at Elvis in his tux, Jess felt like maybe her questions could wait.

"Wanna dance?" Elvis asked.

Wordlessly, Jess fit herself into his arms. She'd forgotten how good that could feel. William Henry Harrison High's most moderately successful third baseman actually had pretty legit biceps.

"Did you know Kim and Teddy were getting back together?" Jess blurted out, unable to stop herself from asking as she watched the reunited couple sway across from them on the dance floor, their eyes closed, matching smiles on their blissful faces.

"Nope. A heads-up would have been nice. I certainly wouldn't have worn my stupid ears had I known."

"You're not wearing—"

"I threw them in a fake tree." Elvis gestured vaguely to the pine forest behind them. Jess laughed. "I'm just glad I didn't wear my bear slippers. But I can't believe he didn't tell me they were getting back together. After all this."

"If it makes you feel any better, Kim didn't tell me anything, either."

"I guess it's not surprising. I feel like I haven't known anything about Kim and Teddy—or anyone else, really—for months."

"You know nothing, Elvis Rodriguez," she teased. "You never have."

He laughed, and then they swayed in silence for a moment, circling around the gym, which somehow managed to look decent, despite its preposterous assortment of decorations. Jess wasn't even sure exactly what everything was supposed to be. She saw a painting of a bear, a pink Cadillac, a baseball diamond, and a whole mess of black balloons.

Maybe the theme of the prom was just Random.

"I'm really sorry about your hair," Jess apologized. "I should never have asked Manny to shave you. That was awful of me."

"I forgive you," Elvis said magnanimously. "I might even get an undercut."

"No you wouldn't."

"You're right," he said. "I wouldn't. I was just trying to make you feel better."

"You don't need to make me feel better." Why was he being so nice to her? She didn't deserve it.

"Well, I kind of do. I did turn those sprinklers on you."

"I knew that was you! 'It's Raining Men'? Seriously, Elvis?"

"It was a thematic choice! It was raining! I'm a man!"

"You're ridiculous." Jess laughed. "I still haven't figured out how you did it."

"That's on a need-to-know basis. And you don't need to know. But you should know, by the way, that Manny never ratted you out for your part in the whole shaving attempt."

"He's a good kid." Jess readjusted her hands at the back of Elvis's neck, relishing the feeling of being close to him again after so long. "Even if his loyalty can be bought for a king-size Snickers."

Elvis laughed again, and they danced in silence for a few more turns around the room.

"So . . . what does that mean for us?" Elvis asked hesitantly.

"What? Kim and Teddy getting back together? Nothing?" she said, feeling sadder than she'd thought she would. "I don't know, Elvis. I mean, I know you're not going to Barnard next year," she teased. "And I don't want to do long distance. So I don't really see where that leaves us."

They danced in silence again. Jess felt an uncomfortable, unfamiliar sensation pricking at her eyes and tickling the back of her throat. Was she going to *cry*?! No way. Jess categorically refused to cry. Particularly over Elvis, who was, for all his good qualities, still the kind of goober who would eat corn off the cob and in no other form, and the kind of goober who actually *wanted* to be called E-Rod. But for a moment in time, he'd been her goober, and that meant something.

"You are the most remarkable woman I've ever met, Jessica Howard," Elvis murmured.

"You're pretty remarkable yourself, E-Rod."

Elvis came to a complete stop in the middle of the dance floor.

"Jess," he said excitedly. "Did you just—does this mean—?"

"There's still one baseball game left in the season, right? Who knows? Maybe it'll catch on."

"And maybe you'll come?"

"Maybe," she said, nestling herself back into Elvis's arms as he started swaying side to side again. "Maybe I'll even make you an E-Rod sign or something."

Maybe she would.

Much stranger things had happened at William Henry Harrison High.

CHAPTER SIXTY-NINE

PRINCIPAL MANTEGHI
PROM

Against all the odds, it appeared as though everything might actually be okay.

Principal Manteghi *did* wonder if she'd gone soft, however. She'd basically let Sophie get away with a fairly serious act of vandalism that the principal was 99 percent sure Sophie was responsible for. And although Sophie had already raised several thousand dollars for the parking lot fund, Principal Manteghi did question whether or not she'd done the right thing in essentially turning a blind eye to Sophie's crime. Just like she questioned whether or not having Toby Neale create posters—school-approved posters, of course—as prom decorations was really an appropriate punishment for his own less expensive expressions of vandalism. And she'd still never caught who was responsible for SnakeGate. Or issued any form of consequence for the all-school food fight. Or the sprinkler situation.

There was no doubt about it. Manteghi had gone soft.

But as she looked around the gym at her beloved William Henry Harrison High, all she could feel was . . . happy.

Despite the four disparate themes, the gym actually looked really nice—mostly thanks to Toby and his punishment-art. In fact, there was something sort of charming about having the prom in the gym instead of in the more elaborate venues of recent years, and you couldn't deny that the four different themes were certainly creative.

Except for the one with the *LIFE IS MEANINGLESS* banner. The principal wasn't entirely sure what was going on there. She made a mental note to ask Mr. Guzman on Monday who had been responsible for that quadrant, and to make sure the students involved were scheduled for time with the guidance counselor. Principal Manteghi wanted all of her students deeply invested in the meaning of life, just as she was deeply invested in all of their lives.

Her students. Principal Manteghi looked at them now, all the seniors, dancing together in the middle of the gym where all four quadrants met. For the first time in weeks, Principal Manteghi didn't see a single pair of teddy bear ears, or Team Kim red, or HeartBeats felt hearts, or AntiKaT buttons. Even Lawrence Goulet appeared to have abandoned his *KIM AND TEDDY NEVER EXISTED* sign. Once again, they were all just her students. Principal Manteghi couldn't believe they'd only be in her school for a few more weeks, and then they'd be heading off into the real world, to make mistakes and cause problems and find out who they really were.

Principal Manteghi missed every senior class when they graduated. But she had a feeling she'd miss this one maybe a bit more than usual. Despite all the headaches they'd caused her.

No matter their faults, they were certainly a unique group of individuals.

"Hey, Principal Manteghi!" Emma Gertz and Amelia Asaad bounced over to Principal Manteghi from the dance floor, Emma brandishing her cell phone in front of her. "Can we take a selfie?"

"Of course," the principal acquiesced, smiling into the cell phone screen.

"Thanks." Emma put her phone away. "I think Mr. Guzman's trying to get your attention."

As Emma and Amelia bounced back onto the dance floor, Principal Manteghi saw Mr. Guzman waving at her from the DJ booth. She walked over to meet him.

"Nice tux," Principal Manteghi said, surprised that it wasn't as loud as she expected behind the speakers.

"You too," he replied.

"What can I say?" She shrugged. "I love a good pantsuit."

The music switched to a new track that the principal didn't recognize but her students clearly did, as they screamed their approval and even more dancing bodies surged into the middle of the room.

"I think your first prom is definitely a success, DJ Mr. Guzman."

"You think?" he asked hopefully. "I know it's a little . . . unconventional . . ."

"I think being unconventional is one of William Henry Harrison High's greatest strengths. And besides," she added softly, "look how happy the kids are."

You could practically smell it in the air, the sense of joy, almost as strong as the BO and body spray. Principal Manteghi looked from smiling face to smiling face, until her eyes alighted on Kim Landis-Lilley and Teddy Lin, dancing in a thoroughly uncoordinated fashion right in front of the DJ stand. Those two had certainly caused Principal Manteghi quite a bit of trouble, but as she watched them dance together, all she felt was happiness for them. Because at the end of the day, that was all Principal Manteghi really wanted: happiness and success for each and every one of her students.

Although a bit more order in the hallways next year certainly wouldn't hurt.

"We're going to announce prom court," Mr. Guzman said. "I thought you might like to do the honors."

"Prom court?" Principal Manteghi had totally forgotten about that. She was slightly concerned that an unpopular outcome might cause some sort of riot, disturbing William Henry Harrison High's newfound peace. "Are you sure that's wise? I mean, perhaps we should just . . . just . . . let things be?" she finished weakly.

"I think we'll be okay," Mr. Guzman said. "I mean, it's like you said. Look how happy the kids are."

Principal Manteghi looked at her seniors. They certainly didn't *look* like they were about to riot. They looked, in fact, like they were having the time of their lives.

She hoped all her students, wherever they were, were having an equally good time.

CHAPTER SEVENTY

PHIL SPOONER
PROM

Phil Spooner was the luckiest freshman—almost sophomore—on the planet.

First of all, he had spent most of the semester lying his face off, and had somehow emerged unscathed, and with a whole new group of friends. It was the kind of non-consequence that made Phil wonder if they were truly living in an indifferent universe, and all was chaos.

If so, chaos was working out for him.

As his "punishment," Diamond Allen had made him listen to the entire original Broadway cast recording of *Dear Evan Hansen* so he could learn, in her words, "what happens when white boys lie." But it hadn't been a punishment at all. Phil had emerged from that auditory experience with profound gratitude that he hadn't had nearly the consequences Evan had (of course, lying about the motivations behind a popular couple's breakup wasn't nearly so bad as what Evan had done), and a newfound passion for musical theater. Phil thought he might audition for the spring musical next year. Diamond had assured him that there was absolutely no improv in musical theater. In fact, she'd told him, it was frowned upon. Which sounded pretty perfect to Phil.

Sophomore year was going to bring a whole new Phil. A singing, dancing Phil who always told the truth, and would, hopefully, be able to introduce the magnificent Diamond Allen as his girlfriend in the not-too-distant future.

She certainly looked magnificent tonight. The top of her dress was purple sequins, and the bottom was a purple skirt like a ballerina might wear, and she was luminous, glowing in the light of the disco ball Phil had helped her hang from the ceiling of the Allen family's finished basement. Earlier today, Phil and Diamond had pushed all the furniture to the sides of the room so that there was plenty of space for dancing. And now, almost the entire freshman class was down there, dancing under the disco ball as Diamond's curated anti-prom playlist blared out from the speakers attached to the enormous TV. Of course, going to prom hadn't been an option for Phil, as he was still years away from being a senior, but he couldn't imagine the *real* prom being any better than this.

The mood shifted as Ed Sheeran crooned out from the speakers, changing something in the air of the basement.

"Dance with me, Spoony?" Diamond asked, and Phil circled his arms around her waist so fast they practically left a trail behind them, like in the videos of fighter jets Phil had seen at the National Air and Space Museum.

Maybe Phil was going to kiss her.

Tonight.

As Diamond snuggled against his chest, it certainly seemed like it might be a possibility.

"Hey, guys." Evan Loomis was standing in front of them, adjusting his tie nervously. "Have you seen Olivia Landis-Lilley?"

"Nope," Diamond murmured.

"You know, Evan," Phil said, "if you like Olivia, you should just be honest. Ask her out. Go for it. Tell her how you feel. Honesty is the best policy."

"You are so full of it, Spoony." Diamond chuckled. "Sounds like somebody learned his lesson, though."

"Do you guys know if she's coming?" Evan insisted.

"I don't think so. Sorry, Evan," Diamond said sympathetically. "She told me she had alternate plans."

Alternate plans. Phil couldn't imagine what those could be. As he held Diamond in his arms and steered her around the basement, he knew there was absolutely nowhere else in the world he'd want to be.

But he hoped that wherever Olivia was, she was having fun.

CHAPTER SEVENTY-ONE

OLIVIA LANDIS-LILLEY
PROM

"Do you think people are having fun at prom? Even though it's weird and in the gym?" Daisy asked.

"Probably." Olivia hacked away at the cookies with a metal spatula. "I think we burned these."

"I knew we should have just eaten the dough raw." Daisy picked up a burnt crisp that Olivia had liberated from the cookie tray and examined it critically. "Bleagh. These look disgusting. I can't wait until we're seniors so we can go to the prom."

"I guess we could have gone to Diamond Allen's anti-prom party," Olivia said.

"From the pictures I've seen so far, it looks nicer than the actual prom." Daisy snorted.

Olivia and Daisy had scrolled through Diamond's Instastories earlier. Yes, Diamond had a truly glamorous basement, but the far more shocking bit of news they'd gleaned from Instagram was that it looked almost like Diamond and Phil Spooner were *involved*, which was absolutely bonkers.

Then again, it had been kind of a bonkers semester.

Not that Olivia had any plans to discuss Phil Spooner's dating life—or anyone else's—at all. She'd had enough gossip about relationships and breakups to last her a lifetime.

"We can still go to Diamond's, if you want," Olivia said.

"Nah. We'd have to get dressed up if we go to Diamond's. I'd rather just hang out with you in my sweatpants. Man"—Daisy crunched into a cookie—"these things are *bad*. They taste worse than they look. How does Kim *never* burn the cookies when she makes them?"

"Because Kim probably remembers to set the oven timer. We should make a new batch. Here. Have some more cheese." Olivia passed Daisy the block of cheddar. Daisy bit into it like a banana.

There was really nothing better than being a gross cheese monkey with your best friend.

"I'm so glad you started eating dairy again," Daisy said through a mouthful of cheese. "Your vegan phase last year was the worst."

"Yeah. Remind me to never get performance-enhancing diet tips from Tom Brady again. Sorry, pea protein. Whey protein is just superior." Olivia got up to start pulling together everything they'd need for a fresh batch of cookies. She hoped they had enough chocolate chips left. They'd kind of gone overboard with the chips on their failed batch. Maybe that had been part of their mistake.

"Do you think *they're* having fun?"

"Who?" Olivia asked.

"You know. Kim and Teddy." Daisy held up her phone. Olivia could see Kim's Instagram account, Teddy and Kim beaming under the disco ball in the gym in their formal-wear. "I can't believe they got back together. After all that."

"After all that." Olivia dropped the ingredients and a new mixing bowl off at the kitchen table and sat.

When Teddy had emerged from the limo to pick Kim up for prom tonight, Olivia had been surprised. But then, as she'd watched her moms—who must have known this was coming, as evidenced by their lack of surprise—snap a bil-lion pictures of Kim and Teddy in front of the fireplace, Olivia was struck by the inevitability of it all. Of course they'd gotten back together. They were Kim-and-Teddy, and that was the way of the world.

"It's kind of romantic, really," Daisy said.

"Kind of."

Olivia didn't really know *what* she thought. Her sister had turned their whole school—their whole *lives*—upside down, only to end up right back where she'd started. Which prob-ably should have annoyed Olivia, although maybe this meant fewer people would want to talk about Kim. Maybe Olivia would go back to being a semi-anonymous freshman.

Almost a semi-anonymous sophomore.

Was Kim having fun? Olivia wondered. She tapped on Daisy's screen, bringing Instagram back to life. Kim certainly looked like she was having fun. Much to Olivia's surprise, she found she wasn't annoyed by Teddy and Kim's cuddliness. She just felt . . . happy. Because Kim was clearly happy. And maybe it was sometimes annoying, to have an older sister who looked like a Disney princess, who never burned anything, who never forgot to do her homework, or turned anything in late, or was ever anything less than perfect, but Olivia still loved Kim, annoying as she was. And she wanted Kim to be happy.

"Come on," Daisy said. "Eat some of this cheese, because I don't want to hear you complain when I finish it all."

Olivia hoped Kim was having fun.

She certainly was.

CHAPTER SEVENTY-TWO

KIM LANDIS-LILLEY
PROM

Prom was so much better than Kim had ever imagined it would be.

Jess had forgiven her for not telling her she'd gotten back together with Teddy, no one was staring at her or gossiping about her anymore, and finally, there were no Teddy Bears or Team Kims or HeartBeats or Anti-KaTs. There was just Kim and Teddy and the rest of the senior class, dancing together and taking pictures and unable to believe that in a few weeks, they'd all be in different places.

"Teddy!" Kim exclaimed, stopping in her tracks in the middle of the last slow dance of the night, lifting her head up off of his chest like she'd been shocked. She couldn't believe she'd forgotten, but in all the breakup and makeup madness, not to mention all the prom excitement, somehow, it had totally slipped her mind. "College!" she cried.

"Um . . . yes? College? I'm sorry, I don't follow." His adorable nose wrinkled with confusion. Kim bopped it playfully, just because she could.

"You must have decided where you were going. I did."

"I did, too." Teddy's eyes widened with delight. "This means we can tell each other where we're going finally, right? I picked—"

"Wait!" Kim clapped a hand over his mouth. "This is a big moment. We need to make it a big moment. Let me get my planner."

"Kim, you don't need your planner to make something a big moment. Also, you have to be the only person in the history of time who brought a planner to prom."

"You never know when you might have to schedule something." She grabbed ahold of Teddy's hand. "Come on!"

Hand in hand, they wove their way through the dancing couples, running toward the chair in the HeartBeats quadrant where Kim had stashed her purse. Eagerly, she pulled out her planner and two of her favorite pens, the Uni-ball ones with gel ink that always wrote so smoothly. She tore two pieces of paper out of the Notes section in the back and handed Teddy a piece of paper and a pen.

"Write where you're going to school," she said. "And on the count of three, we'll show each other."

"Kim—"

"Please?" she wheedled.

"Okay, okay." He scribbled something quickly as Kim neatly wrote the name of her school, wondering if they'd end up anywhere near each other. Wondering what would happen if they hadn't. "Ready?" Teddy asked. Kim nodded. "Okay. Here we go. One . . . two . . . three."

Heart hammering in her chest, Kim flipped her paper over. She looked at Teddy's paper and gasped. Stunned, she heard her pen clatter to the floor and watched her paper drift slowly away.

"You're kidding, Junior." Teddy laughed, and the sound made Kim so happy she worried she might burst. He was looking at her like she was his favorite thing, his absolute favorite thing in the whole world, and she knew she was looking at him exactly the same way. "I can't believe it." He laughed again, shaking his head, his dark hair flopping in front of his eyes in a way that was so familiar, it made her fall in love with him all over again.

"I can believe it." She reached up to smooth Teddy's hair away from his face and kissed him quickly, before Mr. Rizzo could give them a demerit for PDA. "Some things are just meant to be."

CHAPTER SEVENTY-THREE

DUSTIN ROTHBART
PROM

In the past five weeks, Dustin Rothbart had somehow accumulated 234 demerits. Typically, such a staggering accumulation would have prevented him from graduating, but at his disciplinary hearing, Principal Manteghi agreed that the last month had been anything but typical. Instead, he'd be serving his detentions every day after school and on Saturday mornings until he graduated, and tonight, he'd opted to forgo prom in order to serve four consecutive detentions. But as he listened to the music waft down the hall from the gym, Dustin wondered if he might have made the wrong choice.

A particularly raucous chorus of cheers punctuated the silence of the detention room, startling Ms. Powell as she looked up from the papers she was grading. She narrowed her eyes at the door, then turned her focus to Dustin.

"Are you happy with your choices, Mr. Rothbart?" Ms. Powell asked primly. "I hope this has been an instructive lesson that crime doesn't pay."

Had Dustin even committed a crime? He didn't know. To be perfectly honest, he had no idea how he'd racked up quite so many demerits. All he knew was that ever since Kim Landis-Lilley and Teddy Lin had broken up, the teachers had thrown around demerits like confetti, and somehow, most of that confetti had landed on him.

He supposed he could have railed against the unfairness of it all. He could have cursed Kim and Teddy for what they'd done to him, even though it had only been their fault indirectly. But he didn't want to spend the end of the year all bitter and miserable.

Instead, Dustin Rothbart just bopped his head in time to the music.

There would be plenty of dances for him to go to in college.

He couldn't wait.

ACKNOWLEDGMENTS

I wrote most of the first draft of this book lying down, fighting bouts of first-trimester nausea, and trying not to barf into my trash can. Now I'm writing the acknowledgments with the world's cutest baby in my lap. A lot can change during the process of creating a book, and I'm so grateful for everyone who helped make this one possible.

Molly Ker Hawn, you're not only the best agent, you're the best person. I'm so lucky to have you in my life and so happy to be working with you.

A huge thank you to everyone at Scholastic—I am so proud to be part of the IreadYA family. Matt Ringler, my school best friend and my incredible editor: Thank you for giving me the gift of not just one prom, but four! Thank you for diving into the demerit deep end with me, and for never forgetting poor Dustin Rothbart. Shelly Romero, thank you for your insightful notes, for fixing my Google Translate Spanish, for understanding the importance of Selena, and for being the ultimate Nico stan. Thank you to Maeve

Norton for another gorgeous cover—the lip gloss is literally popping.

Thank you to all the readers, bloggers, librarians, teachers, and booksellers for your continued support, and most especially to my beloved Book Cellar.

Writer friends are the best friends—I'm grateful for dumplings with Gloria and cookies with Crystal and Shakespeare Skype sessions with Molly, and for all of you who I don't get to see nearly as often as I'd like. Everyone should move to Chicago.

Thank you to Dad for always thinking the best will happen and to Mom for helping me prepare in case the worst happens. Ali, I'm not sure how you're still surviving as a teacher, but I'm beyond impressed and so glad we can always chat about the ups and downs of education life. I wrote another pair of sisters who are nothing like us.

Max, I literally couldn't function without you. You're crushing it with the positive affirmations. And the dinners. And getting the baby to sleep. And the fact that you're vacuuming right at this very moment. Basically, you're crushing everything.

And last, but certainly not least, thank you, Ezra. You're the best distraction.

ABOUT THE AUTHOR

Stephanie Kate Strohm is the author of *It's Not Me, It's You,*
The Date to Save, The Taming of the Drew, Prince in Disguise, and
Love à la Mode. She graduated from Middlebury College with
a dual degree in theater and history and has acted her way
around the United States, performing in more than twenty-
five states. She currently lives in Chicago with her husband,
her son, and a dog named Lorelei Lee.